For Rave

A COLLAPSE

OF THE MIDDLE ORDER

With kind regards

B Mahendon

13 December 2002

A COLLAPSE

OF THE MIDDLE ORDER

by

B Mahendra

Blackie & Co
Publishers Ltd

A BLACKIE & CO PUBLISHERS PAPERBACK

© Copyright 2002
B Mahendra

The right of B Mahendra to be identified as the author of
this work has been asserted by him in accordance with the
Copyright, Designs and Patents Act 1988

First published in 2002

A CIP catalogue record for this title is
available from the British Library

ISBN 1-903138-62-0

**Blackie & Co Publishers Ltd
107-111 Fleet Street
LONDON EC4A 2AB**

Part One – The First Day's Play

I

A burst of gunfire had not, for once, woken Liz that morning. Almost by instinct she knew it was not yet 7.00, for Phil was still asleep. He did not require the ministrations of an alarm clock; an inner mechanism, endowed by nature, did the deed efficiently, reliably and without need to be wound up. Nights without number in recent months Phil would storm off to bed, and Liz, in diverse states of anger, resentment, disappointment and self-pity, would not even bother to set her alarm clock. It was she who always paid for lacking a finely-tuned natural mechanism; Phil would be up fresh, ready to embrace the virginal day, memories of the fraught bedtime banished to some inner attic of his unconsciousness, while Liz, waking late, tired and fretful, would instantaneously recall the events of the previous night and be effortlessly fatigued.

It was Friday but there was no school that day. Phil would go away to the Test Match and she would have the day largely to herself. Anticipation of the peace and calm to come soothed her for the moment. Then, the clatter of cutlery also informed her that Marie-Antoinette, their servant, was attempting to lay the table for breakfast. Liz's unexpected confidante, Marie-Antoinette had seemingly been deprived by the combined efforts of nature and upbringing of a delicate touch. In fact, she moved with all the grace of a bull that lacked hand-to-eye co-ordination. When they had first met, her clumsiness had reminded Liz of the elephant of her fantasies, but now, after a few months in that country, a familiarity with those beasts had made Liz aware what graceful creatures they really were; the cow elephant the more so. This had led Liz to revise her opinion of the comparative clumsiness of the beasts of burden, and she had resolved to compare Marie-Antoinette not with a cow but, largely in tribute to a festeringly resentful view of the male gender, a bull.

A bull it was that dropped a saucepan in the dining room. Liz, by now awake, alert and anticipating clumsiness, was unaffected by the clanging pan, but the noise, though muffled by the walls, was sufficient to penetrate Phil's sleep-preserving defences; he stirred but did not waken. Not for the first time Liz was consumed by an envious marvel at his ability to get and retain sleep, which, she did not doubt at all, contributed in large measure to the maddening calm he would display during the rest of the day.

There was no school that day as a holiday had been declared in honour of the Test Match. It was not so much an act of generosity on the part of the school as a means of pre-empting the mass absconding on the part of the boys that was bound otherwise to result. The school would hardly have been able to punish those boys going absent without leave when one of their very number, Roar, was making his debut on the national side. Phil had been given tickets by their friend, Bubb, who

2

managed *Roll Britannia!* – the innovative and trend-setting organization that promoted British culture. Both Phil and Liz had been invited, but Liz had declined the proffered tickets on the not unreasonable grounds that, while she did not know enough about cricket to hate the game, she was certain she would dislike the events she was told were ancillary to the contest but played an integral part in creating the atmosphere. On this occasion Phil had not attempted to change her mind as he once had done back in England, when he tried to get her to accompany him to a club match in which a friend of his was playing. It had been during the days of their courtship when Phil was wont to be hinting at hidden depths to his character, spirits from some vasty deep that could be summoned if only Liz had inspiration to call them. Back then, Liz, curious about the character of the man who pursued her with a zeal that had not been apparent in other men, had attended the match with him. Until then, as far as his personality went, Liz felt that only the more mundane spirits had been delivered to the surface by the unwitting conspiracy between subtle projection on his part and a necessary curiosity on hers. An elaborate interest in sport would, on the face of it, have been thought to be out of character for Phil, which was why, Liz had decided, when the charitable constructions of courtship days had eventually yielded to essays in post-marital cynicism, he had brought it up. Phil had said his friend Bob would be playing on that Saturday – splendid chap, oldest friend, who would be enormously thrilled to have the support of friend and friend's future wife; it was the first occasion on which Phil had mentioned marriage.

"But I know nothing about cricket," she had protested.

"Oh, you will learn it easily enough. It is easy to pick up. I'll help you."

He had then picked up an orange from a fruit bowl, grasped it in his left hand, and showed it to her, saying, "I used to bowl a quite useful chinaman."

"A chinaman?"

"Yes. You do it like this. You tweak the ball like this, you bring your arm over like that and, as you let go, you flip your wrist like that. That's how you bowl a chinaman."

Liz had thought she had heard nothing more grotesque and offensive than that, and had enquired no further. In the event, she had gone with little enthusiasm with Phil that Saturday afternoon. It had rained and she saw no cricket. Since then she had remained totally innocent of the mysteries of what appeared to be a comprehensively unfathomable game which, to the likes of her, seemed to exist solely to occupy an inordinate amount of newsprint and time on the airwaves. An orphan girl, deprived of fanatical male relations, she had had little opportunity of learning about the game. She had heard of women who had mastered its intricacies, even acquired prowess at it, but she had no wish to be of their number; any regret she felt for not being initiated into its rites was no more than a nun's for acquaintance with male company.

Now she firmly decided she would not accept the tickets Bubb had offered. She knew Phil would have preferred more impressive company than Bubb could supply him with at the match, and this knowledge merely fortified her resolve to stay away. Her resolve had, at one time, been very nearly undermined by Emmeline, the headmaster's wife, who had said that the Test Match, leaving aside the pseudo-chauvinistic fervour of the participants and even more of the supporters, would nevertheless be a grand social occasion, a kaleidoscope of local colour, where people of significance would go to see and be seen. And there were not many such occasions free of trouble and strife, with a truce thrown in, these days. Emmeline was convincing and persuasive, but Liz decided not to be convinced and persuaded, finding her present mood not up to the promised promiscuity of socially elevated intercourse.

The artifice of civil war had distorted and deformed that country. Liz had not seen and heard what she had hoped for when she had agreed to accompany Phil to his job teaching English and History at this school thousands of miles from England. Phil had believed this might prove the turning point in his career, enabling him to get away from the hothouse that education in England had become, and let him work without hindrance, able to do the job he had been trained but not allowed to do, as well as to see another country, craft a life style more congenial, and think unstressed and unpressured about what he hoped would be his lasting monument – a work on the political history of seventeenth-century England. When the chance had arrived, he grabbed at it with almost unseemly enthusiasm. Liz had accepted what amounted to a fait accompli; agreeing to go, she had constructed reasons for so doing later. It did seem their lives needed more zest, novelty and freedom from wearisome routine. What Phil wanted for his career Liz felt they needed for their marriage. Since they would not conceive of starting a family in the tropics, a breathing space was acquired in that respect, too. In any event, Liz did not want any children until a secure basis to their marriage could be established.

From a time a month or two into their marriage, she had started to question the founding premises of their union in a way Phil was not capable of doing. They seemed, to Liz, to have agreed to marry all right, but, with hindsight, they appeared to have been at cross purposes on what exactly had been agreed. An acquaintance of hers, a solicitor at an evening class they both attended on Women's Dilemmas, had pointed out to Liz that the analysis she had been engaged in was, in fact, a respectable approach to the law of contract. One that had been brought about on the basis of an agreement that was premised on cross-purposed intention was a contract by mutual mistake, she had learned, and this insight, adding legitimacy to her commonsensical musings, had also been strangely comforting. Moreover, having learned also that such a flawed contract was void or voidable, Liz was thankful to go away to this troubled faraway land to test her assumptions. Enlightenment had not come either in respect of her marriage or that country, but that morning she was sure of one thing: she was not going to a cricket match to seek it.

Now there was light but not yet heat to the day. Liz lazed in bed in those fleeting hours between the sun giving warning of its potential and when it came to fulfil it. She looked out of the window and saw that the mountains were clearly visible where, for months past, all she had been able to observe was smoke from burning rubble masking the hilltops. When she eventually decided to come down to the kitchen, Marie-Antoinette had evidently succeeded in preparing breakfast.

"Breakfast will be laying in five minutes, Missy."

Once upon a time, so Marie-Antoinette had assured Liz, she had been the most beautiful girl in her village. Her father having been a village headman, she was also the most sought-after by suitors. Men, it seemed, had fought over her with their bare hands. One man had walked over burning embers in order to impress her, succeeding only in scorching his soles so badly that he was unfit for any work except to become a priest – a line of work in that country in which one so employed could put one's feet up. Another had walked on water – or, at least, tried to swim – and had been dragged by the currents to the village on the opposite bank, beyond the pale of civilization as Marie-Antoinette knew it. Fate, she had then observed, had intended that incompetent swimmer never to truly belong to her own people. Fate, however, had it in for her, too. The father she worshipped died, and beauty, unaccompanied by paternal patronage, as Marie-Antoinette was to sagaciously remark, boiled no rice. She ended up having to accept the nearest reasonable offer of marriage, at the hands of a man who said he was a sanitary inspector.

They had gone to live in the neighbouring village, for that was where his family lived and where he had his work to do. Soon it became apparent to her that her sanitary inspector was a man who went down sewers to investigate and repair. Whenever they had visitors, she had to burn joss sticks and incense to mask the smells of work he would bring home with him. Half her housekeeping money went on what people thought was an impressive investment in objects that were aids to devotion. Thereby she also quickly acquired a reputation for piety, and she felt ashamed for in no way did she regard herself as devout. On the contrary, she harboured regrets, she possessed ambitions to rise in the world, and she was ashamed of her husband. She felt most guilty about the last sentiment in particular, for in his own way her husband was a kind and thoughtful man, though one never wholly at home above ground. She thought he carried a furtive air about him, and this she attributed to too much companionship with subterranean rats. In moments of bitterness she would complain that night soil had warped his soul. The village headman's daughter had herself to become furtive and secretive whenever she went back to her own people, and she had to invent a status and riches that she could aspire to only in fantasy rather than realistically foresee herself ever having. The man of the sewers gave her first one daughter, then another, and then a third. Then he contracted Weil's disease, spread by a germ passed by rats in their urine, and died following fever, jaundice and kidney failure. In the manner of his death, there was an extravagance he had never betrayed in life.

Three daughters, she had bitterly mused in widowhood, to bring up and endow – the sewer man having taken the easy way out. Guilt and self-recrimination at these unworthy thoughts had in no way eased entirely with the passage of time, and only aggravated her pain. She struggled, found menial employment and, through her late father's connections, became a cook to the gentry. Her social ambitions were in some ways appeased by being allowed to work in homes she would once have hoped to own. Her own daughters had by then grown up and she was now on the threshold of grandmotherhood. Some semblance of peace and contentment had thereby, with the promise of this enhanced status, devolved upon her. Her satisfaction would be complete if the truce declared for the Test Match could bring forth a grandchild which would, if God was minded to make amends for the miseries He had inflicted in her middle life, turn out to be a grandson.

Listening, as she often did, to the story of Marie-Antoinette's life had given a new perspective to Liz's own, and had also drawn the two women close.

"How's your daughter?" she asked.

"No baby coming out yet, Missy. We all hoping it will come out during peace period."

"It must happen quickly."

"Baby come out when baby want. Oh, they having mind of their own, Missy."

"So, you think the baby decides when it will drop...er...in?"

"No doubt about that, Missy. Fate decides all things."

"Oh, I see. What is fate planning to give us for breakfast?"

"Lots of good things, Missy. The young must eat well to prosper."

"I'm glad you think we are still young and going to prosper, Marie-Antoinette."

"Yes, no doubt, Missy. But I'm speaking more of the young sir."

"Oh, him? Don't talk too loud. His head will swell even more."

"But he is a nice young sir. He is going to do hundred against English. Fine hundred. Honour to his motherland." She dropped her voice to a whisper. "And save headmaster sir from horrible, horrible fate."

"What are you going on about, Marie-Antoinette? Young sir doing hundred against English. What do you mean?"

"Didn't Master sir not tell you, Missy?"

"Master sir. Young sir. We seem to have a surfeit of sirs."

"Missy don't know? But Master Roar is coming for breakfast."

"Master Roar?"

"Him who is playing today."

"Yes, yes, I know he is playing. But coming to breakfast? Who asked him?"

"Why, Missy, Master sir. He tell me yesterday. He call me and tell me, Marie-Antoinette, I want pawpaw, mangoes and mangosteens tomorrow for Roar. We give him send off on behalf of school. Missy, he not tell you?"

"Of course, not."

"I think it not wise."

"I'm glad you are on my side."

"All those fruit, Missy. They terrorize the tummy. Tummy explode. Master Roar's tummy too upset for making hundred runs. We play bad. Not wise."

"Yes, I see. But Phil's mind is too subtle for deviousness of such directness."

"Anyway, we win, I think, Missy, if umpires' stars in proper prospect and in conjunction."

"You mean, if they are bribed?"

"Oh, no, no, Missy. We not bribing umpires. Umpires just playing for the motherland."

"Just playing for the motherland?"

"Just playing for the motherland. It's only human, no?"

"Blessed are the run-makers."

They were joined by Phil, who had come into the dining room with a newspaper in his hand. Once again Liz marvelled that a man could settle so easily into life thousands of miles away with barely a habit out of place. He glanced without awareness at the laid table. If Liz had hoped the extra place that had been laid would stir some guilt-tinged memory, she was to remain disappointed. Phil settled into his chair and behind his newspaper in the manner that has stirred many a mild English housewife through the ages to serious thought of manslaughter.

Marie-Antoinette had withdrawn into the kitchen, carrying with her the demeanour that suggested awe and coquettishness, in equal measure, in the presence of her master. She had left behind a large jug containing the milk of a young coconut, a fluid whose gelatinous texture, sweetly salt-ish taste and floating debris from the insides of the coconut had become a staple breakfast drink for Phil and Liz. While Phil abstractedly sipped his drink, Liz, in no mood to communicate in the absence of explanation or apology for Roar's imminent presence without prior notification to her, withdrew and followed Marie-Antoinette into the kitchen.

"Things calm outside, Marie-Antoinette?"

"Things as calm as the wind will allow, Missy. But the High Priest, he has gone."

"Gone?"

"Kidnapped. By the terrorists."

"Really?"

"They say it happens last night, Missy."

"Oh, things will be tense then."

"No knowing what will happen, Missy. If they kill him, peace period will also finish."

"How did you get to know?"

"There's talk everywhere, Missy."

"Rumour?"

Marie-Antoinette looked reproachful.

"What for saying rumour or for real, Missy? In these times, these people will believe anything." She made an expansive gesture with her arms. "Everything."

"I hope he is safe and is found."

"The terrorists are real savage, Missy. Last time they saying, if they get the High Priest, they slaughter him. Take his skin and make slippers. Dance in the temple compound in them. Feed his body to the sharks."

"The sharks? Isn't the sea far away?"

"Not if you put him in the river, Missy. It will run to the sea. The body will be all rotten. The sharks enjoying that."

" Not before breakfast, Marie-Antoinette!"

"They don't care when they eat bodies."

"I meant, not before our breakfast, Marie-Antoinette."

"Sorry, missy. But the people saying that."

"The people must not believe rumour. They must find out for themselves what the truth is."

"No, Missy. Rumour better. Rumour agree with what people hope will happen."

"You shock me, Marie-Antoinette."

"Sorry, Missy. People have smell of death and destroying going up their noses. They want to see dying and killing. When rumour agree, they drink it up like hungry baby at mother's breast."

"And the fact the High Priest might be dead is not important?"

"Not so important, Missy. We can always have another High Priest. But if he alive and found, there won't be trouble. We grow old without war and death. We have no revenge. Our heart misses it like the cow misses her dead calf. We get sad. We want trouble to end our sadness."

"I can only hope these are not your views, Marie-Antoinette."

"Who can say, Missy? We are all one and one all."

Further philosophical discourse, seasoned with the promise of controversy, was forestalled by the ringing of the doorbell. Phil, who had started on his milk-soaked rice cakes – another of their breakfast staples – got up and went to the door as Liz walked back to the dining room. Phil's face was calm and untroubled, and Liz, not yet seeing any evidence of the hoped-for embarrassment or guilt on his face, pursed her lips. He returned with Roar, the young hero. Not yet eighteen, Roar was already mature and self-possessed as few English boys of that age could be. Indeed, no English boy of that young age could even dream of being in the England team. The local newspapers, spared a fresh supply of horrors by the truce declared in honour of the Test Match, had spent several column inches over him. Phil and Liz already knew of his coconut palm and rubber ball to willow and leather progress.

They exchanged pleasantries and sat down. For a moment, Liz felt impelled to allude to the unexpectedness of the honour he was bestowing on them by calling on them on the morning of the most important day of his life, but then her better nature asserted itself. She wished in no way to discomfort Roar. Her knowledge of cricket was so scanty she could not estimate what the result of breakfast-time embarrassment might be, but she knew racehorses sweated gently in the paddock before a race and she feared cricketers might possess sensitivities on an equine scale.

Phil was more adept at small talk, at any rate with men.

"Nervous?"

"A little."

"Slept well?"

"Yes, after praying to the Goddess Mar."

"Is there a goddess bestowing prowess at cricket?"

Roar looked surprised. "Oh, no. She is the Goddess of War. She helps out in any battle."

"Is that how you see the contest?"

"That's the way to get in the mood."

"I suppose you have a point there. Psyched up and so forth."

"You must not get it wrong. The battle is not just against the English. It is a general battle. For the country, for my people, the school..."

"Not to mention Uncle Grunt."

"Well, he is depending on me."

"The young hero saves the old coward's skin, eh?"

"Mr Grunt has been kind to me and my family. They are only simple farmers, you know."

"How on earth does a simple farmer's child end up as a test cricketer?"

"It is a religion with us. We play it everywhere, you see. We start with a rubber ball and the fronds of the palm. Everyone plays."

"Why not football? It's so much simpler."

"Football is not for gentlemen. The players don't wear long trousers. Cricketers wear long trousers. They are gentlemen. In our village we are born poor but we dream rich. We play cricket and dream of being gentlemen – rich, leisured, sportsmanly, a life of easy pickings." He smiled roguishly. "Just like at first slip."

"Life needs a long stop, too. Don't your studies matter?"

"It's a gamble. Studies, I mean. You may or may not get anywhere. But God has given me talent. I must exploit it. I must be a cricketer."

"I hope for your sake you do well today."

"You supporting England, no?"

"No. Today I'm neutral. I have the neutrality of the man who hasn't the courage to make up his mind. I will be like Switzerland."

Roar looked mystified, and then his face relaxed, breaking out into a beam.

"You are being a gentleman, you know. Not taking sides against your hosts. You are a true cricketer."

Liz had been listening to what appeared to be literally men's talk, noting with interest how Roar had stopped calling Phil 'sir'. Phil was invariably 'sir' to the boys, and she remained 'miss'. Roar had dropped the title for Phil, but in his shyness persisted with hers.

They were interrupted by the doorbell being rung with peremptory insistence. Whoever was without appeared to be in some emotion; the ringer was soon revealed to be Bubb, manager of *Roll Britannia!*

"Dammit! Sorry I'm late. Place was invaded by the police behaving like so many mosquitoes."

The speaker was a little red-faced man with a surprisingly dark moustache, a nearly bald head, and a boyish face. He looked like the popular caricature of a bookmaker, but one in mufti – a man who ought to have been dressed in a check outfit but who had been saved by a rudimentary sense of propriety. A bald head and a boyish face appeared to be nature's attempt at preserving a semblance of trustworthiness in a soul otherwise sorely disadvantaged by its lack. Now he appeared to be in high emotion, but – thought Phil – with Bubb one was never really sure whether the emotion displayed was ersatz or real. He was capable of erecting emotion the way other men could conjure up charm.

Phil thrust a cup of tea into his hand and tested him.

"Didn't know you had ventured into serious crime, Bubb."

"No laughing matter, I can assure you, my friend."

"Were they looking for something or was it just you they wanted?"

"They weren't after a white man's blood. And it wasn't a mistake, if you ask me."

"Someone put them up to it?"

"I'm sure of that."

"Can't say you haven't been sailing close to the wind. Anyway, I hope they didn't find anything they were looking for...what exactly were they looking for?"

"I think they were looking for a person..."

Bubb's absurd histrionics goaded Liz into an intervention she had not wholly intended.

"Perhaps they were looking for the High Priest."

Bubb looked uneasy but quickly regained composure.

"How did you know that...he was missing?"

"It is common knowledge. You know how it is. Telegraph, telephone, tell-a-woman."

Bubb turned abruptly back to Phil, as if her levity was not warranted in the circumstances."

"The rumours are spreading all right," he said grimly.

"Will it mean trouble now," Phil asked.

"If the Panthers have got the High Priest, it is the sandpit for him, for sure."

"He wasn't a fan, exactly, of theirs?"

"Don't be absurd. Only last month, in a sermon to the faithful, he called for their extermination. The nation and the race would consider it a noble act, he said, at least in the translated version that came to me."

Liz decided to try to redeem herself. "Do you think the truce will hold, Bubb?"

"It all depends on the old man's authority. As long as he is there, peace will prevail, – for six days at any rate."

"I hope he doesn't drop dead during the Test Match," said Phil.

"That would be inconvenient."

"Talk of bad taste stopping play."

"Any excitement could finish him off. A few romantics here would love for their country to win and the palpitating heart of the old man to come to a twitching halt."

"End of match. End of President. End of peace. There's a fearful symmetry to it, don't you think, Bubb?"

The question was left unanswered. Bubb, tiring perhaps of this burst of animation early in the day, turned his attention to his cup of tea. Phil and Liz felt themselves to be alone for the first time that day. They looked at each other. The silence grew.

Liz started formulating a plan with cunning. Phil, unoccupied by tea or any Machiavellian musing, cracked first.

"We are off to the match."

"We?" asked Liz sweetly.

"Yes, Bubb and I."

"But I'm coming, too."

"You...?"

"Yes."

" But...you can't. We haven't got tickets for you. You said you didn't want to come." Phil sounded feverish

"You can get tickets for me, can't you, Bubb?"

"This is most awkward," muttered Phil

"I'll see what I can do," said Bubb, venturing to the telephone in the sitting room.

"Why did you have to spring it like this?" demanded Phil, unappeased. "I thought you were not interested in cricket. You certainly weren't when I tried to teach you."

"The germ of knowledge you planted might have sprouted late," replied Liz mildly. "Anyway, I gather it is the social occasion of the year."

"You put us all to trouble just to show off to all those women."

"I may want to show off to the men, too. Anyway, it is Bubb who is taking the trouble."

Bubb returned, looking as if he had just seen a heavily backed favourite in which he held large sums of the punter's' money being decisively beaten.

"It is fixed. There is an extra ticket."

++++++++

II

"See him there? That's Bark. He'll do anything to betray Mr Grunt and have him sacked."

"Sounds like a quisling to me."

"Is that what you say in your language, child? But in any language it must mean 'traitor'. To think, my father paid for his education."

Liz found herself seated by Emmeline Grunt, the headmaster's wife, Phil having gone over to be with Bubb. She was glad of this arrangement, for she was sure she could not have stomached seven hours of Phil's presence even if she had not been out of temper with him. A spouse's curiosity, which transcends indifference, even outright dislike, could espy Phil lolling about with a mug of beer while Bubb, though similarly encumbered, had not lost any time in making the acquaintance of his neighbours in the seats around him. Liz had heard that Bubb's ability to do business in even the most unpromising of situations had acquired a legendary status. Getting her a ticket at the last moment was but a trivial example of his powers. Rumours of shady dealing had filtered in and out of the British community, fuelled by the usual heady mix of envy, malice and incredulity. If Bubb's rumoured reputation was to be taken at anything like face value, he would be, while incidentally watching a cricket match, concluding a deal to sell torpedoes to the local navy, and following it up with another to sell the ships necessary to fire them from.

Emmeline Grunt was a large, handsome woman who reminded Liz of a stately home built on human lines but one now falling through inanition and improvidence into a gentle decline. Emmeline's pride was matched only by her unconquerable loyalty to Mr Grunt, the headmaster of their school, and to her race, the *Nones*. Mr Grunt had in recent years become a beleaguered man, a *None* in a school, city and country dominated by the *Ings* and, to a lesser extent, the *Ers*. The school itself he had every right to expect to be, given its Anglican foundation, a liberal and humane refuge from racial and communal prejudice. He was a gifted man, evidently destined for great things, but held back by an accident of birth into a community that formed but a small fraction of the population. The school, apparently above conflict of this kind, had made him headmaster. But bigotry had seeped in from the beginning of his reign – seemingly by some process of osmosis from outside – and he now found the foundations of his support rotting and subsiding. It had been said he had been spared only because he had overseen the emergence of an epochally successful cricket first eleven, captained triumphantly that season by the prodigious Roar. Mr Grunt's position, it was fair to say, seemed to depend entirely on the success of Roar and the steadfast loyalty of the formidable Emmeline.

Liz's attention, which had been usurped by the contemplation of Bubb's commercial acumen, was restored by Emmeline's remark that the ingrate Bark's education had been paid for by her father.

"Man of humble origins, was Bark?"

"He did not have so much as a coconut shell to drink from, child. He dressed in clothes thrown away by beggars, so poor he was. My father took pity on him. Fed him. Clothed him. Put a roof over his head. Sent him to school. Now Bark is a big man. He forgets everything. The stomach that is full remembers not the aching void that was filled."

"That's a picturesque way of putting it. But why has he turned against your people?"

"Money. Also, envy. Our people can't bear to see others of our people doing so well. He has hated Mr Grunt from the moment he first saw him."

"When was that?"

"At our wedding. I think, child...come closer, I'll tell you...he was thinking he would marry me. When my father arranged for Mr Grunt to marry me, Bark was furious"

"'Hell hath no fury...', eh?"

"You see, my father thought, charity is one thing; giving your only daughter to a bankrupt's son as a bride is quite another."

"So that was how he became so poor."

"Not poor, child; penniless. His father drank. Business went down. Went bankrupt. Jumped in the well."

"What about his mother?"

"The woman had to sell sweets in the street". Emmeline smirked and dropped her voice to a whisper. " If you ask me, she sold more than sweets. I'll like to see his face when one day I ask him about that."

"What does Mr Grunt think about this?"

"He's not worried. He can look after himself. But, if Roar does well in this match, no one can touch him."

"We had Roar for breakfast this morning."

"He's a nice boy. So obedient. Mr Grunt is like a father to him. We are hoping...come close, child; I'll tell you...he will marry our daughter."

"Really? That'll be a good catch."

"That's what our enemies will also be saying. A test cricketer marrying the headmaster's daughter."

Unobserved by them, Phil, having finished his beer, had returned to the bar carrying his and Bubb's empty mugs. The trip involved walking by Liz's and Emmeline's seats. He succeeded in startling them.

"Enjoying yourself, dear?"

"We are," said Liz, shortly.

"Can you understand the game? It is a bit recherché."

"We can manage. Mrs Grunt here knows all about cricket, don't you, Mrs Grunt?"

Phil evidently did not credit Mrs Grunt with such arcane knowledge.

"It's like this. There are two teams. One bats and the other bowls. When..."

"Go away, Phil."

Phil went away, anticipation of cold beer getting the better of any desire to annoy his wife. When her irritation had subsided, Liz turned back to Emmeline.

"I forgot to ask you, Mrs Grunt, but how did you come to learn about the game?"

"We all learn about the game. It's nothing. It comes naturally. Just like the facts of life."

"I'm sure the birds and the bees have little use for it."

"We all learn the game. It's just like war, you know, only the rules are a little more complicated than in war."

"You mean the killing is more straightforward in war?"

"You mustn't say things like that, child, especially these days. It is the idea, you know. Confrontation."

"I think it is a form of sublimation. Public school boys, trained for and then deprived of a real war, can still play at this war game."

"It builds character also."

"How?"

"You learn to take defeat like a man."

"Trouble is, we are women."

"All the more reason, child, to learn to take defeat like a man and not keep complaining about the pitch and the umpiring."

"You won't make a very convincing feminist, Mrs Grunt."

"Feminism? Pah! If God had wanted us to be feminists, He would have given us muscles and narrow hips. No, God made us as we are for a purpose."

"To be at the mercy of men."

"No, child, you have got it all wrong. God made us women to get the men to do everything for us."

"Someone said the weaker sex is stronger because of the weakness of the stronger sex for the weaker sex."

"Very wise man who said that."

Emmeline broke off to cheer lustily. "Good shot!" she yelled.

All Liz could see was a red object hurtling towards them. She had sat through the morning trying to fathom the mysteries of the gentlemen's game. She was too shy to ask Emmeline to explain and, in any case, her neighbour appeared to be too enthusiastic a follower to have the patience or the tact to instruct a novice. Fairly early on, following the sound of a muffled crack, as if a rifle was being let loose on a poacher in the distant jungle, the stadium had erupted in frenzied cheering, making a noise that reminded Liz of parliamentary proceedings she had heard on the radio when a child. Emmeline had lent voice to that din, while half hurling herself from her seat in order to shout the better.

"Lovely shot! A beauty! They won't be able to find the ball now!" She yelled, then dissolved in giggles.

By connecting Emmeline's volcanic eruptions of enthusiasm with those of other spectators, Liz surmised they were being inspired by a nationalistic fervour; that, when they cheered, the England team had suffered some disadvantage. The first hour had been subdued on the whole, yielding murmurs, a couple of mass groans, and on one or two occasions a sound like a hiss that ended in a sharp intake of communal breath. She suspected that this might have signified delivery from imminent peril. After that quiet hour, however, things had begun to liven up. The local side seemed to be doing well, as far as Liz could tell by monitoring Emmeline's movements and ejaculations in the seat adjoining hers. The vigour of the spectators' responses surprised Liz, who had imagined cricket to be a marginally more animated version of chess or snooker. Once or twice Emmeline and the stadium had uttered a quite terrifying 'boo', a sound Liz had last heard at the cinema coming out of the cupped hands held over the mouth of Tarzan. From Emmeline's visage, Liz guessed that this indicated strong disapproval. On a couple of other occasions there was a collective mournful sigh, a pause, some applause, then heads turning to each other and nodding in collective wisdom. There was a feeling of relaxation at these times, akin to that which breaks out when a court of law adjourns, but these periods did not last long for, following a few shouts of what sounded like encouragement, the combat was rejoined and the tension restored.

For lunch, Liz, who had no idea how one found anything to eat in those surroundings, shared the sandwiches Emmeline had brought with her. The crowd milled around, there was chatter, and various impromptu bands struck up a catholic medley of the latest popular songs, marches and waltzes, as well as tunes that had won many a war for England. She also saw Phil and Bubb moving to the bar again, and after a quite considerable delay, for both the bar and the lavatories were crowded, they emerged to walk back to their seats. Now Phil held one filled mug, Bubb one in each hand. Their seats were directly behind that of Bark, which he occupied when not disporting himself in the stadium.

Phil and Bubb, neither of them normally to be counted among the fanatical enthusiasts of the game, nevertheless saw in the match an opportunity to express the discreet pride that Englishmen have. Phil, who remained a historian by hope, remarked that, in cricket, he could see why England once had had a revolution but not much blood had been spilt. However, that morning the two men had not had much to cheer, the balance of advantage lying with the home team; as is customary, England having squandered a few chances.

"We must break through first thing. That's our best chance," Bubb had said.

"Do you think the wicket will play more easily with time?"

"It damned well won't," snorted Bubb. "These buggers would have prepared it so it will break up by the fourth day."

"They seemed above gamesmanship and deviousness."

This elicited another sound of contempt from Bubb.

"I tell you that they would have fixed the coins with heads on both sides. This is the East, remember. Or else, a magician would have helped them win the toss, whatever was called. They had to win the toss and bat first. Their spinners must bowl last. Our only chance is to break through first thing, when the dew is still fresh on the ground and gives our quickies a chance."

Bubb's cynicism found further expression as play progressed, while Phil wondered if the dropped catches might also be attributable to the malign influence of the indigenous sorcerer who could make tails appear as heads. However, except for a few groans and a few suppressed expletives, Bubb had little initial opportunity to vent his feelings. This came when, just before lunch, an appeal by Freeman, the England fast bowler, was turned down. At first the relieved cheers of the sea of brown faces around them had smothered the dissent of the pair of Englishmen.

"Did you see that?" howled Bubb.

Those cheers had overwhelmed that remark and the several injudiciously uttered words that followed. When play and calm resumed, Bubb, losing all inhibition, had bellowed, "These bloody blighters have bribed that blind bastard."

Apart from emotion – which had been vented twice that day – Bubb seemed also to possess an alliterative eloquence that it had not hitherto been suspected he had in his repertoire. Phil did not have time to admire his companion's way with words, for they were instantaneously confronted with menacing stares and implacably hostile gazes. Their neighbours had until then been placid and had left them alone. The match, after all, had been moving at the dignified, not to say funereal, pace associated with the game; the proceedings had not merited much by way of fervour. Actually, Phil and Bubb had even been rather pleased with themselves and able to assume some superiority after the reception that had been accorded to the black England fast bowler, Wilberforce, when he appeared on the field to start the England attack.

The crowd, finding its resources of congruity stretched by this spectacle of a black man playing for England, displayed ribald merriment when Wilberforce started to measure his run.

"Who is that?" asked an incredulous voice.

"What is that?" responded another, sending the crowd into hoots of laughter

"Slavery!" someone shouted when the laughter had subsided.

"The match should be in the jungle."

"Up the trees."

"Will he get a banana when the drinks come up?"

Each remark was punctuated by a communal cackle. The taunts continued for a few minutes into play, then at the end of his over and then again at the commencement of his new one. But Wilberforce silenced them with his turn of speed. He beat the bat repeatedly and the batsmen were obviously uncomfortable. Bubb's prediction of early-morning dew was being realized and a wicket was foreseeable with every ball. By then, such was the respect Wilberforce had managed to extract from those present that, when he bowled his first bouncer, an event normally giving rise to a reflex of jeers and protests, the crowd only murmured meekly. The taunts were not heard again. Observing the scene elevated Bubb and Phil.

The crowd ignored them thereafter until Bubb's outburst. At once the placid, gentle faces took on looks of hostility, even savagery. At first hand Phil was educated on how that beautiful, heaven-blest land of legend could, when circumstances augured ill, turn upon itself. Its constituent people seemed to be able to slip off their civilizing mask whenever they perceived any challenge, however trivial. His lesson in history and contemporary politics quickly absorbed, Phil sensed real, physical danger. Bubb, realizing the enormity of his unplanned verbal outburst, had retreated into a carapace of silence. Phil followed him. Images flashed through his mind, irrational, absurd and bizarre, such as are found in times of profound stress. Horrors of the recent past persecuted him —

beatings, lynchings, sandpittings, necklaces, just the plain brutality of the newspaper reports, the stuff of a thousand gossip-ridden or rumoured stories, personal accounts, semi-veracious official bulletins, all milled in his head. But the natives did not speak; more importantly, they did not act. The tension remained, charged and awaiting detonation. Then, fatefully, Curry at mid-off chose that moment to let a drive go through his legs. No cricketer worth his salt – and of diligent application to the coaching manuals – should suffer that indignity. As Phil blessed him for demonstrating this latest falling-off from traditional standards, the stadium erupted in hooting laughter. The imagined assassins surrounding Phil and Bubb gave themselves up to uncontrollable mirth. Phil sensed deliverance as Curry looked with scarcely borne embarrassment at the grass burning under the noonday sun. Good humour had been restored. The two Englishmen were now the recipients of appreciative looks and grins. If previously they had been held responsible, for, at best, a breach of good manners or, at worst, an insult to an entire nation, they were now being congratulated for being by some means the instruments in the staging of an incident of comic ineptitude on behalf of the entire English nation.

Thereafter, as the match resumed its familiar meander, Bubb, having grown restless after attempting a couple of tentative moves towards Bark in the row in front of him, finally tapped him on the shoulder. Bark was a squat man, very dark and the owner of a toothbrush moustache. In the diplomatic silence of his mind Phil had catalogued him as a ruffian. Bark nodded to Bubb and then leant over, whispering conspiratorially.

Soon afterwards it was lunch.

"Interesting-looking chap you were trying to speak to," commented Phil as they made their way to the bar tent.

"Yes, that was Bark."

"What does he do?"

"Oh, this and that." Bubb fell silent for a moment, then said, "I think I'll get him a beer and loosen his tongue." Bubb had an expert's understanding of the flow of speech that succeeds the dissolution of discretion in the solvent of alcohol. He added, "I'm trying to find out more about the High Priest. Bark must know if anyone does."

Phil by now had come to know Bubb well enough not to be surprised at this intelligence. Why the manager of *Roll Britannia!* – concerned as he should be with the dissemination of modern British culture to the less privileged – should also interest himself with the vanishing of an exalted cleric in his host country, still less when the disappearance was not acknowledged officially and was merely the subject of rumour (relayed in Phil's instance by his cook), was a matter of specific puzzlement only to Phil, who had heard of Bubb's involvement in a large number of affairs which required strenuous exertions of the imagination to be called cultural.

Liz saw Phil and Bubb, accompanied by beer, making their way back to their seats. Play recommenced for the afternoon session and Liz, softened by the sun even in those covered stands, felt drowsy; might even have nodded off. Emmeline, her enthusiasm undimmed by food and the heat, continued with her raucous interest in the incidents of the game. A din above the ambient clamour roused Liz.

"What is happening?"

"I think they are fighting, child."

"Over what?"

"Nothing. Probably the drink has got to the brain. Oh, I say," shrieked Emmeline, her voice rising in the tones of girlish mischief, " they are thumping Bark."

"Really?"

"They are really punching him. Come on, give him a few more."

"What is happening?"

A voice behind them, hitherto unheard, piped in.

"He was not out."

"Who wasn't?" asked Emmeline sharply

"Shrieker shouldn't have given him out," another voice added. "The ball was going down the leg side."

"The bugger must be blind."

"Or bribed."

"Neo-colonialist mentality, if you ask me."

"What is happening?" demanded Emmeline

"Umpire Shrieker gave Growler out."

"Shouldn't he have?"

"No, he shouldn't. Growler was not out. He was playing forward. And the ball was going down the leg side."

Liz remained thoroughly bemused. But curiosity gnawed her and she ventured to seek a simple explanation. The excited Emmeline, like several others, was now standing on her seat and waving her arms.

"Is it bad?" Liz called above her. "I mean, Growler being out."

"Very bad. He's our most experienced batsman. We'll collapse now."

"Oh, I see." murmured Liz.

"But wait...Growler is there... Why is Growler still there?" Emmeline asked, shouting at the rows behind her.

"He was called back," said the voice that had earlier queried the umpire's visual acuity as well as his sexual orientation.

"Sainsbury called him back. A real sportsman, Sainsbury," said the voice that had previously disputed the umpire's financial rectitude.

"When all is said and done, they still have manners," said the man who had put a political gloss on the umpire's interpretation of events.

"Some of them, at least," said a more cautious spectator.

"At least when they are sober," remarked one who had been reading the football reports in British newspapers.

Emmeline, who now felt she had to instruct Liz in these mysteries, turned to her.

"Sainsbury called back Growler."

"Why did he do that?"

"Because he is a sportsman. He knew it was not out, so he overruled the umpire. Real sporting. The match is open again. If our middle holds."

Liz, feeling she should contribute to events, seized her chance.

"They have stopped punching Bark."

Emmeline agreed in tones that conveyed disappointment.

"But they are still shouting at him. Waving their fists. Go on, give him one. For my sake," she pleaded.

"What has he done?"

"I overheard these people. It seems Bark did not like Growler being called back. Started shouting that we could stand on our own feet. We didn't need their charity. Didn't they realize we had been independent for two generations? We are not the Falklands, you know. And so on. Just like that creature to bring up patriotism when we are in the middle of a crisis. So they thumped him. He got a bloody good hiding, I must say."

"Were they thumping him for his bad manners?" asked Liz, still mystified.

"No, child. We need Growler there to score for us. What is the point of patriotism when it boils no rice?"

She turned as the din recommenced. The unfortunate Bark, having been given a brief respite during which only verbal abuse was showered upon him, was being set upon again. Punches, kicks, the odd drinks can, even a bottle or two followed. Bark appeared to be fighting for his life, patriotism not having proved a sufficient refuge for him. He would surely have been badly mauled, even perhaps killed, had not a man of impressive bearing come to the edge of the mêlée and parted the crowd as if he intended to be Bark's saviour. The crowd retreated respectfully as the man went up to Bark, took him by the arm and led him away.

"But that's Mr Grunt," shouted Liz.

Emmeline had been rendered speechless by this turn of events. By the time she found voice the crowds had withdrawn to their seats and the cricket had resumed.

"Mr Grunt...", was all she could stutter, but Liz saw tears flowing down the headmaster's wife's face. Moments later Liz found Phil standing beside her.

"Hello, dear. Not too upset, I hope, by the fracas."

"I was enjoying it, actually. Good thing Growler was called back. He was not out really, don't you think?"

++++++++

III

The dinner for the two teams was held that evening at the Imperial Hotel, an institution that had seen off the Empire but still managed to retain an innate dignity. All national functions of any significance were staged there. In times of peace the President or the Prime Minister would have hosted the occasion, but the peace that had been called for the six days of the match was thought too tenuous for these dignitaries to be risked. The President, a Cambridge Blue in the 1920s, was believed to have insisted the England tour go ahead, personally guaranteeing the safety of every England player and official. Having made the country safe for Englishmen, it might have been expected that he would pay them the additional compliment of being present at a dinner given in their honour, but it had been known for months that no Government minister, given that their enemies were lying everywhere, could feel safe, even within the walls of the old Imperial.

The man chosen to be host was, in fact, the inconsequential Minister of Culture, whose portfolio, much like Bubb's, embraced culture in its widest sense. This minister was believed by most to be the most expendable member of the Cabinet. He belonged to the *None* community, but was of such low caste his status was unfathomable. He carried no clout, had no influence outside his community, and was an MP and minister solely so that fellows of his caste would feel represented and deliver without question their votes to the Government. He was of use, therefore, so long as democracy existed, but voting and elections now appeared to be historical relics and democratic practices were thought unlikely to resume in the foreseeable future. In any event, the minister was not a young man, so his future value was limited. It therefore came as no surprise that he had been ordered to attend, despite his acknowledged ignorance of all sport, and represent the nation.

All this intelligence had come to Phil and Liz from Bubb, through whom they also found themselves invited; otherwise, there was no compelling reason for a schoolmaster and his wife to find themselves at a function like this. But Bubb had used his influence on a man at the Ministry of Culture who himself was on a reciprocal social list at *Roll Britannia!*

They had all been puzzled earlier in the day as to how lax security had become at the Test Match. But that evening the authorities seemed to have resumed their wary watch on terrorism. Armed policemen milled around in the luxuriant grass of the old Imperial's gardens. The car park had been isolated and wrapped in barbed wire. Passes were scrutinized carefully and faces fitted to names. A rare white skin, coupled with an exotic name, was a considerable advantage in these circumstances. Motor bicycles and push bicycles had been banned, these being the favoured mode of transport of the two most lethal terrorist organizations, the Lions and the Panthers. The

Lions were especially feared in the period of the truce as they had opposed the staging of the Test Match. They were opposed to the game of cricket, in any event, believing it to be an unacceptable relic of the colonial past. When they eventually seized power, they proclaimed, they would make compulsory the indigenous sport in which a rubber ball is thrown to a person wielding a wooden club, which is used to strike the ball, whereupon the striker runs to his right to a base, replacing another who runs to another base also on his right. The rules and implements were simple and the game was popular in the villages from which the Lions drew their support. No one had dared yet to inform the Lions that the old imperialists and their accomplices might also possess a version of that game.

If the Lions were expected to make trouble in the week of the truce, the Panthers, who represented the minority *Er* community, and who were a considerably more opportunistic organization than the Lions (who were wont to put ideology above everything else), were expected to behave themselves. The Panthers had as their avowed aim the creation of a separate state for the *Er* people and were not averse to putting the Government in any bad light, however dimly perceptible to the observer, to further their objective. Having learned that – in general – if the weather held, the umpires were not got at and the locals did not suddenly discover a horde of bowlers of genuine pace, then England, being the stronger team, could reasonably be expected to win, the Panthers resolved the match would go ahead. It was they who had taken the initiative regarding the truce, an offer that at first had been dismissed as a cynical ruse to win time to rearm and regroup. Upon reflection, however, the Government, equally in need of respite and a boost to its image, which lately it had been able to burnish only by making murderous examples of its opponents, had cautiously agreed. The result had been a considerable coup for the Panthers and for this reason, if for no other, the Lions were expected to disrupt proceedings.

The *Ers* were locally believed to be the darker-skinned people – a belief also commonly used in identifying potential Panther membership – although Phil, Liz and Bubb, not to mention the entire England party including Wilberforce, would have been hard put to distinguish between the shades of colour in the native complexion. But that evening the *Ers* became the favoured local community as being those least likely to disrupt a Government-sponsored event. Like the whites, they were waved into the hotel grounds and ushered into the building after perfunctory inspections of credentials.

The England team stood around in little groups, not knowing very much what else to do besides drink from their glasses. The locals were in an immeasurably worse plight, for their religion and strict official instruction forbade alcohol in any form. Bubb had been hoping to introduce Phil and Liz to

Thistle, the England manager. Bubb and Thistle, who already knew each other, having met before in unspecified circumstances, renewed their acquaintance.

"Fancy meeting you here, Ken," Thistle had shouted across the room.

It was the first they knew that Bubb had been christened 'Ken'.

Meanwhile, Liz had been observing how elderly the England team seemed in contrast to the local, who, though altogether more youthful in looks, appeared to be just as mature as the visitors. She had heard this maturity being attributed to the effects of the tropical sun and heat, which, it was suggested, seemed in these climes to mature individuals as if they were fruit and vegetables – quick to grow, mature and ripen, after which they declined, shrivelled and fell. The propensity to accelerate physical ageing was a property legendarily claimed by the sun, but could the effect on human emotional maturity really be as marked, she wondered.

"What are you doing now, then, Ken?" inquired Thistle.

"Oh, this and that. Mostly that."

They both laughed.

"Keeping out of trouble?"

"Up to now."

"Something big here, is it? What is it? Bridges? Dams? Construction?"

"Actually, I run *Roll Britannia!*"

"What?"

"That's the outfit. I'm the bloke in charge of spreading British culture hereabouts."

Seizing the opportunity presented by his successful attempt at rendering Thistle speechless, Bubb introduced Phil and Liz to the manager.

"Couple of my friends here. They are teachers in a school nearby."

"Pleased to meet you. Thistle, England team manager. Were you at the match?"

"We were. Things not looking too good."

"The early advantage is theirs. There is time yet to assert ourselves, though."

Liz was interested to hear this. She had left the ground early with Phil and Bubb in order to avoid the rush, and also to be able to dress for dinner. She had not been able to ask Emmeline, who had stayed on, what the score might be but was, nevertheless, puzzled at the absence of the enthusiasm which she expected to have punctuated the closing stages. This she had put down at the time to the lack of passion generally to be found in the game of cricket. She refused to ask Phil what the result might have been as they dressed in silence. A discreet inquiry of Marie-Antoinette was not possible, as she had left early to tend to the daughter in labour. Liz continued perplexed, but knew of no practical or dignified way of finding out. It would seem extraordinary to ask people at dinner the result of a match she herself was supposed to have attended earlier in the day, and she wished she had possessed the foresight to listen to the radio.   And now she was hearing Thistle saying they had time to assert themselves.

"Sure," said Phil, "but the wicket is not going to play easy all the time, is it?"

"We expect it to start turning on the third day."

"We need then to get a good first innings score."

"Yes.   We plan to bowl them out first thing tomorrow, get stuck in, and see it at least to the end of the third day."

"Oh, so you do have a plan, do you?"

Innocent as the words were, Phil's tone of voice made Thistle grimace.   Liz, listening wondering how to break into the conversation and assuage her ignorance without making a fool of herself, was gratified to see Phil manage so effortlessly to offend someone he had just met.

"Do you think much is likely to happen next?" she asked tentatively.

Thistle seemed relieved to speak to someone apparently so innocent. "A lot will depend on the weather.   There was some moisture first thing but the atmosphere was a bit too clear for our liking. We need cloud cover."

"Are the local team any good, do you think?"

"They are pretty formidable on their home territory, with their own crowd behind them. But I must give their umpires due credit". He dropped his voice.   "That fellow Shrieker is so bad that both teams are at equal risk.   That's only fair." He giggled.

"We have a boy from the school playing in the team."

"A schoolboy? Really? Who is he?" Thistle was all curiosity.

She pointed to the local team, who stood by themselves sipping their fruit juice.

"It is him. The tall boy holding a mug of passion fruit juice."

"What the hell is the colour of passion fruit juice?"

"It's orange."

"But you said it was passion fruit juice."

"That is right. Passion fruit juice is orange."

Thistle spotted Roar. Drawing a piece of paper from his pocket, he scanned it with impatience. "He hasn't batted yet. Excuse me, I must have a word with the boys."

Phil and Bubb, who had wandered away to mingle with the guests, spotted Bark in a far corner of the room. When they reached him, Phil discovered that a black eye on a dark person is not always obvious. Bark's bulged but could not easily be put beyond physiological variation; only the grazes and bruises betrayed the history of recent violence suffered by the proprietor. Phil stayed a discreet distance from Bubb and noted that Bark did not seem too pleased to see Bubb, but nonetheless made no attempt to move away. His defensive exertions earlier in the day seemed to have rendered him weary and, no doubt, he had mixed feelings about renewing contact with the man who had supplied him with the beer that had given him the unwonted courage to stand up and defy the will of the multitude in the stadium. Bark had not enjoyed the resulting exercise in practical and vigorous democracy.

Phil overheard Bubb's solicitous greeting to Bark.

"Not to worry. I'm in one piece," replied the stoical Bark.

"I'm glad. I was hoping to have a word with you at the match but, then, after that business, it didn't seem appropriate."

"No."

Bubb, realizing an investment in a couple of beers was insufficient when it came to eliciting information of a grave nature, applied some leverage.

"It's about..." he started, before breaking off and dropping his voice to an intimate whisper while looking cautiously around, "... you know who."

Bark stood impassively, rubbing parts of his face in turn. Looked at from a distance, Phil could not help thinking that he looked uncannily like a black version of the late Chancellor of Germany who had given so much inconvenience to so many in so short a time. The moustache, the plastered hair, the wild eyes, the wounded look and the unpredictable movements had all been replicated. This was in a land that believed in reincarnation, a process that was said to take place over centuries, but Phil, for a fanciful moment, wondered if the spirit world had short-circuited the process and dropped this potential monster, harbouring as it did every known grievance, on that troubled land

"What about him?" asked Bark eventually, through clenched teeth, due to resentment or damage Phil did not know.

"Where is he?" Bubb asked anxiously.

Bark deliberated for a few moments.

"He is all right."

"He is?"

"Yes."

"Do I have your word he'll come to no harm?"

This was clearly the wrong approach, for Bark, hitherto smouldering but static, now made a move and stalked off. He might have wished to walk out of the hall and, perhaps, the hotel but, at its entrance, he was hurled to one side by a couple of armed policemen who had just entered leading the ministerial cortège. Phil knew the Minister of Culture by reputation as being a man of the people. He was, accordingly, dressed in the utmost simplicity, in a quasi-Gandhian outfit with shirt accompaniment. In effect, it was as if a bed sheet had been wrapped around him; his legs were covered; he wore shoes. The man could have passed himself off as Bark's brother and, further, Phil knew he belonged to the *None* community. *The Pedigree,* the local counterpart to *The Tatler,* had long speculated that the minister's anomalously dark skin was indicative of his lowly origins, even perhaps to be located in the *Er* community. That journal had recently run a series, as it did from time to time, on the relationship between complexion and communal membership. It seemed to be repeating the received wisdom that the *Nones* had the lightest skins and the *Ers* the darkest, with the *Ings* somewhere in between. But, within each community, the magazine speculated authoritatively, there were gradations. Thus, it was possible for a lowly member of the *None* community to be darker-skinned than one high up among the *Ings*. This intelligence must have reassured the minister, whose political position was owed entirely to his membership of a low caste among the *Nones.*

As the minister entered, the guests rose and the band, drawn from all the services to avoid charges of favouritism and minimize the risk of disaffected plotting, shuffled and struck up the national anthem. Phil recalled how, soon after they had arrived in that country, at a dance held by the local Byron Society, he and Liz had found themselves dancing. The music had stopped, to be followed by a melodious tune that had procured another dance from them. After a few minutes Liz had stopped in mid-step, whereupon Phil realized they were dancing alone, seemingly to the national anthem. He had later learned to whistle it inaccurately and unmelodiously until asked to desist by Liz on the grounds that his efforts were causing offence to Marie-Antoinette.

When the music ended, the minister sauntered to his table with Bark in close attendance, looking not unlike a sniffer dog attached for protection. When the minister had taken his place, Phil, Liz and Bubb sat down at a table near him; they could not help noticing that all those placed closest to the minister were foreigners or those who were very darkly complexioned. Bark sat beside the minister.

The truce had made the catering easier, for food could be brought up from the coast without fear of convoys being bombed en route. In past months Bang Bang prawns, to take one example cited by restaurateurs, had acquired a novel meaning on account of lorry loads from the sea being blown up. Liz had been curious about the menu and her anticipation was not disappointed. The starter followed the serving of a local liquor, *arak* – served to foreign guests only, the locals being expected to endure an officially teetotal evening – which was distilled from coconut sap or fermented rice. It looked like a rice wine – very pale, very dry, and a fair approximation, when tasted, to a bone-dry sherry. To accompany this came a dish of devilled crab served in its shell, spicy, lachrymogenic and crusty. Tears poured down Liz's face as she spooned the crab, but, as she was deeply suspicious of the purity of the iced cold water – Bubb having warned her that hotels were wont to collect tap water in bottles and stick them in the refrigerator, thereby offering chilled comfort to potentially lethal germs – she soon emptied her glass of wine, which was generously re-filled. Soon she found her head attempting to slip its moorings.

The crab shells were replaced with dishes of crisp pancake, the centre of which was filled by a fried bull's-eye egg. These were bland and crisp, and Liz was grateful for this emollient to her smarting tongue. This dish in its turn was succeeded by a main course consisting of a whole lobster in its shell from which the flesh had been removed, fried with herbs and spices and then replaced; the meat was now of a dark hue, and it sat on a bed of rice surrounded by deep fried prawns. Boiled yams, fried aubergines, poached lady's finger and a curiously lean vegetable, very like a bamboo shoot served in a sauce of its own juices and coconut milk, sat beside the lobster dish. There were several sauces, and a side dish made up of dried fish and onion with spices and herbs was also served. It was a rich and satisfying course that went with an astringent Chablis. The sea, it appeared, had been trawled and had yielded up her riches without protest. Water was taken around by the uniformed waiters but Liz, ever mindful that even the old Imperial might be subject to retrenchment and sharp practice, stuck to her Chablis, preferring a temporary loss of sobriety to permanent chronic sickness. After a brief respite, a sweet dark congener of crème caramel, made with the crystallized juice of the palm tree and virginal eggs, was served. Despite a feeling of repletion Liz campaigned through the sweet with compulsive relish, glad that only tea was to come.

The busy buzz of conversation was interrupted by the chairman of the Cricket Board asking the guests for their attention; when that was given, he introduced the guest of honour. The minister rose with an obtrusive glass of tomato juice and drank from it before commencing to speak. The assembled local press made a note of the minister's sobriety even in the face of justifiable temptation. He peered at his audience, first scowled and then beamed as if seeing a dyspeptic pang pass by. His momentary suspicion could be put down to his usually being a butt of jokes and a figure of fun, partly as a result of his office and partly through his own background and perceived lack of refinement. Despite the apparent innocuousness of his liquid refreshment, he swayed slightly.

"Honoured guests from over the seas, ladies and gentlemen. Our country is facing many…difficulties, not least from those who would like to destroy us. They call themselves…after animals but they are not animals, for, if they were – listen to me – they would…behave with the nobility of animals. They are behaving just like human beings, they…are doing things that only human beings can do. They destroy. They kill. They…subvert. They maim. What animal will do this wantonly? No – listen to me – they are…not behaving like animals at all. So, these men and women in lions' and panthers'…clothing, listen to me, we will see through your clothing, we will strip away your…masks and we will destroy you."

He paused to refresh himself with his tomato juice, and Phil idly wondered if the tomato could ferment if left to do so. Apparently fortified, the minister resumed.

"Our two countries have long histories. We go back a long time. Our country goes...back a long, long time. We had a civilization when Europe was full of barbarians...without speech and dressed in skins. Yes – listen to me – we had a noble civilization...that was laid waste by these Europeans after they had found gunpowder. We are a...noble people and a peaceful people. We preferred peace and art and culture and...meditation to war and war-like activities. So, we did not go in search of...gunpowder. It is an easy thing to make. Our children do it in their laboratories and...these terrorists do it everywhere. But we did not go in search of it. So, we were...unilaterally unarmed. Our art and culture and noble civilization were no match for...these savages from Europe with their gunpowder. Our gentle people were overrun...might was right. And then we recovered. We got back our independence. We...planned things. But those foreign ideologies came to these men in wolves'...clothing. They try to destroy us again. But we are ready. I tell you, and you listen...to me, we are ready this time. We have all the gunpowder we need this time. We...have friendly governments like Britain giving us gunpowder now. The enemy...be warned. We are keeping our gunpowder dry, but we will let it loose."

He paused to take another sip. Phil and Bubb exchanged glances. "I knew he...would compliment us eventually," murmured Bubb.

"Our two nations have many things in common. We respect animals. We have our sacred animal and our visitors pay homage to them, too, in their...own way. They have the animal in their own home, they treat it like a...member of their own family; they feed it, they look after it. They have a...Royal Society to protect animals, but, I tell you and you listen to me, their...own children have only a national society. That is how much respect they have for animals. Their own Queen has several animals in her own home...and she takes them wherever she goes. That is how much respect there is...for our Sacred Creature. So, let me tell these people who have no respect...for our Sacred Creature, that we cannot do business with them. They may...have gadgets and factories and powerful economies, and they may promise...us aid and help and even offer us gunpowder, but I can tell anyone from the...Republic of Korea at this gathering that, until they end this pogrom, this...holocaust, of the Sacred Creature, our two countries cannot have...diplomatic relations."

He paused to thump the table with his hand for appropriate effect.

"Do the Koreans play cricket, too?" whispered Liz.

"I'm sure they are working on a transistorized version of it," said Bubb, making Phil giggle and the minister look up before continuing.

"Let it not be said that our concern is only for animals. Our two nations practise charity to our kind, too. Our human rights records are an example...to the world. We lead the way in fairness and justice. We give the less...fortunate a start in life. Only today we saw the England team playing a...black man. Even the negro from Brixton has a place under the British...sun."

He paused to look defiantly at the gathering, as if inviting contradiction.

"Today we were given an example of sportsmanship, also a feature of the...shared heritage of our two nations. The splendid England captain, quite rightly called Sainsbury, summoned one of our batsmen back who had most unfortunately and incorrectly been given out."

Bubb leaned over to Phil and confided, "It is the shrewdest move an England captain has made abroad in recent years. Marvellous PR. The umpires have to play fair by us now"

The minister looked up at them sharply and then returned to his text. But he could not get any further. A loud bang convulsed the atmosphere. Liz lurched and then saw the minister stagger, his chest stained red. There were only a couple of screams and an eerie calm followed. But another bang, not as loud as the first, went off and this time pandemonium ensued.

"The alarm!" someone shouted. A waiter, who had in the meantime dropped a tray of jugs and tumblers, ran to get the fire alarm to sound.

"Switch off the lights!" someone else yelled, and the room went dark. Things might have started to settle thereafter if nothing else happened, but another bang, loud as the first, went off. Now the guests were in a state of profound panic.

"Lie on the floor!"

"Under the table!"

"Oh, my God!"

"He's hurt!"

The gathering scattered. Phil, pushed off his chair, lay on the floor. Bubb found himself seated on the lap of the Board chairman's wife; weeping quietly, she uttered no protest. Liz made her way under a neighbouring table, crawling on all fours. It was pitch dark and she did not stop until her head collided with another. The other let loose what sounded like vituperation in the local language.

"I beg your pardon," said Liz.

The voice stopped cursing and, when it resumed speaking, it was in tones of exhilarated relief.

"Oh, it is one of you. I'm so glad. I'm so relieved", it said. She could not make out the face in that intense dark underneath the table, but the voice seemed vaguely familiar; she then realized it had been perorating only minutes before.

"You are not badly hurt, then?"

"No, no, not yet. I thought those buggers had come to get me," said the minister.

"But I thought you had been shot."

"No, no, not yet."

"There were blood stains all down your shirt."

"No, no, that was just the tomato juice. Problem for the washer woman, not for me." He burst out laughing.

It was still dark but the panic was more controlled, only the occasional scream being heard.

"You are a visitor. Been long here? How do you like our country?"

"I…like it better by day and in light."

The Minister barked a short laugh.

"These things are temporary. A minor matter. I think these people are celebrating the truce, you know. Nothing to worry about. Nothing to panic about. The match will resume tomorrow as if nothing has happened."

Liz seized her chance to seek enlightenment.

"The match goes on? How many days?"

The minister sounded surprised.

"Of course it goes on. Goes on for five whole days. Lot of man-hours wasted. Not a suitable game for a developing country."

He would have given her a lecture there and then but the alarm faded and the lights came back on.

Part Two – The Second Day's Play

I

Liz sat in their dining room drinking coffee. It was 5.00 in the morning and the cool of the night was giving way imperceptibly to the first hint of the heat to come. A few hardy crows had begun a raucous chorus in the trees outside, but soon gave up as if hushed by their more decorous fellows. Liz's coffee was of the instant variety and foreign-made; preferable to the local powder, which was akin in consistency and colour to dried chilli powder and as harsh and corrosive to the stomach as yet unlined by food. This was her second cup that morning, in the hour after Phil had retired, weary and out of temper. Liz herself had had a long and unaccustomedly eventful day, and a long night to follow it, but found she was not ready to be restored by sleep. It was that way with her if the customary hour for bed had passed; it was as if a timing switch had been set and could not be altered – she had to await the next cycle. Defiance of nature was futile; only a dispiriting failure would ensue. She consumed caffeine, therefore, to hold fatigue at bay.

They had returned home late. After the excitement of the blast at the Imperial, most of the guests had felt impelled to linger and share their experiences. That it had been due to fireworks, let off presumably by a group of disaffected mischief-makers, had not become apparent to the guests until they had picked themselves up, dusted themselves down, inspected one another, glanced at the still-intact ornate furnishings of the Imperial and been reassured that damage to persons and property could have been infinitely worse. Yet, for all that, the disarray had been considerable, and the stampeding guests had been able to provide the assembled photographers with evocative pictures for what might otherwise have been a thin, peacetime issue of the newspapers on the morning after. When the all-clear had been given, the minister had insisted on holding a press conference and being filmed by television cameras, his red-stained shirt and robe conspiring to achieve a bloodless publicity coup, to the breakfast-time annoyance of his colleagues who had sent him into that place solely in order to avoid the danger of being shot at themselves.

The management of the Imperial, conscious of that great hotel's history and its role in past campaigns of warfare – it had been a rendezvous for British officers in the Boer War, the Great War and the Second World War; four Victoria Crosses decorated the men among those who had fallen, and their names were listed in the Roll of Honour mounted in the foyer – insisted on serving brandy to the survivors of that night's action. The exigencies of presumed warfare meant the official prohibition on alcohol was rescinded so that local guests could accept the Imperial's gracious gesture of reparation. The minister himself had risen and announced that, as a tribute to the two great nations' never-ending battle against evil, he was ordering that brandies be drunk.

Not a little shaken, Phil and Liz had returned home well after midnight. They had not spoken, but both were preoccupied and needed the comfort of silence. Until that night the civil war, involving as it did the issues of communalism, race and language, had been a distant happening. They had felt as if they were observers, spectators even, who could have been watching some war film. The issues were as remote to them as, say, the causes of the Peninsular War or attitudes to the Kaiser. If they had been moved, as they sometimes had been, by stories of individual heroism, sacrifice, savagery and brutality, those transient emotions had been washed away by the waves of tedious anxiety that broke upon the routine of a young couple. But that night, they both felt, all that had changed; they had now been co-opted into the *dramatis personae.*

Back home, Phil had poured himself another brandy, but, when he had offered the bottle to Liz, she refused. The feelings of post-prandial nausea, suppressed by the blasts and the events that followed, had been revived as the crisis had receded; further alcohol would have been unnecessary provocation to her system.

"I'm going to make coffee," she had said, eliciting a disdainful look from Phil. He was of the decided opinion that nothing kept sleep away as successfully as coffee.

In the kitchen she found that, at that moment, she could not stomach coffee, either, so she boiled the water, poured it into a mug and dissolved in it two teaspoonfuls of bicarbonate of soda. She then rejoined Phil for the couple to continue with their silence.

It was cool then – in fact, the chilliest part of the day. The sun had long departed but its warmth would linger for several more hours after it disappeared, to dissipate slowly before a new sun rose to heat the land again at dawn. It was quiet, too. Their house was detached, situated several yards from the dormitories in which the boys slept. The only noise to be heard at that hour was of some solitary bird of the night as it winged its way to a tryst somewhere towards the hills. They had not appreciated such peace outside for several months. Guns and bombs had been cast aside for now; the sounds of destruction had been stilled. For that moment, the couple, engaged in their dialogue of silence, moved to forget about one another, and each listened intently to the world outside clothed in its specious calm.

Half an hour later Phil went off to their room, leaving Liz in her chair in the dining room. As he went, he appeared as if he were about to say something but aborted the process. As she sat wondering, she was suddenly jerked upright, causing her to spill the by now tepid fluid over her lap, as the school bell went off. Normally it was meant, in the hurly-burly of the day, to signify by its sounds to staff and boys when each period of study was at an end. Rung by the oldest servant in the school – he had succeeded his father in post and had served for over fifty years – it was last pealed after prep each weekday; it had no business going off at that hour to shatter the pre-dawn calm.

Legend encrusted that bell. Howling, the current incumbent in the post of bell-ringer, if accosted on a day before he had gone to drink, would, for the price of a glass of *arak*, recount how he had once, a long time ago, apprehended two boys in the act of illicitly ringing the bell at night; it had been on the occasion of the school's big match. One boy had grown up to become the Prime Minister while the other was now the Bishop. They had been spared punishment on account of the occasion being a very special one, and Howling, otherwise a ferocious prosecutor, had been prepared to overlook the misdemeanour, mitigated as it was by high spirits. The bell was off limits to all except Howling, and its venerable structure, which had seen generations of boys metamorphose into men by its sounds, seemed to many to encase in alloyed steel the ageless values that the school upheld. For the duration of two world wars, which had run their course in faraway places, Howling and, before him, his father had also assumed the grim burden of tolling the bell whenever the school had learned it had lost one of its sons on the field of battle. But now, as the noise of violence cultivated at home reverberated in Howling's ears, he did not have to undertake that additional grim duty; old boys of the school did not die fighting civil wars.

To Howling, the bell was as much an extension, an appendage, of his body as it was also a virtual family heirloom. He had no son, so when he had tolled his last peal no blood of his would course in the arms that would be called upon to continue performing what to him was a quasi-devotional act. But Howling contrived to avoid thinking that far ahead. Indeed, in more recent months, being much preoccupied by what he perceived to be the change in timbre of the tone that emanated from the old bell, he had consulted matron in the sick bay in case his hearing had approached terminal decline ahead of his body. But matron had put his mind at rest by assuring him that she, too, had noticed the sound had changed but feared to mention it lest it be thought her hearing was going with age as well. Sombrely they had discussed the issue and had concluded that the extraneous, alien sound of gunfire and bomb had made an impact on the bell, that it was no longer itself, and that it also probably pined for the old days as much as they did; always provided, of course, that it was not their own ears that had been affected by the clamour of violence from without.

But to Phil and Liz, as they ran to their respective windows, the bell's tones sounded alarmingly clear and stark. By day, from any window facing the quadrangle, they had an unobstructed view of the bell. By the murky pre-dawn light they could discern a solitary figure pulling at the rope. The figure did not appear steady and even to their untutored eyes it seemed to lack the sobriety necessary to effect a bell sound satisfactorily. Without need for conscious thought on their part they simultaneously concluded that the figure could not represent Howling, who, whatever degree of drunkenness might have afflicted him, was always singularly capable of tolling that bell – indeed, was believed able to make it ring even when only a sleepwalking automaton. Proof for their view was adduced in the shape of a silhouette of another figure that was seen advancing – shouting and waving its hands – on the unidentified bell-ringer. This was unmistakably Howling, running in protest. They watched as Howling made vigorous remonstrance, and then, feeling tired again as the stray excitement of the incident palled, and somewhat disapproving of the inopportune schoolboy prank, they made as if to withdraw.

No sooner had they attempted this than they became aware of a detonating altercation. Howling, normally to be trusted to despatch any such miscreant with summary justice, appeared now to be out of his depth. The voices outside, though still indistinct, grew louder. From their windows they noticed that the lights had gone on in several houses and that two or three housemasters were looking out of their upstairs windows. Outside they saw that a third figure had by now joined the squabbling pair. One of this trio, presumably the loser in some three-cornered bout that had evidently taken place, was lying on the ground. Phil and Liz still could make no sense of the yet unresolved fuss. This was, after all, no monastery but a school full of red-blooded youths with a natural propensity for healthy mischief. No one could have appreciated this better than Howling from his vantage of years at the school, and Phil cursed him with feeling for keeping him away from his bed. Despite the vigorous noises still issuing from the scene, they were preparing to withdraw from the windows yet again when their ears were assailed by a violent knocking at their front door.

When Phil opened the door, Emmeline Grunt, in a large tent-like housecoat and sporting great distress, stood outside.

"It's you, Mrs Grunt. What's the matter? Come in."

"What has happened?" called out Liz as she made for the door.

Mrs Grunt struggled to find speech.

"It's R...Roar. He is ringing the bell."

"What?"

"It's Roar. My God, he's drunk!"

"Good God!"

"What are we to do? The shame."

Phil rushed out into the quadrangle, in a far corner of which stood the bell. Liz and Mrs Grunt followed at a more decorous pace. They came upon Mr Grunt remonstrating with Howling, with Roar seated on the ground with his head in his hands.

Howling, taking no notice of the recent arrivals, continued with his savage denunciation in a local language while Roar looked up, pointed in turn to each of the spectators and burst out laughing, his bouts of merriment petering out as the residual alcohol overpowered his system and he collapsed once more.

"Come with me," ordered Mr Grunt, advancing on the boy.

"Bugger off!" shouted the newly emboldened Roar.

Mr Grunt shrank back as if to avoid a viper spitting venom.

"The language! My God!" wailed Mrs Grunt. "He's so drunk."

"Yes, yes, we know he is drunk," replied Mr Grunt impatiently. "But we don't want everyone to know about that. We'll take him to our place. Come with us, Roar."

Roar remained inert, now disinclined even to swear drunkenly at his headmaster. Howling came up to him and pulled him roughly by the arm. Roar repulsed his advance.

"Don't be rough with him. Let me try," volunteered Phil.

"No, sir. He needing thundering slap. That put the drink out," advised Howling, finding the English tongue.

"No, you silly man. The boy has had a hard time," scolded Mrs Grunt. Soothingly she turned to Roar. "Come with us, Roar."

Roar did not react to Phil at first, but gentle tugging on the latter's part coupled with cooing encouragement in the background from Mrs Grunt led to gradual success. Like some wounded calf elephant Roar got ponderously to his feet;

unsteady, tottering, swaying, but eventually reaching the upright.

"That's right, steady," said Phil taking his arm. Roar followed uncertainly.

"Bring him to our house," ordered Mr Grunt.

They followed behind the odd couple, Howling bringing up a resentful rear.

"He pull my bell," he complained.

Mrs Grunt stopped and gave her voice a vigorous airing in a native tongue. Even to Liz, who was almost totally ignorant of the language, what she said sounded impressively clear, crisp and convincing. She was glad she was not at the receiving end like Howling, who shrank like a salted snail and was visibly reduced.

"I told him, if he said anything about this to anyone, he'll be sacked, thrown out of his cottage and his pension cancelled," said Mrs Grunt grimly, turning to Liz and feeling she ought to translate the gist of her remarks.

"It is not like Roar at all," said Liz.

"It is not him, child. It is our enemies. They have put the evil eye on him, you know. They are so jealous of his success, and what it means to us."

"But how did he get to drink? I mean, we saw him at the party. He was drinking fruit juice, I'm sure of that. I even pointed him out to someone."

"Somebody must have given him drink."

"Well, they gave us all a brandy after the bomb...the fireworks went off."

"Not one brandy, child. Many brandies. I tell you what I think. It's that cunning devil Bark, I think. I'm sure it is. It must have been Bark."

They had by now reached the headmaster's house, the five of them, Howling having dissolved noiselessly into the night. Roar was now more amenable and, when Phil had laid him on the sofa, he moulded himself onto its contours.

"What do you do for a drunken man?" Mrs Grunt whispered to Phil.

"I...I don't know. Not much, I expect. They are usually allowed to sleep it off. That's the best thing." He turned to Liz for support, but she possessed little first-hand knowledge of the management of acute drunkenness.

"Can't we somehow get the alcohol out?" asked Mr Grunt. "I mean, the trouble comes only with the alcohol reaching the brain."

"I think Mr Grunt means an antidote," suggested Liz.

Phil turned sharply on her. " I gathered that. He's hardly expecting Roar to be held upside down and the drink shaken out of him. We could send for a doctor, of course."

Mrs Grunt seemed startled into further speech.

"No, no, not a doctor," she pleaded.

"Why ever not?"

"You won't understand. He is an *Ing*."

"I think we can trust the doctor," intervened Mr Grunt. "He's been with the school for years. He's an old boy."

"You can't trust anyone these days. He's an *Ing.* He'll spread stories. He'll harm you," wailed Mrs Grunt.

"They have their ethics. They can't talk about their patients in public. They will be struck off."

"But Roar is not a patient. He's only drunk."

"I think we will send for a doctor," persisted Mr Grunt.

"No, I won't allow it. Enough trouble has been made already. All this is your fault. Why did you have to save that man Bark at the match?"

"He was getting hammered. He might have got killed."

"So what?"

"Haven't you got any mercy, woman?"

"I have only your interest at heart."

"Tell your heart to listen to your head. You might learn some Christian charity that way. But you must know and, if you don't know, I'll tell you. I need Bark."

Phil and Liz had been listening with some embarrassment to this domestic altercation, fully aware that, but for the transient grace of God, they could have swapped places with the Grunts. By now Roar appeared fast asleep, but, intrigued by Mr Grunt's last remark, they remained behind and settled to watch a first-class argument catch fire.

"You need Bark!" retorted Mrs Grunt with incredulity. "Don't talk cock."

"Don't talk to me like that."

"Why can't I talk to you like that? You are not my headmaster.," replied Mrs Grunt heatedly.

She turned to the awed couple and, pointing a derisory finger at Mr Grunt, said mockingly, "He needs Bark! The man is doing everything to destroy him, and he says he needs the man. Where are your senses? What you need is for your head to be opened and for a loose screw to be found and tightened."

Mr Grunt pursed his lips and screwed up his eyes in the face of this onslaught from his wife in front of outsiders.

Sighing, he said, "I need him because he brings me luck."

The quiet tone of his voice seemed to halt his wife in her tracks. He turned to address Phil and Liz.

"On the surface of things, Mr Bark seems to be against me and seeking my downfall. But we cannot go just by what is on the surface. I have analysed the situation and I have also taken expert advice. Mr Bark brings me good fortune and there is no doubt about that."

Mrs Grunt recovered her voice.

"Who gave you expert advice?"

"The Master Mystic."

"You consulted him?"

"I did. I showed him my palm and he also cast a fresh horoscope and gave me a reading. Mr Grunt, he said, there is a short, dark man whom you see as your enemy. Be assured: that man's actions can only bring you benefit. It is written in your stars."

Phil and Liz, who had till then not wished to intrude into this private confrontation, now felt able to speak.

"Really?" asked Phil.

"How is that possible?" queried Liz.

The headmaster seemed pleased with the interest he was generating.

"You see, it is like this. Our lives and our actions are governed by our own stars. You accept that?"

"Yes," replied Liz readily, while Phil remained circumspectly silent.

"But, you see, that is only half correct. Our stars cannot act solely in isolation. What really happens is that our stars interact with the stars of other people we get involved with. Does that make sense to you?"

"Oh, yes," replied Liz.

"So, it stands to reason, does it not, that, whatever might be the superficial actions of an individual, what really matters is how his underlying stars are influencing the stars of others."

"You mean, things may be good or bad on the surface, yet underneath the exact opposite may be happening?"

"Exactly. A man might appear to be your sworn enemy, yet his mere presence in your circle may be influencing your fortunes in a beneficial way."

"Is that how they see things here?"

"That is correct. We must not go by superficial happenings alone but must seek a deeper understanding."

Phil, whose respectful attention to his headmaster's utterances had hitherto been tinged with scepticism, found the last point of interest.

"I suppose it is like the consciousness and unconsciousness. Events in the consciousness may be the exact opposite of what is desired in the unconsciousness."

As Mrs Grunt spoke, her voice had not entirely been relieved of tones of scorn.

"Talking about the unconscious," she said, "don't you think we might all get some sleep? We have been up all night and there is a very busy day tomorrow...today, I mean."

"He's sound asleep," remarked Liz, looking at the reclining Roar.

"Poor boy. And he is expecting to bat today. I hope he will be well," Mrs Grunt said to them, and then, pointing to Mr Grunt, added, "You must ask him what good fortune is coming to him when Roar is made drunk by his enemy the night before he plays his first test innings."

Leaving Roar with the Grunts they returned to their own home, for Phil to go to bed and to sleep and for Liz to sit in the dining room and line her stomach with coffee. With sleep no longer attainable, all she could do was to await the dawn.

At six o'clock she was joined by Marie-Antoinette.

"Good morning, Missy. You up with the crows. You not sleeping well, Missy?"

"Not sleeping at all, Marie-Antoinette."

"Oh, my, my. Poor Missy. Was stomach upsetting by rich food?"

"That was the least of it. There was the blast from the fireworks."

"Oh, they playing the fool, Missy. Real war stopped for moment, so like boys they play-acting."

"It was frightening when it happened."

"Not to worry, Missy. No harm done. Big hotel still standing."

"Things calm outside?"

Oh, very calm, Missy. All so peaceful. Fish and vegetable lorries coming up without problems."

"So the markets will be well stocked."

"Yes, Missy."

"And your daughter, I forgot to ask?"

"Water no burst yet. Only waiting and seeing possible."

"I hope it will be quick."

"I hope so, too, Missy. But it is first baby. Take time. But if we lucky baby born before match over."

"You don't suppose the peace will last?"

"No, Missy. This is the drought before the monsoon pouring down. Gunfire start as match stop."

"You happy with how the match is going?"

"They say on radio we doing well. But four more days left. Plenty more balls."

"Tell me, Marie-Antoinette, what do you do to make a drunken person sober?"

"You get drunk, Missy?"

"Not me."

"Master sir get drunk?"

"Not him. I am just asking generally."

"Not much to do, Missy. Time must pass. But in our village we grab drunken man and make him drink lots and lots of water."

"He'll be sick."

"That's why water poured down, Missy. Water bringing up *arak* and toddy and drinks, and man getting less drunk and going to sleep."

"Bit strange they have not discovered anything simpler for such a common condition."

"You mean, Missy?"

"I mean like aspirin for headache."

"But, Missy, headache come afterward. It is God getting revenge for man's stupid behaviour."

Marie-Antoinette left to busy herself in the kitchen doing myriad things that Liz could not imagine needed doing. It was a mystery of insoluble proportions to Liz that, in a kitchen here that was almost as well equipped as one in England, the two of them together found more occupation than the average English housewife; a kind of tropical Parkinson's Law seemed to apply.

Wearily, Liz sat watching Marie-Antoinette go about her work. More solid physical vigour than conspicuous intelligence or imagination was in evidence. It seemed appropriate, in a land where the heavy-footed bullock still resisted the subtle creep of mechanization, that primitive methods continued to pervade the kitchen. Several cups of coffee had put Liz on edge, and irritability was now becoming grafted onto fatigue as she observed the clanging in the kitchen.

She was startled into attention by an intemperate knocking on the front door. Going there, she found Mrs Grunt, fully dressed now and also wearing concern on her large and mobile face.

"Oh, my God! Roar..."

"What's happened?"

"He is very sick. He is groaning, child. He is in an awful way."

"I'll come."

She hesitated and then, making her mind up, rushed to waken Phil. For once he was grumpy, large quantities of drink and excitement having deprived him of his refreshing quota of sleep. However, moving swiftly into his clothes, he accompanied his wife to the Grunts'. There they found Mr Grunt solicitously standing beside a recumbent Roar, who was holding his head and uttering pathetic groans.

"His head is bursting, he says. When we gave him an aspirin he was sick all over," explained Mr Grunt.

"He can't see at all. And his stomach is jumping up and down," said his wife.

Phil had no trouble making a swift diagnosis.

"He has a hangover."

"Oh, is it serious?" asked Mrs Grunt.

"Not serious at all. It will go away in a few hours."

"But he'll be batting in a few hours," protested Mr Grunt.

"What can we do?" asked his wife.

"You see, it is caused by lack of fluid. Dehydration," explained Phil. "The alcohol has mopped up the water in the body. He needs to take in some fluids."

Mrs Grunt ran to the refrigerator to pour a tumblerful of water.

"I think he'll need much more than that."

"He'll be sick if he drinks more," countered Mrs Grunt.

"Isn't there something else?" asked Mr Grunt.

"Something hot and spicy might work," suggested Phil, working from first principles.

"Like what?"

"A raw egg with chilli, perhaps," offered Phil recklessly.

"My God!" cried Mrs Grunt, shocked. "He'll get blisters everywhere inside."

Liz, who had been observing this irresolution, suggested they bring in Marie-Antoinette. This was an unexpected proposal and no one could quickly think of an objection. Marie-Antoinette was actually found lurking outside the headmaster's front door and was able to accept Liz's invitation with alacrity.

Once they had reached Roar, Marie-Antoinette took charge of proceedings.

"The poor boy," she clucked. "Why did he have to do it while playing in important match?"

"He didn't do it," retorted Mrs Grunt. "It was done to him."

"God, what a sin. Who will be so cruel?"

"Never mind all that," intervened Mr Grunt. "What can you do?"

"In our village we see men all the time like this, especially the morning after pay day. It is the poison in drink that cause headache, bellyache, heartache and so on..."

"What do you do?" demanded Mr Grunt impatiently.

"We give them a little more to drink."

"What?"

"A little more, only a little more."

"But where can we find something at this hour? We do not touch it ourselves," rasped Mr Grunt.

"If I could be of help," offered Phil.

"You keep drink in your house?" asked his headmaster.

"Only a little for medicinal purposes."

"Thank you very much. It was a very kind offer. But I do not want the rules of the school broken. It is all right for you. You are a visitor and some of our honoured visitors cannot sometimes help it; they need a little medicine now and again. But we have had enough trouble already. Lot of embarrassment to the school. The Board of Governors will be very upset. They may want a few sackings if we are not careful. So, I cannot accept your kind offer. We must use only a legal source of alcohol. But I think I know what to do."

He withdrew into his study and re-emerged after a few minutes with a sealed envelope in his hand.

"Marie-Antoinette," he called out. Turning to Phil, he asked, "I hope I can borrow her for a few minutes. Marie-Antoinette, go to the chaplain's room and ask him to come here. And make sure he brings the bottle unopened."

As Marie-Antoinette sped off with the note, Mr Grunt turned to Phil and Liz and, with that twitch of muscle that was his approximation to a smile, said, "I don't want the diluted stuff he gives to the boys in chapel. I said it was for medicinal purposes."

++++++++

II

Feeling fatigued after these unexpected and seemingly endless series of bizarre incidents, Liz decided she did not wish to attend the second day's play in the Test Match. She thought it advisable to rest, and, in any event, there were costumes to be gathered for the old-boys'-day inter-house drama contest to be held at the school that evening. Moreover, Emmeline had told her that she felt her place as a wife that day was to sit next to the headmaster. Mr Grunt, despite the appearance of calm control and authority, had evidently been

77

shaken by the recent turn of events, and his wife's desire was to lend support by his side. Liz suspected Emmeline's real concern might be more to prevent her husband's charity getting the better of him; on the second and subsequent days, Mrs Grunt would ensure that the hated Bark was left to suffer whatever fate had planned for him.

Phil and Bubb took the places they had occupied the day before. A cloudy covering over the ground already promised more for England on that second morning; Thistle's prayers had evidently been answered. The England fast bowlers could reasonably be expected to be revitalized in these conditions, and an England breakthrough seemed foreseeable – and before the morning had grown much riper.

But hardly had they sat down to negotiate their opening mugs of beer when Phil felt a tapping on his shoulder. It was his headmaster, and Phil rose to acknowledge him.

"Could I have a word with you?"

Phil accompanied him out of the stadium and to the verge of the car park.

"We have a big problem."

"Sorry to hear that."

"It is Roar."

"Hasn't he recovered on the communion wine?"

"He is better. But he is still...what would you say?...lethargic, reflexes not working too well, co-ordination suspect..."

"You mean, he may not be up to it."

"This is a Test Match, you know. All your cylinders must fire."

"True. But, you see," said Phil, dropping his voice, "a hangover takes time to go away."

"You can't ask the Test Match to wait while what you call a hangover passes. It is only rain and bad light that can delay play. Have you anything to suggest?"

"What about a doctor?"

The headmaster raised a warning hand.

"No doctors. If the school doctor can't be trusted, how can we trust anyone on the ground?"

Phil thought for a moment.

"Would you mind if I consult my friend Bubb?"

"Bubb?"

"Chap I'm sitting with. He manages *Roll Britannia!*"

"You think he might know a British doctor?"

"He might."

With the headmaster's approval Phil approached Bubb.

"You mean the chap is ill? Why don't they get a doctor?"

"There are complications. They don't want a local doctor involved."

"Don't tell me the little bugger has caught the pox. What about the England physio?"

"I think it is his mind that needs a bit of stimulation, not his body."

"I tell you what. I'll take a look at him."

They went back to the headmaster.

"You mean, you want to examine him yourself?" he asked. "Are you medically trained?"

"I've done a bit of healing in my time," replied Bubb cheerfully.

The headmaster took the two men into a side room annexed to the local team's dressing room. Roar was lying on a divan on his side, his eyes closed, his hands to his head, which was covered with a wet towel, looking for all the world like a beauty of a bygone age awaiting revival by smelling salts. He did not look at all like a man who could get the hundred runs hoped for by Marie-Antoinette.

"How's the sleeping beauty, then?" asked Bubb.

Roar opened his eyes and purred softly.

"Where's the pain, then? Tell uncle Bubb."

Roar pointed to his head. Bubb inspected him closely and, then, straightening, drew Phil to a side and whispered, "If I didn't know the strict customs around here I would have bet the blighter was recovering from a good old soaking of his insides."

"I'm afraid you would have been right."

"The little beggar! When did it happen?"

"Last night. He has received some first aid."

"Only time is of any curative value in these cases. But you have no use for that. Time being of the essence, I propose a drastic remedy."

The headmaster intervened anxiously.

"Remedy, Mr Bubb?"

"It's nothing. I carry a few tablets with me. Here they are." He took a small package from an inside pocket and, handing it to Roar, said, "Take it and you will feel like a new man."

They returned to their seats but, when the time came, no player appeared on the ground. The hour being early and the good humour still unsullied, the crowd generously granted that play was being determined by the umpires', and not the ground, clocks. The playing conditions, the cloud cover apart, appeared perfect. A few more minutes went but there was still no player stirring. The good humour soon began to evaporate, and a slow handclap commenced. The insidious clapping provoked officialdom, and an apologetic voice promised play soon. The handclaps were now translated into boos; small ones at first, but they grew in sound and, eventually, vociferous full-throated ululations shook the rafters. Officialdom returned and said in mitigation that play would be extended at the end of the day. This remark served only to inflame the crowd, and for a few minutes giant boos dominated all other sounds of expressed displeasure. It was more or less a fraud for, as everyone knew, in all tropical countries the sun sets rapidly, fleeing as if to keep a date somewhere else. Light is quickly lost and the ball soon becomes unplayable. Rarely does play continue even to six o'clock. By now, communal anger had completely driven out any remaining vestige of good humour but, fortunately, it was too early in the day for too many illicit bottles of beer and arak to have been consumed. Nonetheless a few habitués gathered armfuls of cans and bottles to throw at the edge of the boundary. More of the spectators turned to music and the bands in the stadium struck up incongruously jolly tunes. Phil and Bubb listened to repeated renditions of *For he's a jolly good fellow, It's a long way to Tipperary,* and *Roll out the barrel.*

"What's happening?" inquired Phil.

"Perhaps there are a few more hangovers we don't know about," suggested Bubb.

"There must be a good reason for the delay. I was at a match once when one umpire was taken ill and they spent ages looking for a replacement."

"Not as easy as changing misshapen balls, I expect."

"Do you think Shrieker might be having a hangover?"

"I hope not. He had trouble enough seeing when he was presumably cold sober."

As the first half hour passed with still no sign of impending play, tension rose still further among the crowd. To help defuse this a juggler took up a position on the boundary edge in front of Phil and Bubb; some yards to the left of him, a man in drag and on stilts paraded himself; to the right, a man with a small monkey on each shoulder started singing tunelessly but without seeming to annoy the monkeys unduly. The atmosphere soon took on the elements of a funfair; the crowd broke out of their seats, and the restraints and dignified formalities of a cricket match were in danger of being lost. As if in some desperate attempt to restore order, the public announcer reappeared, but he was roundly booed. Unabashed, he stood at his station and, when the noise subsided, asked Mr Bubb to report to the England dressing room.

As Bubb rose in his seat the spectators broke into cheers in which Phil, in a spirit of mischief, joined.

"Twelfth man!" someone shouted.

"He'll play a match-saving innings."

"Good luck!"

In the midst of this laughter, Bubb, normally so self-possessed and confident, looked embarrassed. Wearing a cotton short-sleeved shirt with a loud floral pattern, his red face and bald head gleaming in the heat, he made his way through the crowd.

"Now they have got their hero, play will soon start," announced the man in front of Phil, and they all laughed again.

Left alone, Phil felt in need of the company of a drink, but was too shy to move lest he provoke further ribaldry. He fretted for a few minutes longer but, then, able to contain neither thirst nor curiosity, got up abruptly so as to forestall mockery and succeeded in moving out without exciting comment. On his way to the bar, to his surprise, he glimpsed Bubb's figure through the open door not of the England but the local team's dressing room. He appeared to be in negotiations of some kind. Intrigued, Phil postponed the purchase of his beer and made his way there himself. Although no one made as to challenge him, he thought it prudent to stand outside the door and eavesdrop on what now appeared to be animated discussion involving Bubb, Thistle, the local team manager and umpire Shrieker.

"Tell us what is wrong with Mr Freeman," demanded the local team manager, Baying.

"Tell us," echoed Shrieker.

"Freeman is indisposed," said Thistle defensively.

"But you can tell us what is wrong with him."

"I've told you, he has an upset stomach."

"Where is he?" demanded Baying.

"He's at the team hotel."

"He's at the hotel because he has an upset stomach!" cried Baying derisively. " What nonsense is this? It is like going to hospital for a cold."

"Or going to the doctor's for a scratch," put in Shrieker.

"Look, Mr Thistle, if we all stayed at home for an upset stomach, nothing will get done in this country. Upset stomachs are as common as flies."

"Or ants."

"Yes. Flies or ants. Was Mr Freeman drinking?"

"Oh, no. Freeman does not drink to excess. He took just a drink or two to be sociable."

"Then, perhaps, you would like to complain about the food that was given last night. It was too rich, perhaps."

"Or infected."

Thistle looked exasperated. "Look, Mr Baying and Mr Shrieker, we are not complaining about the food or drink or indeed our treatment. It has been excellent. Your hospitality cannot be bettered, in fact. We have rarely enjoyed ourselves so much. But Freeman is not well. He is not fit to play. We are asking to be allowed a substitute. The rules allow that."

"Aha, Mr Thistle. These are not rules. They are laws. Very different thing. The laws allow the other team a discretion. We are exercising that discretion. Are we not right, Mr Shrieker?"

"Quite right, Mr Baying. The team opposite has a discretion. It can say yes or it can say no to a request for a substitute."

"But it is usually agreed to on the nod; isn't that so, Bubb?" Thistle turned pleading to Bubb.

"It certainly is. There is usually no problem about allowing a substitute."

"But these are not usual circumstances, Mr Thistle. Yesterday your team, and I hope I am not being rude saying this, did not field very well. Perhaps you have second thoughts about Freeman. Perhaps you want fielder who will stop the ball rather than letting it through his legs."

"May I remind you that it was Curry, not Freeman, who let the ball go through his legs. And why would we need someone who, in any case, cannot bowl? We would be mad to let go Freeman, who is our main bowler."

At this point, as the voices ceased, Phil looked up to see Thistle and Bubb conferring in earnest whispers. Bubb spotted Phil and beckoned to him. Phil entered the precincts of the dressing room – territory that he had always been told should be treated as consecrated – uneasily. The two local men looked sharply at him but Thistle, with whom Phil had not got on terribly well the night before, seemed relieved.

"Can you help break this deadlock?" asked Thistle.

"I...couldn't help overhearing part of your conversation just now," said Phil in some bewilderment," but why don't you just show Freeman to them?"

"There you are," said Baying in triumph. "Your own side says so."

"Freeman is too ill."

"With a stomach upset? Come, come, Mr Thistle. In this climate stomach upset is either so trivial you take no notice or so serious you are fighting for your life in hospital. No one lies in his own home with it."

"Or his own hotel."

"Surely some trained person can take a look at him," suggested Phil innocently, only to be astonished to elicit a look of pure hatred from Thistle.

"Our physio can take a look at him," offered Baying.

"There's nothing wrong with his muscles."

"We can get down a doctor, then. Can I send for one?"

"No. I'm not letting any of you disturb Freeman. I must say, I'm very disappointed at your attitude. A simple request turned down."

"Only at our discretion. We are keeping within the laws of the game."

"And I, as the umpire, say the laws must be obeyed at all times."

"Very well. We shall take the field with ten men. But we shall not agree to make up for lost time at the end of the day."

"That's all right, Mr Thistle," said Baying sweetly. "We have got our runs. You must get yours in your own time."

Thistle stormed out of the dressing room; Phil and Bubb followed. He marched in the direction of the England dressing room and the two expatriates, their services still not evidently discharged, went behind him.

A small, expectant crowd awaited them there. Sainsbury – tall, bearded, uncertain – looking not unlike an earnest social worker, stepped anxiously forward.

"Any luck?" he asked.

Thistle shook his head. "They want to see him."

"But why?"

"They suspect a fiddle."

"For God's sake, we just need a substitute fielder. He won't be batting or bowling."

"You can't shake them. Freeman seen, substitute yes; Freeman unseen, substitute no."

"What are we to do?"

"Play one short or concede the match."

"I suppose we can't appeal to the umpire's' sympathy."

"No luck there, I'm afraid. Shrieker was actually egging Baying on."

"Damn!"

Thistle turned to the group. "You boys have any ideas? Ken, you were always good in a tight spot. Haven't lost your touch, I hope."

"No, I hope not. But, Thistle, why don't you take up Phil's suggestion and show them Freeman. They see him and you get your substitute.

Thistle pondered things and then slowly shook his head – a motion that reminded Phil of a monitor lizard surveying its prey.

"We can't do that. Freeman is not here."

"Not here? Where is he?"

"He's gone. Taken away. Kidnapped."

"Good God! Who...when did it happen?"

"Last night. Or, more precisely, early this morning."

"How do you know he was kidnapped?"

"Keep your voice down. No one else is supposed to know about it. The Panthers have got him."

"The Panthers? You mean they just came in and seized him?"

"It didn't happen exactly like that. Well...it is a long and somewhat embarrassing story. It was like this. At the party last night I got talking to a lady...your wife, I believe...who said a boy from your school was playing for the locals. We thought we would have a lark. I told the boys. They seized the lad soon after the blackout...you know, soon after the alarm went...and purely in fun...a lark, you understand...we offered...we gave...well, we persuaded the boy to have a drink or two..."

"How many?" demanded Phil.

"Well, a few. Anyway, that is not the point. The boy was a virgin as far as drink was concerned...untouched by drink, as it were... How were we to know, and, anyway, it went to his head. He became merry and then he became drunk. Then he became dead drunk. We stopped before he became dead, thank heaven, but I admit we had gone much too far. In a strange land, too. Who knew if there could be some law against making people drunk? We thought we could be locked up, flogged, deported, humiliated...you know what the press would have done with a story like that? We panicked. We didn't want to leave the boy lying there in case he choked or something. We would have become murderers as well as common or garden felons."

"The 'we' is strong. I take it you were heavily involved yourself, Thistle," said Bubb severely.

"I admit it. But it was only a lark. I swear we didn't force much by way of the booze. It was just the boy was unused to it."

"I wonder how many wronged women have had that said against them."

"But, look here, it could have happened to any of us anywhere. It just had to happen in this bloody country. Anyway, what were we to do? We could hardly have carried this semi-corpse back to his team-mates. And, in any case, they had all dispersed. There were about half a dozen of us with this inebriated, comatose schoolboy. We didn't even know where his school was. It was utterly chilling."

"What happened then?"

"We saw this man standing outside the entrance to the hotel. He looked like an ordinary-looking native, short and dark, but with a distinctive moustache, like young Adolf if he had got at the boot polish."

"Bark!"

"Beg your pardon?"

"That was Bark. We know him."

"Do you? Really? Well, he's bound to know where Freeman is."

"What do you mean?"

"We found this chap looking at us with interest. We had wanted to keep the whole business under our hats but, as the minutes ticked by, the situation was looking increasingly hopeless. In desperation we called him and told him...at least, told him the boy had got drunk. Could we safely get him back to his school if he knew where it was?"

"And Bark agreed?"

"Well, he said he knew where the school was, but he couldn't take him himself as he was going in another direction, but he would find someone who could drop him off. He went away. And a few minutes later an estate car with a couple of chaps inside pulled up. We loaded Roar onto the back seat. One of you come, they said, to keep an eye on the young gentleman. We'll drop you back here, they said. It seemed a reasonable enough request and, in the circumstances, it was the least we could do. Freeman volunteered to go, and they sped away. Well, he didn't come back to us. We thought he might have been dropped off at the team hotel. It being late, we didn't bother to check. This morning the maid brought me a note. It read: 'We have got English Man. He kidnapped. He killed if you tell Police. Be quiet and win match if you want to see him again. Boys with Panthers.'"

"Better get going if you wish to see Freeman alive," muttered Bubb. "We have lost nearly an hour already."

Phil and Bubb left the troubled Thistle and went back to their seats. The intrepid public announcer informed of a start in a quarter of an hour's time, drawing jeers, ironical cheers and another round of slow handclapping.

"Good God!" sighed Phil. "What are we playing at, do you think?"

"One down with hangover but he will recover. Poor Freeman – I hope he gets out alive."

"They want England to win to save his neck. Hostage to the impossible, I would have thought. By the way, we have no drink."

"Oh, it is only three quarters of an hour to lunch."

"Can't wait that long. Dehydration can cause thirst as well as a hangover, you know. Won't be long. Just going for a couple of beers. Want to see how our protégé Roar makes out."

When play commenced, England fielded only ten men, but straightaway a determination, absent before, was perceptible. With their backs to the wall, and the fate of their absent colleague hanging on what the rest of them could achieve, there was a new purposeful aggression about them. The historian in Phil did not have to go back more than a couple of generations to seek out a parallel in the nation's history. The bulldog spirit wakened in him by Clio saw Hardy and Wilberforce, the two remaining fast bowlers, attack with vigour, even spite. A wicket fell before Bubb had even returned.

"There you are. Thistle can be a man of his word," said Bubb as he passed a mug to Phil.

Before he had sat down Wilberforce clean bowled another. Bubb remained enthusiastically on his feet, raising and recklessly waving his mug. Phil got to his feet in support and for a full minute the two Englishmen cheered and shouted tasteful encouragement while the locals looked on indulgently.

As they sat, Phil observed Roar arriving at the crease. He peered anxiously but Roar, at any rate from a distance, looked none the worse for wear. Torn between wishing Roar to succeed and wanting England to wrap up the innings, he turned as Bubb spoke.

"Your chap is at the crease."

"I hope for his sake he gets a few."

"He's looking surprisingly good, I must say. None of that parboiled look that comes with a hangover."

"Your pills must have worked."

Personal relations, Phil decided, must take precedence over blind and – at that remote distance – indirect allegiance to country, and he resolved to support Roar. This satisfied him for a few minutes until he realized that this was probably how Philby, Maclean and Blunt, not to mention hundreds before and after, had argued. Admonishing himself for becoming absurdly melodramatic, he turned to the cricket to see Roar striking Wilberforce over the latter's head and into the sightscreen.

Tumultuous applause greeted the young lion's defiance.

"He's all right!" shouted Bubb, cheering.

It did not end there. Roar, who seemed to have little idea of the dignity appropriate to the occasion, lashed and struck and heaved as if he were playing in a house game. The crowd were rendered delirious. The two England fast bowlers, who were attacking with speed and guile and were used to respect, at least in the first hour of the playing day, looked outraged. The middle, which had been desolate only a few minutes before, now hummed with action.

But Roar's performance proved to be a solo effort. Although he had sped to thirty, the England bowling, deployed skilfully in relation to the other batsmen, sliced through the local team's middle.

When Roar was left undefeated at the end, any thoughtful local who had detached himself from patriotic hysteria would have acknowledged that they had collapsed comprehensively. But for the moment the cheers were for Roar, and both Phil and Bubb, while relieved and exhilarated by England's ruthless dissection of the local team's middle and lower orders, joined in the acclamation.

"Splendid show that," said Bubb.

"It was a sight for sore eyes. He acted like a man possessed," concurred Phil.

"Well, he was inspired, that was for sure."

"He looked half dead this morning. What a transformation!"

"A semi-miracle, wasn't it?"

"What do you mean?"

"Well, raising the half dead must merit semi-miracle status, mustn't it?"

"You mean..."

"They never fail," said Bubb complacently. Dropping his voice, he continued. "You should have seen old Weeley at my office on the morning after his somewhat extravagant stag night. A dose of my specific and he made the wedding speech to end all wedding speeches. The guests thought the ghost of Churchill had gatecrashed."

"Good God, Bubb!" exclaimed Phil, scandalized. "Don't tell me..."

"Shush, my boy. There is no dope test – yet – in cricket."

+++++++++

III

Having stalked and captured a couple of hours' sleep after lunch, Liz felt refreshed and altogether in the mood to gather together the costumes needed for that evening's school inter-house drama competition. This event, given by the boys and bringing the old boys' day to an end, had been an annual feature, but the turmoil of the world outside had led to its more recent suspension. Until now a peaceful, curfew-less evening could not be guaranteed sufficiently in advance, if at all, for the event to be arranged. Now, the school, like many others elsewhere, grabbed the opportunity afforded by the truce, in its case to plan and stage the competition. The President of the Republic, an old boy, had declined his invitation to attend with much regret – sentiments which were believed to be sincerely felt, for his loyalty to his old school was second only to his attachment to his old Cambridge college. The Prime Minister, another dutiful old boy, had gladly accepted the invitation to deputize for the President. The entire England cricket party had been invited, and Bubb would, of course, represent *Roll Britannia!*

In the respite offered to the capital of that beleaguered country it quite promised to be the occasion of that evening; the whiff of nostalgia alone was expected to draw the public in. The night before, the old Imperial had filled the belly and also provided unplanned incidental entertainment; that night, the school, which professed high thinking and plain living, would aim to treat the mind. Fishcakes and prawn canapés would, of course, be served.

For Liz, who occupied an uncertain slot in the school's life, preparation for the drama competition gave an opportunity to be fully accepted into the fabric of the school, in the same way she knew Phil had already been. In that country, even more in that school – hidebound by tradition as it was, as befitted an institution rumoured to have been modelled on Harrow – status and position were all. Phil, as a master, was accorded all privileges *ex officio.* He was, in fact, treated as an honorary old boy; his place in the scheme of things did not have to be located; everyone knew where he stood. Liz, as a mere wife, felt she had to walk the metaphorical yard behind.

Oddly enough, she had first heard of the impending event from Marie-Antoinette, who had been hired to help out in the school's kitchens that evening. Liz confirmed the rumour by checking it out with Emmeline Grunt. Following that, she lost no time in inviting herself whenever Phil had to attend a meeting of the drama committee. Drama itself was taken seriously at the school. In the nineteenth century and well into the twentieth, the school thought nothing of staging for public consumption each year a couple of plays in the original Greek. With independence and the coming of democracy, the school responded to change by substituting the language of a later empire, and for a couple of generations the high spot of the school's year was the annual Shakespeare play. When the civil war dealt the Bard the same blow it gave the rest of the nation, that tradition, too, had gone by the board.

The senior English master had invited Phil to select the scripts for the fifteen-minute productions each house would put on. There were five houses at the school, named after the great English cathedral cities of Canterbury, York, Norwich, Lincoln and Winchester. Given the influence of the Church on the school – the Bishop was the chairman of the Board of Governors of the school and the presiding spirit on these occasions – the scripts, the senior English master had warned, had to be what he called 'suitable'. An authentic old boy would have sensed what was suitable in his marrow; Phil anticipated a little more difficulty. There were a few guidelines. Shakespeare, for instance, would not be questioned, whatever act of whichever play was chosen. He had been performed so many times that familiarity with him had engendered a complacency even when, objectively looked at, it could have been queried if some of his pieces were suitable for playing by boys many of whom were barely in their teens. But, like the Bible, Shakespeare could do no wrong. On the other hand, any work from this century was suspect. So much Phil knew, and he was additionally grateful for the intelligence that came his way that the wisdom of making a young Englishman the arbiter of the scripts had been closely questioned. Cautiously the headmaster had also made up a committee of censors consisting of himself, the senior English master and the chaplain. Of these, Phil had confided to Liz, he feared most the chaplain, a fat, dour Australian who played rugby and sang its songs but who, on his first tour of the school library, had raised his eyebrows alarmingly. It had been muttered that the instruments of a classical education might provoke alarm in those who had been deprived of one.

Liz, who had decided to suspend hostilities for the duration of the drama contest, attached herself to Phil as he went about choosing the scripts. She advised they needed to keep things light in deference to the generally prevailing atmosphere of relief and respite. The boys themselves, naturally, had expressed a desire for scripts with numerous female parts, notwithstanding the inconvenience and dislocation such choices would lead to in an all-boys school. They had also expressed an antipathy for those authors whose works had been imposed on them as set books, but exempted from this injunction Shakespeare and Shaw, whose *Pygmalion* commanded universal support.

In the event, Phil and Liz decided that a scene from *My Fair Lady* was preferable on the ground that the audience would possess greater familiarity with the film version. As for the particular scene, several boys from Canterbury house had suggested the one featuring Ascot, giving them as it did a chance not only to play the Ascot gavotte on a tape recorder but also the prized, though less commendable, opportunity to cry quite lawfully, "Move your blooming arse!" to an audience including the Bishop, the Prime Minister, their headmaster, their teachers and their parents. Phil turned down this scene, however, for its lack of legitimate dramatic appeal. Liz concurred reluctantly, for she had fancied working on fancy costumes, but, on reflection, she had to concede that clothing a dozen boys in fashionable period costume entailed a task that was likely to be incommensurate with any possible reward. The boys' next preference was for the scene in which Alfred P. Doolittle celebrates his stag night, with all the potential it afforded for making noise and indulging in horseplay. Liz herself preferred the scene at the end when a reconciliation is brought about between Professor Higgins and Eliza Doolittle; but Phil with, so to speak, his casting vote picked the earlier scene in which Higgins and Colonel Pickering discuss the vagaries of English pronunciation, and linked it to the later scene in which Eliza laboriously learns to utter proper sounds. To link the scenes for the audience, Phil brought back Pickering as narrator and thereby created the device by which the gist of the story could be compressed into fifteen minutes. Liz had to admit this was a neat trick.

She was not the only one to be taken by the script, for Squealer, the Canterbury housemaster, reported himself delighted.

"Fine idea. Very fine, indeed. The judges will be most pleased," he said to Phil.

"Why do you think so?" Phil had asked, intrigued, for, decent enough chap though he was, Squealer could not quite be accommodated within the ranks of drama critics; indeed, it could have been suspected that, but for universality of the knowledge regarding the film, he might not have recognized the piece at all.

"The judges will like the idea of talking properly," Squealer explained. "You know, we spend our whole working lives trying to get these boys to read, write and speak properly. And here you are, in fifteen minutes of an evening's entertainment, without a cane or detention book anywhere to be seen, getting the idea across to everyone. My dear Phil, you are a genius!"

For Norwich house, Phil selected – with the approval of Liz – an excerpt from the first scene of the last act of *A Midsummer Night's Dream*, which promised an authentic performance by the boys of the actions of the rude mechanicals. The play itself had been the set Shakespeare text in the fifth forms, and the excerpt was popular, given the flourish of trumpets at the beginning of the scene and the opportunity it brought to act as animals. The censors insisted on deleting, "this dog, my dog" for fear of offending native susceptibilities; it was not that the old boys could not see a dog as

Shakespeare did, the senior English master assured Phil, but, as he put it, in this age of the common man one tried to accommodate the sensitivities of the multitude. He went on to congratulate Phil on choosing as a script a piece that laid so much store by punctuation. Phil was mystified.

"You see, when Theseus says, 'this fellow doth not stand upon points'," explained the senior English master.

"Oh, yes, I hadn't thought of that."

"And when Lysander says, 'he knows not the stop. A good moral, my Lord: it is not enough to speak, but to speak true.' It could be the motto of the school, don't you see? Norwich are halfway to success with the judges already."

Appreciating by now that entertainment in the school was a deadly serious business, Phil got down to selecting a piece for Lincoln house. He felt like daring the audience with a Restoration comedy, and recalled a rendering of the *The Country Wife* he and Liz had once enjoyed in England. His initial choice from the work's second act he discarded, reluctantly, as references to dogs abounded. Stuck, he turned to Liz, and she suggested he do what he had done with *My Fair Lady* – namely, amalgamate several scenes. Phil thereupon slaved at the script and produced it in front of the censors.

While the headmaster read through without comment, a scowl encroached on the fat Australian chaplain's face; the senior English master said nothing.

"An old-fashioned play, this," said the headmaster at length. "How it brings back memories, Mr Smallbone. You are too young to remember the scourges of the past. Do you remember the plague?"

"No, headmaster."

"I remember it very well. It happened in our village, you know. People fell like trees in the monsoon winds. Rats, you know, carry the disease."

"England has not had the plague in modern times, headmaster."

"Is that so? But it is no bad thing to have the odd epidemic now and then, you know. People then appreciate the workings of God." He turned with a twitch to the chaplain.

"Perhaps I should not be speaking for God when we have the specialist among us."

"Anyone can speak for God, headmaster."

"Have you any scourges in Australia, chaplain?"

"Not that I know of. I suppose myxomatosis does not count."

"I think the idea of illness in a play is a good one, especially when the play refers to a plague of the recent past: smallpox."

"Smallpox, headmaster?" inquired Phil.

"I see in this script several references to smallpox. An excellent idea, that. Better than the ordinary plague, which is carried about by rats. Smallpox, gentlemen, goes from humans to humans, carried from their mouths. It is symbolic, for it is like rumour. We shall reach the audience with this symbolism. Not one of those in the audience would have been untouched by the effects of rumours. Mr Smallbone, I congratulate you. You have found the perfect play."

An uncomfortable silence descended on the other three men. The chaplain looked angry; the senior English master looked embarrassed; Phil looked awkward. The headmaster beamed.

"If I may say a few words, headmaster," began the chaplain hesitantly, breaking the silence.

"I do not think Mr Smallbone's script refers to smallpox, does it Mr Smallbone?"

"Not quite. At least, I don't think it does. After all, it is set in the seventeenth century."

"What does it matter?" asked the headmaster airily. "Smallpox, big pox. It is the symbolism. It is the artist's licence. We must allow them their freedom to prick us."

"But, headmaster, it will offend the old boys," wailed the chaplain.

"Will it? That's a good thing in itself," replied the headmaster, the first drops of rebellion bubbling within an oppressed man. "As a man of the cloth, don't you think it is a good idea to put to us God's workings, like a thorn in our backsides, to make us jump up and notice His doings?"

"They certainly will jump up when they hear cursing and swearing on the stage coming from their sons they are expensively educating."

"Cursing and swearing? I don't see any of it."

"But, headmaster, 'pox on you' is a swear phrase. And it does not refer to smallpox."

"Is that so?" said the headmaster doubtfully, and turned to the senior English master. "I say, Mr Chattering, what do you say?"

The senior English master spoke quietly and in diplomatic tones.

"It is an excellent play, headmaster, and it will be rightly appreciated if done by an adult cast. But I fear the chaplain is right. It will give offence."

"Offence!" the chaplain shouted. "It's a shocker! The pox, headmaster, refers to venereal disease."

The headmaster looked stunned. "Good God! I wasn't aware of that. Did it really exist then?"

"It has existed in every age, headmaster."

The headmaster rose and raised his hand as if in an attempt to stem this flow of filth.

"That won't do at all, Mr Smallbone. You have an important point to make but I don't think our old boys are ready to have it made to them just yet. You'll have to produce something else."

Disappointed, and furious with the chaplain, Phil decided to work on a script that would offend the Australian and no one else. He had cast about for a few days when he learned, quite by chance from the librarian, that among the books in the library the chaplain had taken exception to were the works of P.G. Wodehouse. This startled Phil somewhat, but enlightenment came his way once more from the librarian who explained that the chaplain's objections had been on the grounds of the alleged snobbery in Wodehouse's work rather than because of any latent and hitherto undetected lasciviousness. Phil had immediately resolved to find something from Wodehouse, and chose for adaptation the first two chapters from *The Inimitable Jeeves.* With their accounts replete with the feudal spirit and their keen descriptions of the more pernicious consequences of the class system in the love life of the friends and acquaintances of Bertram Wooster, they offered, Phil had no doubt, the perfect irritant to the chaplain. He took the script back to the censorship committee, hoping the fat, red-faced Australian would be silenced by apoplexy.

He had estimated right, for the chaplain was furious beyond words. Later, in calm retrospection, Phil was able to allow that Wodehouse's real genius probably lay in eliminating sex, violence and politics from his stories altogether. As a result his works were supremely appropriate for a public school theatrical production, his characters inhabiting, as the school did, a world that had long parted company with reality.

The headmaster had been thrilled and the senior English master permitted himself a quiet smile.

"Why, Mr Smallbone," trilled the headmaster, "this is a marvellous choice. So entertaining and so clean. In these troubled times it will allow the old boys to relax and get away from the horrors of our lives. I envy the boys of Lincoln house. They are going to win first prize. The old boys won't be able to resist something that reminds them so much of the old days. Well done, Mr Smallbone!"

The senior English master looked on approvingly. Seeing the chaplain's flushed face – and recalling with amusement how Wodehouse had described a character of like facial feature as looking like a tomato struggling for self-expression – Phil could not resist displaying a smirk.

For York house, Phil – with the active encouragement of Liz – chose an excerpt from *The Merchant of Venice,* a work familiar to the lower school. The piece was the courtroom scene from the fourth act, and he was careful to excise references to dogs which occur in Shylock's speech and Gratiano's abuse in the form of 'inexecrable dog' and 'thy currish spirit'. Making discreet inquiries, he found, "...for thy desires are wolfish, bloody, starv'd, and ravenous" locally acceptable. Indeed, the boys pleaded with him to retain the line so they could say 'bloody' lawfully, for once, at school. The entire play, judiciously edited, had been staged several times at the school without adverse comment, and Portia's speech, he found, was a set piece in the school repertory. When, however, he got Liz to read the extract aloud, Phil felt the piece lacked vim, appearing as no more than a Shakespearian cliché. He had begun to harbour second thoughts when he was struck by the notion that, by transposing Shylock's plaintive cry from the third act to his speech for the prosecution in the fourth, he could inject some vitality into it. It did indeed do the trick, for the headmaster was much taken with the script and proceeded to read it aloud.

"I am a Jew. Hath not a Jew eyes? Hath not a Jew hands, organs, dimensions, senses, affections, passion? Fed with the same food, hurt with the same weapons, subject to the same diseases, healed by the same means, warmed and cooled by the same winter and summer, as a Christian is? If you prick us, do we not bleed?"

The headmaster paused. "Mr Smallbone," he said in a voice trembling with emotion, presaging the praise Phil by now had come to accept as his due, "you are a genius!" The senior English master could, of course, be relied on to pass any Shakespeare on the nod, and, as for the chaplain, not locating any sex or snobbery, he could not have cared less.

Having achieved by then a near clean sweep of approval with his first four scripts, Phil decided to chance his arm with the last piece for Winchester house. Keenly aware though he was of the political symbolism, he was nonetheless determined to adapt a scene from *Julius Caesar*. Liz lost interest once she had failed to deflect him from his resolute course. Yet again, the play had once been a favourite from the school's repertory, but not so recently. The play had also been a set text and the boys were even more familiar with the filmed version screened from time to time by the school's film society. Phil selected the opening lines of the third act, on account of the dramatic impact possible to achieve in the space of a quarter-hour. For support he felt he could count on the senior English master and on the chaplain's indifference; the latter, being a rugby enthusiast, had no objection in principle to stylized violence. Phil's vestigial apprehension rested with the headmaster's possible sensitivities faced with what could have been considered as being too overtly political a subject.

"Interesting piece you have here for Winchester, Mr Smallbone," the headmaster had said while perusing the script, and Phil, who had become accustomed to being hailed a genius, felt somewhat deflated.

"Yes, headmaster?"

"But the first line troubles me."

"Let me see, headmaster. But it only says, 'the ides of March are come'."

"Yes, Mr Smallbone. But perhaps you are slightly innocent of our politics. Those words may offend some of our old boys."

"I don't understand, headmaster. They seem quite innocent to me. Perhaps there is some local superstition."

"Ho ho ho!" cried the headmaster alarmingly. "If it is a local superstition we could ignore it. Our old boys are religiously against superstition, especially local ones. It is the politics that worries me. It is an unfortunate line."

"I still don't get it," called Phil from the depths of mystery.

"Perhaps I could help here," suggested the senior English master. "You see, the Prime Minister and the Finance Minister do not see eye to eye. They are also rivals. It is said the Prime Minister feels the Finance Minister's somewhat, how shall we put it, unorthodox financial proposals are merely means to undermine the Prime Minister's position."

"You mean, the PM is being embarrassed by the Finance Minister's plans? Why should we be concerned with political rumour and gossip, even though the PM is an old boy and the guest of honour?"

"If it was just rumour and gossip it would cause some embarrassment but nothing more," replied the senior English master quietly. "But, you see, there was a cartoon recently, in the underground press but widely circulated, showing the PM being stabbed in the back by the Finance Minister with his rolled up budget speech. 'The ideas of the March hare are come', read the caption."

"There you see, Mr Smallbone," intervened the headmaster, "your play is political dynamite."

Phil pondered for a moment, and said, "I'll think about it," as he left. Alone, without even Liz, who had washed her hands of that particular script, to consult, he turned resentful. Here, he said to himself, was one of Shakespeare's better-known efforts, retailing more or less accurately one of the better known incidents in history, and yet, here he was, an outsider taking little more than an academic interest in local political events, being pushed around; he might as well be serving some bigoted local educational committee in England.

He decided to tackle Bubb.

"Well, if you don't want to remove the line, why don't you consider removing the Prime Minister?"

"What do you mean?"

"He is chief guest. Stop him coming."

"How?"

"It can be arranged. Let it be known in the right circles he is going to be shot."

"But this is an old-boys'-day show."

"Lots of old boys desire to shoot the PM."

"Are you being serious?"

"It is not necessary to specify the allegiance of the assassin. These days one can be shot up by anyone."

"Can you manage it?"

"Shooting the PM – no. But scaring him off – yes."

"How do you manage it?"

"You don't simply announce he is going to be shot. You arrange for an astrologer to read his signs and say he is in imminent peril."

"Isn't that taking a chance? I mean, supposing his stars are all right."

"Look, my boy, if you get two astrologers, one will say the signs are good and the other will say the signs are ominous. You take the pessimist along to see the PM. Leave it to me. But remember this."

"What?"

"If there is any likelihood of anyone getting shot or blown up, they'll make sure to send the Minister of Culture."

"Oh, I don't mind him at all. In fact, I rather like him."

"I suppose you are right. He won't be able to spot a symbol if it blows up in his face."

Phil waited to hear from Bubb before returning to the censors, but found he had been pre-empted by the headmaster.

"The play is safe. The Prime Minister is not coming," he announced. "But I still have some doubts. There's too much politics, Mr Smallbone. Too much like the country's politics. I am uneasy."

"It is a historical play, headmaster."

"History is not always a comfort, Mr Smallbone. Now, if it is something harmless like the other plays you are going to do. No, more than harmless, enjoyable, instructive, setting an example to our boys, old and young, it will be so much better."

"But, headmaster, with respect, history is meant to be enjoyable, instructive and set an example to young and old."

"It is unsettling all the same. Would it be too much trouble to ask you to rewrite it?"

"It is by another writer, headmaster."

"A countryman of yours?"

"Yes."

"Is it possible you could put in a word and alter it here and there?"

Phil decided to stand his ground, and the script was accepted as he had excerpted it. Once the decisions had been made, Liz threw herself into making the costumes, helped enthusiastically by the boys themselves. Short though the notice had been, and temporary the respite from the troubles, everyone at the school seemed determined to make the most of the evening.

She had finished making the final checks when Phil got back, early, from the match. He looked preoccupied, but she did not venture a query. They dressed and went in good time to the school hall, the venue for the contest. The old boys themselves, before assembling there, were having a late tea, some of it fortified by illicit whisky conveyed in smuggled personal flasks, in the headmaster's home.

As Phil and Liz entered the hall they spied Bark standing by a side door. They recalled the night before and feared his presence might be a threatening omen. However, the pressures of the next hour drove all such considerations out of their minds. A jolly confusion prevailed as the boys, assisted by their respective housemasters and their wives, their own mothers, the wives of old boys and Phil and Liz, were dressed and propped.

Phil greeted Bubb at the door. "We have the programme printed. The Minister of Culture will speak, but for five minutes only before the competition starts."

"That'll cut him off, for sure, though I don't mind listening to him for hours."

"So would I, but it is a tight schedule. Ninety minutes for the performance. Two hours in all, with the interval included."

"No time for fireworks."

"What do you mean?"

"The minister's oratory seems to provoke pyrotechnics."

"This is no time for levity, Bubb," said Phil severely. "Make yourself useful. You will be required to announce the performances."

"What?"

"Announce the performances. Read out the introduction to each house's scene."

"But I can't do that."

"Why can't you? Just walk on the stage before the curtain comes up and read from the programme. For heaven's sake, *Roll Britannia!* can manage that. After all, it is all British writers tonight."

"Can't you find someone else, Phil. I...I mean, I'm not the man for this. This is an important occasion for them. Get one of the old boys to do it."

"It's too late. I've told everyone you are doing it. Can't wait to talk to you. Must rush to see all is well."

Phil disappeared, leaving Bubb holding a copy of the programme as if it were a stick of gelignite. Shortly afterwards, the headmaster rose to welcome the Minister of Culture, who had come in accompanied by an entourage almost as large as the one enveloping him the night before. It was incongruous to see the minister in that setting: a man who, as a boy, could scarcely have been permitted to set foot in the establishment was now listened to with the respectful good manners of the school that were its selling point to socially ambitious parents throughout that land. Wearing the exiguous national dress, which contrasted strongly with the finery all around, the minister grasped the microphone. Liz, peeping from the wings, thought it was like watching a crow addressing a pride of peacocks.

"Ladies and gentlemen, your headmaster has said I must speak for only five minutes, and, like all headmasters, he must be obeyed. This is an important evening for culture and I am privileged to represent our Government today. Many years ago a minister in Germany said, during the Nazi troubles, 'whenever someone speaks of culture, I reach for my gun'. Tonight I tell you, and you listen to me, if you do *not* speak about culture, I will reach for my gun."

From the inside of his robe he then plucked a handgun and brandished it, to gasps from the audience. Grinning broadly, he ended, "I have nothing more to say, but we will enjoy the evening."

Relieved applause broke out as he sat. For a few minutes afterwards nothing happened. Phil, just about to thrust Colonel Pickering through the curtains to begin his narration of the story so far before Higgins and Eliza came on, spotted Bubb and shook his fist at him. Bubb, spotting the signal, rose gingerly to his feet and stumbled onto the stage.

"Ladies and gentlemen," he announced, "we proudly present *Julius Caesar.*"

Applause, quickly succeeded by guffaws, broke out as the youthful Pickering bound on. The boy, all things considered, thought Phil and Liz, did marvellously, not being put off at all. The acclamation for all the players at the end was well merited. Phil shook his fist with more feeling as Bubb returned to the stage.

"Next we have *Jeeves and the Feudal Spirit*," called Bubb as the curtain rose to display Theseus, his bride and his court awaiting a variety performance. Loud laughter greeted the scene.

"What the hell is he playing at?" muttered Phil.

"Perhaps he is drunk," suggested Liz. "Maybe he had a few quick ones after you suggested he play compère."

"All he has to do is to read from the programme."

They broke off to watch another inspired performance by the juvenile actors. The applause had not quite died before Bubb was up on the platform once again.

"Next we have *Bottom and his Cronies*," he announced to more merriment. An incandescent Phil could just see the curtain go up on grave and toga-clad gentlemen. The laughter became uproarious. Bubb seemed to be putting in for the award for the outstanding individual performance.

When the interval came, Phil ran up from backstage to collar Bubb. To do this he had to come down steps into the yard outside and re-enter the hall through a side door. The guests, in good humour, sought refreshments. Phil located Bubb sizing up a sweetmeat.

"You!" hissed Phil. "What the hell are you doing? You are ruining the evening."

Bubb showed no shame or remorse. "On the contrary. The people are in splendid form."

"That's not the point. Why don't you read the programme in the right order?"

"I was going to explain when you ran off before. I can't read."

Before Phil could recover from the receipt of this intelligence, Bubb had gone. Phil, returning backstage, hoped at least by a process of elimination Bubb would announce the two remaining scenes accurately. But in all honesty he could not deny the theatrical effect of the contretemps.

As he ascended the short steps into the wings, wondering if he would ever learn the limits of Bubb's being, he was confronted by a figure covered in a sheet with holes for the eyes standing a few yards in front of him like a displaced member of the Ku Klux Klan. Phil's temper, already frayed, snapped.

"Why haven't you undressed, you silly boy?" he shouted at the figure. "Your scene is over. The others must go on. Don't you know you must leave the stage when your act is over?"

When the figure did not move, Phil strode menacingly towards it.

"Stop!" commanded the clothed figure.

The voice was vaguely familiar but not at all that of a schoolboy. Phil halted. The figure moved forward and a blunt object was pressed through the sheet against Phil's chest.

"No noise or I shoot. Come!"

Phil was turned around and marched down the steps again, into the yard and into the darkness.

Part Three – The Third Day's Play

I

Once they were within the yard a sheet was placed over Phil and this, lacking a slit or any other opening for the eyes, obliterated any remaining light and plunged him into total darkness. His abductor compounded this discomfort by administering a gratuitous punch to his chest and then proceeded to drag him along. A few yards of haphazard progress later, Phil was pushed to the ground, from where he heard muffled voices, the owner of one of which then commenced to tie up Phil, starting with his feet. Two pairs of hands then lifted him from the ground, turned him to the vertical and placed him on what felt like some narrow seat. He felt rather vaguely as if he might still be above ground. One of the voices then gave a low, sharp order, and Phil felt himself borne forward. He was in a cart of some shape, dragged, on the evidence of two feet pounding on the ground, by a man at work. It then dawned on him that he was being conveyed by rickshaw, an exotic mode of travel, a relic from the past.

Human-drawn rickshaws were still popular with the tourists and were licensed by the Tourist Ministry, the licensees being required, on pain of penal sanction, to take care of the rickshaw pullers in their employ. While a form of bicycle-powered rickshaw was also available for hire, the real romance lay in a ride on the man-drawn variety.

Contrary to rational belief, these were jobs that were much sought after, for the pay was good – or had been good, for their real attraction was to foreign tourists now driven away by the civil war – and the tips plentiful, the Americans especially gratefully generous for being given a taste of the exotic East and prone to reward in scarce dollars. The men – for they were all men, the Ministry drawing the line at permitting women to drag a conveyance in the street – had, in fact, enviable conditions of service, working just two days of the week and resting thereafter. They were almost as well treated as the horses and bullocks that drew the street carts. Also, whilst on duty, they had all to be fed and watered and, after service of a mere five years, became entitled to a full state pension. Unsurprisingly, to become a rickshaw-puller was the aspiration of many young men drawn by what had previously been a tourist boom.

After the troubles began, and mass tourism ended, this work ran dry, and it was possible that it was one of these redundant pullers, hired cheap, who conveyed Phil through the streets. Never before having travelled in one of those contraptions – in his free moments he would have been horrified at being a party to such naked exploitation of human flesh – Phil was now able to appreciate the surprising smoothness of his transit. A refugee from the discomforts and inconveniences of travel by British Rail, Phil, despite his plight, found this form of leisurely progression quite agreeable.

They went silently through the streets, Phil, encased as he was, only dimly aware of the distant traffic; he surmised he was moving down a side street. They passed a chiming clock, possibly perched on a church tower, but he missed the strokes; it could have been 8.00 or 9.00. The night had turned cool, his throat was dry and his body wet, but his mind remained alert. He turned to his situation. Not grasping any obvious motive for his kidnap, he made vague connection to Freeman's the night before. Pondering further, he also connected the faintly gruff sounds of his captor to the abrupt speech of Bark.

Strangely, he felt little fear. If money was the motive, he and Liz had little. He was, after all, a mere schoolmaster, comfortably off perhaps by the standards of most natives but hardly qualifying as rich. He had kept away from local politics, expressing no preference for the Government or the Lions or the Panthers; he had merely laughed at them all. No Englishman had previously been kidnapped, or been hurt or troubled in any way, until Freeman. The only plausible reason he could extract from the recesses of his mind was his friendship with Bubb, the promiscuity of whose interests might have impinged in some way on local sensitivities. He could also not believe the official forces of the state could be involved in his seizure; it had to be the Lions or Panthers, and, given the circumstance's of Freeman's disappearance, it was more likely to be the latter.

After what seemed like three or four hours of travel they reached some kind of destination. The rickshaw stopped and several pairs of hands drew Phil out and took him into a room where light filtered through the cloth covering him. He was laid on a soft mattress. After a silent pause someone untied him and the sheet was removed. The light dazzled and stung his eyes. He shielded them and blinked, noticing a room sparsely, even ascetically, furnished and a naked light bulb swaying gently over his head. There were three chairs, a table and the mattress on which he lay. There were also three men, all strangers to him, plainly dressed and with the demeanour of bank clerks. Phil knew that terrorism in that country was the occupation of part-timers. He felt he was in no immediate danger.

"Mr Smallbone?" asked one of the men, in a greeting that was not unfriendly.

"Yes," replied Phil, and instantly felt his response was inadequate. At the very least, his immediate afterthought suggested, he should have created some kind of scene and demanded to see the Queen's representatives.

The man addressed his two colleagues in their tongue; he appeared to be their leader as well as interpreter.

"You are surprised to be here, no? We are very regretful we had to bring you here like this. We have a purpose. We need your help."

Phil suppressed the urge to enquire why they could not get in touch through the normal channels.

"We have a problem. An unexpected problem. We would like your co-operation. You will help, yes?"

"I will try."

"It is one of your countrymen who is a problem to us. His actions we cannot understand. We thought you might help us to understand him."

If they were referring to Bubb, Phil could not see how he could help; he himself had not started to achieve that comprehension.

"There's a cricket match, no?"

"Yes, there is."

"England team playing?"

"Yes."

"We want England to win. We support England."

He turned to his colleagues with a gesture, whereupon they gave a little cheer of approval.

"We all support England. You support England."

"Of course."

"That is good. England can then win. But, you see, your friend we cannot understand.

He..." the man's brow furrowed, "he...does not seem so sure."

"Perhaps he is not sure England will win. It is not something you can put money on."

"Money? Ah, yes. We'll come to talk about that. But now, your friend..."

"If you will pardon me, who is this friend of mine?"

"Ah, the cricket friend. The other guest in this house."

"Freeman?"

"Oh, yes. Mr Freeman. But we like to see him co-operating more. Wait, we shall invite him to this room."

Phil had to reassure himself it was not all a dream. Supporting England was one thing; hoping fervently England would win was another; but willing England to win was something else. He would happily back the most ill-fancied horse with any money he had rather than speculate on the prospects for English cricket.

They brought Freeman into the room. To Phil, who had seen him on the field and had a glimpse of him at the dinner at the Imperial, Freeman did not, at first sight, appear of the stuff of which heroes are made. He might have been England's leading fast bowler but he was of no more than medium size, compact, nondescript – moderate in all respects. He seemed to represent in person the decline of English cricket.

"Freeman, I take it. I'm Smallbone. I teach here."

"I wish you would teach these buggers something."

"Let's be civil. It is more likely to be helpful."

Freeman spoke with the accents of the West Country, but Phil could not recall which county he played for since, in those days, Yorkshire apart, they all poached each other's players with predatory gusto. His critical words could have been overheard and given offence even though the only guard left with them evidently spoke no English.

"They've been asking me questions. But whatever I say doesn't seem to satisfy them."

"They said they found you unco-operative."

"Puzzles me. I answered all their questions."

"Perhaps they could not understand all you were saying."

"Why should that be? I spoke to their leader, the one who speaks English."

"Perhaps he does not understand the way you speak," Phil said gently.

"Everyone else does."

"It is not their first language. Anyway, that is beside the point. They want some assurance England will win the Test Match."

"Yes, they kept saying that. Sounds bizarre."

"Their desire England should win?"

"Yes. Don't you think so?"

"Not necessarily. The politics of this country are complex."

"Bloody complex. They want England to win."

"It is too complicated to go into. But I can understand why they want us to win. Anyway, let's not argue over that. What can we do to convince them that England are really trying to win?"

"I was damned well doing my best until they snatched me. Anyway, you teach here. What can you tell them about English cricket?"

"I can tell them a few things about English cricket. Not all of them flattering," said Phil, annoyed. "But that is not going to save our skins. Anyway, I'm here supposedly to help make you see sense."

"If they want England to win, they might let me go. We are not going to win with a man short."

"Yes, we played with ten today. They wouldn't allow a substitute.

"I heard about it. They let me listen to the radio."

Their solitary guard had fallen asleep. There was no one else present until the leader returned.

"I see you have been talking, Mr Smallbone. Is your friend co-operating?"

"Mr Freemen is very eager to co-operate. We have been chatting together and we can tell you that we wish nothing more than for England to win."

"That is good. But we need to be sure England will win."

"We talked about that, too. You see, for England to win, Mr Freeman will have to go back and join the team and play. He is an important player. You understand that, sir?"

"How will we know he will keep his word?"

"The rules are like that, sir. The team has eleven players. Mr Freeman is one. If he is not there, there will be only ten for England and eleven for you. England are less likely to win."

"We know nothing about this sport, Mr Smallbone. We are fighting a war for our independence, for the dignity of our people. We do not bother with childish things like sport. But I understand you to say your friend must go back..."

"To join the team. To play. To get England to win."

"This is a complex matter. We must confer."

He shouted an order and his two accomplices returned. They huddled together. Then they paused and, without a further word, one of them took the bewildered Freeman by the arm and led him out of the room.

"Good luck, Freeman!" Phil called out.

The leader turned to Phil. "This is more complicated, Mr Smallbone. We desire England to win. That is why we arranged for the truce in the first place. To see the usurpers of power in this country humiliated in the eyes of the world. You know any history of this country, Mr Smallbone?"

"I've tried to read a little, sir."

"They are all lies. History writers are the biggest criminals. They distort, destroy, damage. They do criminal damage. I know, I used to be a history teacher myself. Used to give these lies out, second hand, like some drug pusher distributing the big dealer's goods. The opium of the people, that is the history our children, our people are learning. So, I thought. And then I acted. The more I searched the more I found. The true history of our people, subjugated in this so-called free and independent and sovereign country. I joined the movement to free our people and win our true freedom. But, you know, what I found? This country, whenever it quarrelled and was divided, could only be united again by foreign invaders. Then the country would get together. But the foreigners would stay on. There would be peace. But the country they united was not the true country. It was separate countries, different countries. So, I thought, we must get a foreigner to come to stop the squabbling, but go away before he did too much damage by bringing the country together artificially. Then God sent the England cricket team to stop the fighting, but to take them away before they brought the incompatible together. In the peace of those six days or so we could achieve a defeat for this country and complete the plans for the full victory of our movement. England must win!"

"If you will let Mr Freeman go, I'm sure he'll do his best and urge his colleagues to do their best."

"That is a problem now, Mr Smallbone. We took Mr Freeman by chance. It was not our plan. But we couldn't let it go. We need guarantee of success. He was a hostage. We need a hostage."

Phil did not like the sound of things.

"We will let Mr Freeman go to win the match for England. You, Mr Smallbone, will stay here till the match is won for England."

Phil was in no state to ask what might happen if England did not win the match.

"We only brought you here to speak to your friend, to make him more co-operative."

"Why me?"

"Why not? You are as good as any. And you could be picked up by one of the supporters of our movement. He helps to protect the Minister of Culture who, I understand, was at your school last evening."

He left Phil to be alone. Time passed and one of the other men came back to escort Phil to another room. This one was more extravagantly furnished and held a bed with signs of recent occupation – presumably Freeman's. The guard returned to mime food being taken to the mouth; Phil riposted with a drinking motion and was handed a tumbler of water.

While he lay on the bed, Phil regretted not sending a message to Liz through Freeman. He hoped Freeman would possess the sense to contact Bubb through the medium of Thistle. He shut his eyes after learning it was 4.00 in the morning, according to his watch, and tried to sleep, wondering if Liz had got to sleep.

Liz, in fact, not having slept for more than a few minutes, had had a restless night. She had been behind the scenes right through the evening and had not noticed Phil's absence. In the hurly-burly of performance no one seemed to have missed the prime mover. The final two scenes had gone without a hitch and even Bubb, whether through chance or inspired guesswork, had contrived to announce them correctly. The judges decided the scene from *My Fair Lady* merited the first prize, but Shylock won his player the best actor's award. The minister handed out the prizes and the head prefect moved a vote of thanks, praising Mr Smallbone's efforts. Liz wondered if Phil should take a bow and was puzzled he did not even appear to be present. She saw Bubb in the audience, so it was not that they had slipped out for a drink together.

The guests drifted away and the boys returned to their homes or dormitories. Liz walked back home and found their car was still in its garage. Baffled, she poured herself a drink and ran a bath. By 9.00 that evening she had prepared a snack for herself and settled to listen to the radio. She resisted a weak temptation to ring up Bubb, whom she had seen leaving with the other guests. Eventually she went to bed but could not find sleep, all sleep-inducing contrivances being of no avail. She rose and switched on the radio, but the local station went off the air at midnight.

Abandoning her with such melodrama, she decided, was not Phil's style. Moreover, not being the most practical of men, he was not likely to get very far without mobilizing assistance. If such a volunteer was not herself or Bubb, who else could it be? And why would he leave during the drama competition that he had himself organized with such care and pride?

In the early hours of the morning, desperately tired but keenly alert, it suddenly came to her that Phil had been kidnapped. The only motive she could initially acknowledge was gain, for, while they were not at all well off, to many of the locals money and the English were still linked with romantic inaccuracy.   But who would kidnap him under the eyes of hundreds of guests, and from the school itself?   He must have been persuaded to go with someone.   She and he had grown apart in recent months; could he have been recruited as an undercover operative for one or other of the organizations that had been spawned?   The Government?   The British Government?   MI5?   The CIA?   Who knew?

Bubb, she decided, must be consulted without delay in the morning.   At four a.m. she abandoned all further attempt at acquiring any more sleep, dressed, went into the kitchen and made tea. Physical activity, she resolved, was the means to set the mind at rest for an hour or two.   Meticulously she set about cleaning the house, starting in the sitting room, then the dining room and finally the kitchen.   Vigorously she washed her clothes, she dusted and she polished.

Shortly after half past six, Marie-Antoinette reported for work.

"Missy up already?   Missy doing all the work."

"Yes, Marie-Antoinette. I felt like doing some work."

"Missy feeling all right?"

"Thank you for your solicitude, Marie-Antoinette.   But Missy did feel she needed to do something."

Marie-Antoinette looked troubled.   Liz could see she suspected serious marital dissension, perhaps even an irretrievable breach.

"You see, my husband seems to have gone."

"Oh, my poor Missy. When he left?"

"I didn't say he had left. He has gone."

Marie-Antoinette pondered matters.

"Men do not go, Missy. Men are made to leave."

"What do you mean?"

"Who is she, Missy?"

"There is no 'she', Marie-Antoinette."

"Why he go then?"

"That's what I'm trying to find out. Last night, during the drama competition, he...he just vanished."

"You were not fighting, Missy?"

"Certainly not. This was in front of hundreds of people."

"How man go like that? He not kidnapped, Missy?"

"I fear he has been taken against his will."

"The police, Missy?"

"No, Marie-Antoinette, that is not wise. Publicity may not be helpful."

"My poor Missy. What are we to do?"

"I'm going to speak to Mr Bubb first thing. By the way, are there any rumours?"

"One or two, Missy. Now no fighting for a few days. So, all rumour quiet. But they saying English cricketer kidnapped."

"Kidnapped? Who is saying?"

"People outside saying. They saying England team playing one short."

"There may be a connection. Get me another cup of tea, Marie-Antoinette, while I phone."

Bubb was sleeping late when his phone rang.

"Good morning, Bubb. Sorry to put you up so early. But something awful might have happened."

"What?"

"Phil has gone."

"Gone?"

"He disappeared, I think, during the competition last night."

"You didn't quarrel or anything?"

"Don't be silly. This was in front of hundreds."

"This is serious. Give me a few minutes. I'll come over."

When Bubb arrived, he found Marie-Antoinette had laid the table. Bubb helped himself to bread, butter and honey; Liz stuck to tea.

"When did you notice?"

"During the prize-giving. He wasn't there. I knew he couldn't have gone with you because you were still there."

"But where could he go?"

"Not far. By himself, that is. The car is still in the garage. We haven't friends...not the kind of friends he would suddenly turn up to see. Bubb, did anything happen at the match? I mean, did you get involved in anything...so that someone had a reason to get Phil?"

"No. Not much. We met the England team. You see, there was an incident, a minor one. The locals wouldn't give us a substitute."

"A substitute? For what?"

"You know, when a player is hurt, another takes his place. The locals said no to a substitute for Freeman."

"That's why England played one short."

"So you have heard about it."

"I just heard from Marie-Antoinette that there is a rumour that an England player has been kidnapped."

"Probably true. Freeman is missing."

"Who took him?"

"The Panthers. They want him to ensure England will win."

"But why Phil? He's nothing to do with the England team."

"You are assuming the Panthers took Phil, too. Lots of things are happening in the country. There are lots of factions. They grab what comes."

"What do they want with Phil? I mean, we haven't got much money, we are not involved...I mean, we are nothing."

"The Lions were planning to disrupt the match. If they can't succeed, they might try to cause a diversion by seizing an Englishman, any Englishman."

"Should we go to the police?"

"No, not yet. For all we know the authorities may be involved."

"You mean the Government?"

"The Government does strange things nowadays. But what motive do they have? They are heavily dependent on us. And they want to keep the truce. But we don't want to do anything hasty. Not embarrass the Government or put the truce at risk. Leave it to me. I'll make some enquiries. We'll decide what to do after that."

"What am I to do?"

"Keep calm. Appear normal. Go to the match today. He won't come to any harm. Anyone who wants him wants him alive, whole and well. He is of no use to anyone if he is harmed."

"Oh God, I hope he is safe."

Bubb got up to go. "I'll start chasing this up as soon as the offices start filling. Maybe I should speak to Thistle and ask him if he has heard anything about Freeman. Hang on, there might be a connection. Do you know Bark?"

"Bark?"

"The dark fellow with a toothbrush moustache. The ebony Führer, he looks like."

"Oh, yes. The one who was beaten up at the match...the one Mr Grunt saved."

"That's him. Thistle described someone like him as being involved in Freeman's kidnapping. He was there last night, wasn't he?"

"I think he came with the minister. I thought he was the minister's bodyguard."

"That is the connection. Freeman and Phil were both taken away when the minister was about. And Bark is holding the High Priest, too. I need to speak to Bark."

As he moved to the door, its bell rang.

"Who is it?" asked Liz excitedly.

She ran to the door, Bubb close behind. There stood outside the imposing figure of Emmeline Grunt. As she began to speak, she espied Bubb at Liz's shoulder. Liz was still in her dressing gown. In his haste to get over, Bubb had thrown a few clothes randomly over himself, had not shaved, and generally looked dishevelled. The reasonable, prudent man, as lawyers call the evaluator of objective fact, could have drawn only one conclusion. Emmeline looked embarrassed and half turned to leave.

"I'll come later, child, when you are more...settled. Sorry it is so early."

"That's all right, Mrs Grunt. Bubb was just calling over to talk about Phil...oh, this and that. Can I do anything?"

"No, no, not at all. It is...I wanted to know if you were coming with us to the match."

"Of course. I'll be delighted to come with you today."

"That was all, child. I will leave you now. You must have lots to do...catch up...see you later. Cheerio, now."

She waved and left awkwardly. Liz and Bubb looked at one another and laughed.

++++++++

II

Liz found herself seated once again beside Emmeline on the third day of the match. Having missed the second day's play hardly seemed to matter to her; nothing seemed to have changed on the ground. But her recent excitement had precluded any opportunity to find out the state of the game.

She should in all truth have felt tired and restless but, curiously, the mood that affected her was that of alertness and anticipation. She looked forward to the resumption of play, if only to ease the tension that appeared to have sprung up between Emmeline and herself. The headmaster's wife, though striving to be friendly, conveyed distance between themselves that morning; there was even an hauteur about her, much as if she might be Dr Schweitzer among his leper patients.

"Happiness, child, is what comes at the end of a long struggle," she had offered without provocation soon after they had settled into their seats.

Liz assumed this was in reference to the encounter with Bubb and herself that morning.

"I would have thought so, Mrs Grunt."

"Are you happy, child?"

"I am as happy as anybody ever is."

"It is a difficult thing to plan, happiness. When I married Mr Grunt I thought happiness was just going to come – an event, you know, the way children come in a marriage."

"Not in all marriages."

"That is so. But that is fate's doing. But those who are childless are benefited by fate, too. They may choose to serve God or their fellow men. That way lies the path to happiness for them."

"Are you saying that, whatever fate ordains, the path to happiness lies in the individual's hands?"

"That's what I am saying, child. Fate has dealt us our cards. We can choose how to play them. We can choose our paths to fulfilment."

"There's a lot in what you say, Mrs Grunt."

"That is the reason we must resist the temptation to gain a temporary advantage, a short-lived pleasure, a cheap thrill."

"Do you really believe fate decides things for us?"

"No, you are wrong there. Fate gives us a chance to show our colours. Fate gives us potential, a piece of derelict land that we can develop by the lives we lead. When I married Mr Grunt, as I was saying, I thought there was to be nothing in my way. He was a most brilliant man. He would succeed whatever the obstacles. Influential people would help him. Fortune would smile on him. Any difficulties would be temporary, an opportunity for him to reveal his true ability and jump over the obstacles. But that was not to be."

"There was something you did not anticipate?"

"Yes, child. I forgot that blood is thicker than water. If you have the wrong blood, all your ability may be of little use by itself."

"Being a *None* is a handicap – is that what you mean? – for which fate has not made allowance."

"No, child. Maybe fate has put the accident of birth with the other challenges we have to face and overcome. But what I am saying is that seeking happiness is a never-ending business, like seeking the truth or making money. It never ends."

"I wish I knew what real happiness is and how one goes about finding it."

"You are young, child. There's life ahead of you. You are having a sojourn here. Accident of birth has blessed you. You are not like us, plagued for our life by what blood ran in our parents. You can seek true happiness if you are not waylaid by cheap thrills and quick fixes."

Liz did not respond but looked towards the seats Bubb and Phil had occupied on the first day. She now saw Bubb with a half-full beer mug and an empty chair by his side. He must have sensed being observed, for he turned and waved.

Play had commenced. Liz was still none the wiser as to its state. She saw it was the local team that were fielding and she heard occasional snatches of polite applause. Emmeline, too, was subdued, there being none of the raucous cheering and earthy dispensation of advice that had characterized her participation on the first day. By lunchtime the ground had been reduced to an unnatural quiet and the spectators to an eerie solemnity.

"We are slipping behind," groaned Emmeline.

"How do you read the situation now?" asked Liz.

"We were doing very well till yesterday afternoon. We got a good score and then we collapsed. We lost the initiative as England made a good start. They are going ahead every minute they bat on."

"You put your money on England, Mrs Grunt?"

"Have to, child. What else can we do? And, to think, England started playing with ten men only. Their top fast bowler, Freeman, was not even there. And yet we collapsed. It is absurd."

"What happened to Freeman?"

"I don't know for sure, child. Some said he had eaten too much. Others said he had drunk too much. But we didn't allow a substitute because they wouldn't show him to us. They are saying he was not there."

"Not there?"

"Not with the rest of the team. Disappeared. I think he got bored with the hard work he was having to do and took himself off to the hills. That's not good enough. No substitute allowed for that."

"You don't suppose he was...kidnapped?"

Emmeline appeared shocked. "Kidnapped? You mustn't joke about things like that, child. Who would kidnap him? For what? No, I think he went off to enjoy himself. Just like that. That's young people for you today. Shirking hard work. Just the same everywhere, your country or my country. But we did not benefit. The other bowlers just wrapped us up. Roar's innings was in vain."

"Roar did well, did he?"

"He did marvellously. Such hitting as we have not seen. He seemed to be like a new man. A pity he ran out of partners."

"You must be pleased, after his ordeal."

"Just as I was saying, child. A cheap thrill like that, just one bit of bad behaviour, could ruin your entire life. I hope Roar has learned his lesson with that."

"You have forgiven him, Mrs Grunt?"

"He must have been in bad company. He was misled. He's too young to know about things like that. But, I say, for your future you must be mindful of all that. One little thing and bang goes your future."

It was lunchtime soon afterwards. Liz was anxious to hear any news Bubb might have garnered about Phil, but could not approach him as Emmeline stuck close to her. The women's lavatories were in the direction opposite to where Bubb sat so that pretext did not avail either. Then, as she contemplated a device to attract his attention, Liz noticed Bubb was waving to her. She gestured discreetly in Emmeline's direction. Bubb nodded, smiled and gave a thumb's-up sign. Instantly Liz felt very relieved. She knew Phil was safe and, for the first time in weeks, she felt happy;

the weariness retreated. For the next few minutes she concentrated on making sense of the scoreboard.

After lunch the atmosphere became noisy, the sounds and the music intensifying as if refuelled by refreshments at lunchtime. The spectators chatted, joked, argued and quarrelled. Liz did not blame them for trying to take their minds off the game. The players seemed to be functioning on their own in another, remote, parallel world, separate from the spectators. Liz herself felt dozy but fought off sleep lest Emmeline put the worst possible construction on her deficient sleep of the night before. As Emmeline herself appeared restless, Liz initiated more conversation.

"Things in the middle seem quiet, Mrs Grunt."

"Yes, child. England are piling up the runs. The match has slipped away from us completely."

"Really? England must be very strong."

"But we missed our chance yesterday when England were one short."

"I'm sure you'll get another chance. Maybe it requires Mr Bark to put in another appearance."

"Don't talk about that creature to me. Still, he failed to make Roar fail."

"You quite sure it was Bark?"

"Who else could it have been? That fellow will do anything to have Mr Grunt sacked. When he came to the contest yesterday evening I was worried. I thought he might wish to spoil it."

"Do you think it went well?"

"It went excellently. The old boys were pleased. They thanked Mr Grunt and they praised him. He thanked them for their kind words and praised your husband. Yes, your husband worked very hard. Is he pleased?"

"I'm sure he's delighted."

"It was such a nice sight, no? We used to have plays every year before the troubles. The school was very famous for it. Lot of our best actors started here at school, you know. There was a tradition of drama at the school."

"Why did it stop?"

"Politics, mostly. The plays the school put on were not nationalistic enough, they said. You know, Shakespeare is not these people's cup of tea. I say, if they watch a little Shakespeare, there won't be any of the troubles."

"I'm sure there's something in that. If people have enjoyable diversion they won't fight, I suppose."

"These people have no hobbies. That is the trouble with them. All they do is eat, breed and fight. How sad."

"I hope you will resume the tradition. Of plays, I mean."

"Thanks to your husband, we may be able to do that. By the way, I don't see him. Is he at the match today?"

"He couldn't...wasn't able to come."

"Possibly he is tired. After all that hard work. But he deserves the rest. Anyway, let him sleep.

He would have fallen asleep anyway if he had been watching this sleepy match."

Within a few minutes the game had been revived from the torpor it had fallen into as a dog ran onto the field. How it had come to be in the environs of the ground was uncertain. As Sacred Creatures, dogs were no longer kept as pets; in fact, it was believed to be an act of sacrilege even to touch them. Perhaps the gatekeepers and ushers, overawed by its status, had let it in without challenge. This particular trespassing representative of the species was not a very prepossessing specimen, being undernourished and the owner of a mangy coat. The irony was that, as humans avoided them out of respect, dogs were now neglected whereas previously, when mere pets, they had been looked after. Not being actively fed, they scavenged, and rubbish did not always supply balanced nutrition. They were unwashed, except by the rains, and ungroomed. Unvaccinated, they were chronically ill and rabies was rampant, giving a secular reason for not going anywhere near them. They came to fear nothing and, elevated above all regulation, cultivated a psychopathic streak. There was no regular breeding, and not one pedigree dog or identifiable breed had been observed by Liz. Some foreigners and embassy staff kept them as pets, but out of necessity these remained secured out of sight.

The sight of the dog removed from the spectators the task of trying to find amusement and warding off sleep. The crowd cheered, some in reverence but more in the spirit of profane fun. The applause egged the animal on and, with a disdain for the laws or propriety, it ran in the direction of umpire Shrieker. Thus confronted, and this time receiving no guidance from his rule book, he ran, to the further delight of the crowd. Having seen him off among the crowd at the far corner of the ground, the dog retraced its path back to the playing area. One of the England batsmen approached it with an extended bat handle but, before he had gone a few paces, a communal hiss had brought him to a stop.

The crowd bellowed at him.

"He mustn't do that. It's a sin," cried Emmeline.

"He probably doesn't realize it is sacred," explained Liz. "What will they do now?"

"This has happened before. The umpires must stop play. The players must leave the field. And a policeman and a priest must persuade the Sacred Creature that it is not on sanctified ground."

"Will they try speaking to it?"

"No, child. You don't know our customs. They do it with the power of the spirit the priest has. That's why the priest is there."

"Will there be a priest on the ground?"

"There might be."

"I saw our chaplain. I suppose he doesn't really count."

"No, it must be a local person."

"Tell me, Mrs Grunt, you are a Christian. The school is Christian. But you accept these customs?"

"Of course, child; we accept the local customs. Christianity will not work if it is not adapted to local needs."

"Is that why you have not been able to keep out of the troubles?"

"The troubles are not to do with Christianity or religion, child. It is to do with people. Christians can kill and be killed like anyone else. Our saviour's message has not yet got through to everyone."

"Don't your Christian beliefs get in the way of accepting local customs?"

"No, not at all, child. Christianity has only been grafted onto local customs. We all – *Nones, Ers, Ings* – accept local customs. Christianity is an extra. It is a matter of faith. It is for the individual. But our communities need something that is common, to try to hold us together, and so we believe in our customs, like worshipping the Sacred Creature."

The Sacred Creature on the field decided to follow the players and the remaining umpire as they trooped off. One could see this representative retained a good measure of the species' cunning, for it went to the boundary, saw the players off, and, then, returned to the field, thereby earning itself a renewed round of applause. A capacity to seek publicity had evidently not been dimmed by lack of intimate contact with humans. Once back, the dog chose to recline. Play had been suspended as they awaited the arrival of the state and the clergy to begin negotiations with what appeared to be a clearly superior power.

Phil had been listening on the radio his captors had given him. In normal times he would tune in more or less absent-mindedly to catch the score, but now, for the first time since ceasing to be a schoolboy, Phil listened to a cricket commentary with studied attention. He suspected his release, perhaps even his life, depended on the outcome of this game. He had to concede that, whereas he would not have dreamed of charging the England batting with such a momentous responsibility, now, when it really mattered, they seemed capable of rising to the occasion. Overnight, having bowled the locals out notwithstanding Roar's late flourish, England had made a cautious but assured start. The next day they had resumed batting, played steadily, took no chances, scrounged and teased and bored for every run, showing in the process a purpose and tenacity conspicuously absent in recent years. The score was being slowly accumulated with the relentlessness of a miser's hoard and was beginning to look impressive and formidable. The return on the couple of wickets lost had been good; so much so that Phil retrieved an appetite at lunchtime to eat the dry bread and soup his captors fed him.

As he settled to listen in the afternoon, England carried on, the score mounted further, and hope began to return to his heart. Then the dog ran on. Phil liked animals, dogs especially, but at that moment he could have inflicted grievous injury on that specimen. As the radio faithfully conveyed the sounds of reverence from the ground, he swore with impatience and switched it off.

The leader came into the room.

"Radio not working, Mr Smallbone? Perhaps it is the batteries. I must apologize. We are having to use old recharged batteries nowadays."

"No, the batteries are okay. The radio is working perfectly well. I simply switched it off."

"England not doing well, then?" he asked anxiously.

"England are doing quite well. It is encouraging. But a dog has run onto the field..."

"Ah, that is a pity. But perhaps England will win after all."

"Fair chance if they can get that animal off the pitch."

"Ah, it is complicated. It always is when the Sacred Creature gets anywhere."

"It is sacred to you, isn't it? I'm sorry if I said anything offensive just now."

"No, no, not necessary to apologize. I understand perfectly. You are a foreigner. Foreigners find it difficult to understand our reverence for the Sacred Creature."

"Do you all worship...the Sacred Creature?"

"You mean, all the communities? Yes, we do. It is the common feature in all our lives, our worship and respect for the Sacred Creature."

"It is rooted in your history?"

"No, no, you are incorrect there. It was not part of our history at all. It was this Government which made it part of our worship. They gave an election pledge, you see, that they would make them Sacred Creatures. Some of the Government party officials, chief among them the present Minister of Culture, had found that in our history the Sacred Creature plays an important part. You see, the founder of our religion was a man, a human being, a prophet, but he was persecuted. When his prophecies became true his life was put at risk, his enemies seemed everywhere, there was a price on his head. One night he hid in a shed with the beasts of burden and he knew his time on this earth was coming to an end. So, he prayed to God to thank Him for what He had given our founder and begged for His mercy. As he was praying, the beasts in the shed started making noises, mooing, braying, bleating, neighing and so on. The owner of the shed would have come out and, discovering our founder, he would have seized him and handed him to the authorities and claimed the prize money which he would have loved, for he was but a poor farmer despite the beasts he had in the shed. As the owner got to the shed, by a miracle our founder had been turned into a dog. He was discovered, but the owner was annoyed at only finding a dog. He took a stick and started beating the dog, but the dog seized the stick and ran away as far as it could, and it ran and ran for several days until it came to another land which it got to by swimming right across the river. When it got to the bank on the other side, the stick that it had carried between its teeth had turned into gold and it was encrusted with pearls and rubies and precious jewels of every kind. The people of this land knew about dogs and were not afraid. But they coveted the stick and thought the dog had raided some nest of jewels. So they took the dog in and looked after it, pampered it and fed it, hoping it would lead them to this store of precious jewels. The dog accepted their hospitality and food and their company. Also, by the nobility of its bearing, it made this wild, uncivilized and savage people behave better. They began to think that whoever among them behaved best would be the one to be led to the treasure by the dog. One by one all the people came to behave properly. The people lay down their arms and turned to alms and pacifism; they gave up eating meat; they abjured violence; they would not knowingly take life; they began to respect all creatures, the Sacred Creature above all. Thus were the *Ing* people civilized and made holy by the Sacred Creature. They had not found material treasure but their lives had been changed forever. They sued for peace with their mortal enemies across the river and in time the whole land became one. The *Ings* and the *Ers* had been brought together by the Sacred Creature. That is the legend."

"But, you say you didn't pay much attention to this legend until recently."

"No. You see, then the *Nones* arrived. They were invaders. They were boat people, expelled from their land, with nowhere to go, so they landed here. They were heathens as far as we were concerned. Some of them converted to us. But the others wouldn't. There was much dissent. Civil war broke out. Only the foreign invasions united us, as I told you. In the process our ancient rights were lost and wrongs were committed. The Sacred Creature became just another animal, just like the beasts that had very nearly betrayed it."

"So, at the last election, the present Government party pledged to make dogs Sacred Creatures again?"

"Yes. And there was uproar in the opposition parties. They said we would be completely out of step with the rest of the world. We were going back two thousand years. The world would laugh at us. If dogs were not controlled, there would be plagues."

"Plagues?"

"Yes...they were thinking of rabies. Terrible condition, human rabies. Everyone who gets it dies. What would happen to the tourist industry?"

"Couldn't the dogs be vaccinated?"

"Oh, no, that is not possible. Dogs could not be touched under the new law."

"So what happened to the pet dogs?"

"They had to be let loose. Many of them starved to death because they had forgotten how to forage for food. But the people applauded the Government's action. By a stroke of the pen an ancient tradition had been restored. Five hundred years of foreign rule need not have been."

"How will they get this dog off the pitch?"

"Ah, that is a problem. Lot of people say, when a dog goes anywhere, it must be left alone to decide in its own time what it wants to do."

"You mean, it could be there till nightfall?"

"It will get hungry, of course. Even divine creatures must answer to nature. But some people say it is proper for the High Priest to come and bargain with it."

"Only trouble being, you have the High Priest."

"No, you are wrong. We don't have the High Priest. We meant to invite him to confer with us, but he has gone elsewhere."

"Mr Bark has said he knows where the High Priest is."

"Did he? When did he say this?"

"I was with a friend at a party a few days ago. He asked Mr Bark where the High Priest was. Mr Bark wouldn't say where, but he did say he was safe."

"A friend of yours interested in the High Priest? It wouldn't be Mr Bubb, would it?"

"It was Mr Bubb. Do you know him?"

"We know him well enough. We contracted with Mr Bubb to deliver the High Priest to us."

"Really? So Mr Bubb knows you."

"Mr Bubb knows of us."

Phil was now convinced Bubb must know where he was. Bubb had suspected Bark's hand in Freeman's disappearance and he had been right. Bark and Bubb seemed to be as thick as thieves.

But Phil did not wish to discuss this angle with his captors just yet.

"But we haven't finished discussing how the dog is to be got off the pitch. If there is no High Priest..."

"Any ordained priest will do."

"What do they do? Order the dog off?"

"That's not possible. Utmost respect must be shown to the Sacred Creature at all times. The priest will arrive with a female Sacred Creature that is in season. I told you, even divine creatures have to answer the calls of nature. If the Sacred Creature is of the male kind it will respond to this call. The people at the ground have to cover their eyes, or they will be cursed forever."

"Good God!" said Phil, and muttered, *sotto voce*, "I hope the mutt is a randy old sod."

It must have taken the better part of an hour for the priest to arrive with receptive female canine company. The commentary had, out of respect, gone off the air; music from the studio took its place. Phil switched on at regular intervals but, to his deepening frustration, was treated only to solemn music.

At last, after the dog in the field had been lured by those effects of nature that never fail, the cricket came back on. The break in events proved as unnerving to the England batting as it had been to Phil. Within a couple of minutes of the resumption a wicket had fallen; another followed soon afterwards. Then the third wicket for the day went down. The tea interval that followed conspired to break up concentration once more. Phil became anxious as the advantage accrued during the early part of the day began to be frittered away.

To take his mind off things, he tried to recall the meetings he had witnessed between Bubb and Bark. But, if the latter had been in the pay of the Panthers, what was he doing keeping the High Priest for himself? Was he playing a double game? Where was Bubb in all this? Could he have helped kidnap Freeman? For that matter, could he also have been involved in Phil's own seizure? His mind started to whirr like a manic engine, and he was relieved when the tea interval came to an end and he could revert to earlier anxieties concerning the England batting.

The break not unnaturally made matters worse for the England batsmen. The last five wickets were surrendered without appreciable resistance. Freeman, released and savouring his liberty, struck out boldly for a handful, but the rest made for the usual doleful tale. Phil had to turn the volume down as the sounds rose with each England mishap. The spectators, driven into retreat earlier in the day, now sprang reanimated. Quite apart from their joy at England's discomfort, the collapse to them was also proof of divine intervention. The Sacred Creature appeared to have stepped in when the nation found itself in peril, and this delivery could be deemed to be little short of the miraculous. Phil, normally the most passive and phlegmatic of observers at a cricket match, struggled to contain his anger. Silently, and somewhat to his surprise, he found himself cursing these superstitious savages whose impotence in the face of stray canine trespass had ruined, perhaps irretrievably, England's chances. When the last England wicket fell, to tumultuous uproar, he switched off the radio with an impatient flick.

The leader came into the room upon the sudden cessation of the sound.

"Has the Sacred Creature come back?" he asked with mockery in his tones.

"No, it did enough damage with one appearance."

"You do not look happy, Mr Smallbone. England not doing well?"

"Not well at all. We have thrown in the towel, I'm afraid."

"I do not understand. What has happened?"

"It is a collapse, I'm afraid. It is a collapse of our middle order."

++++++++

III

It had been Marie-Antoinette's idea that they pay a visit to the carnival that evening. Liz had returned from the match in Emmeline's company; during the entire day the latter had seemed determined not to permit Liz to wander beyond her range of vision and into temptation and turpitude. Then, having seen the local team make a brisk and promising start to their second innings, the two women had left just before close of play. Liz's spirits, already cast down, were further aggravated by Emmeline's voluble expressions of satisfaction at the local prospects. She had started to fear again for Phil and wished she could speak to Bubb.

Once home she rang Bubb, but he had not returned. Despairing, she sat in the kitchen and put her head in her hands, too weary even to make herself tea. For two nights running she had not managed to get to sleep. In a sense she feared sleep, not for itself but for the terrors that would envelop her upon waking. Not being able to get to sleep was a nuisance; not being able to sleep in peace and restful calm was a pity; but the feelings of futility and self-pity and regret that descended as she woke she found almost unbearable.

Unseen by her, Marie-Antoinette was busying herself outside. She had been called away at midday when her daughter, yet again, appeared on the verge of labour. But it turned out to be another false alarm. She had stayed with her daughter but her thoughts had turned to her mistress. That morning, she had not liked the look of Liz; indeed, for some time she had not liked the look of the marriage of the young couple for whom she felt devotion as well as responsibility. To Marie-Antoinette's mind, influenced as it had been by the hearing of a thousand infidelities in her village, a man gone missing was a man who had, in all probability, bolted from his wife. And there was invariably a third party. Who, she wondered, had her master found?   There had been no inkling in that respect, for sure. The dissension between the couple was palpable but they had given nothing away. Had they come to this land to run away from their problems or had the land given it to them? Marie-Antoinette found no answer, but a pang of resentment not unmixed with envy for the putative third limb of the imagined triangle drove her back to her mistress's side.

"Poor Missy. Missy looking so tired. I make Missy a cup of tea," she said as soon as she emerged in the kitchen.

"Thank you, Marie-Antoinette. I didn't know you were still here," replied Liz, who had been dozing on the kitchen table.

"I go home earlier, Missy. But daughter still not ready for baby. It is another damp cracker."

"You mean it was another false alarm?"

"Yes, Missy. First babies are so unreliable."

She handed Liz a cup of tea.

"But Missy finding about Master sir?" she enquired anxiously.

"Nothing heard, Marie-Antoinette. No one knows. And I'm advised not to go to the police."

"The police, Missy? That no good. Police not interested in case like this."

"That's what I'm told. Apparently it happens all the time now."

"That is so, Missy. The modern world like that. No discipline, Missy. No respect. People doing what they want. People behaving like animals."

"Animals hardly go round snatching one another."

"It is terrible for Missy. But in our hearts we must wish him to be happy."

"Happy? I had hardly thought about that. It's his safety I'm concerned about."

"He'll be safe, Missy. These young people giving all the pampering he wanting. But they don't care, Missy, for those left behind."

"What do you mean, young people? Do you know where he is?"

"I not knowing, Missy. But is perhaps young person he fancying."

"He's been kidnapped. He has not run away from me. He's been taken. Seized. Snatched. Bark's friends have taken him."

"Kidnapped, Missy? My God! What for?"

"I wish I knew."

"No crying, Missy. But, my God! Master sir kidnapped. He not harming anyone. He not terrorist. He teacher. My God!"

"I'm so worried. What will they do to him? They took Freeman and demanded England must win the match."

"No, no crying, Missy. England can win the match. Master sir will be safe."

"I wish I could believe that. But our record is not good."

"Not good, Missy. But we having hope. England winning till Sacred Creature stop play."

"Talk of the game going to the dogs."

"Missy smiling again. Missy must have hope. Missy must take mind off things. We go to carnival tonight."

"What do you mean?"

"Carnival in esplanade, Missy. Grand affair. Everything there. Roundabouts, giant wheels, fortune tellers..."

"Oh, I'm in no mood for carnivals, Marie-Antoinette. I'm so tired. I've not slept for two nights."

"You sleeping very well tonight, Missy, after going to carnival. Missy seeing things, enjoying and then sleeping."

"But how do we go? I don't feel like driving."

"We go by the walk and the bus."

Thus persuaded, Liz went with Marie-Antoinette. The day had cooled and their walk was a pleasant one. In the street the people, now spared a curfew for a third successive day, made the most of that Sunday. Several were on their way to the late-night shops, to stock up to face the shortages that would be inevitable when the match and the truce came to an end and the war resumed. Others simply chatted in the street, while yet others transacted business. A man tried to interest the two women in boxes of matches, a woman tried to sell them raw, sliced mangoes with an accompaniment of spices or, if they preferred, olives. A fruit-seller gloried in produce that had been scarce only a week before: mangosteens and rambutans, luscious exotic fruit hinting of romance and mystery – incongruous given the recent mundane bloody history of the land that grew them.

The buses were crowded. When she had first arrived, Liz had been fascinated watching the bus conductors trying to pack their vehicles with all the finesse employed by sardine-packers. Little thought was evidently given to the comfort of the traveller, even less to his safety. Those obtaining seats on a bus were in a minority; others stood, occasionally contriving to place both feet on the floor of the bus, sometimes making do with one. Some adventurous young men preferred to retain a precarious toehold on the footboard. The two women now went to the bus stop, but had to let several buses go by for there was not the remotest possibility of finding a seat on any of them. Their queue inched forward and, after an hour, they managed to board a bus that commenced its journey from that stop and, for that reason, started empty. Marie-Antoinette paid for the tickets with money Liz passed to her. They took their seats and observed the procedure by which the bus was filled. Those standing after all the seats were taken were made to creep up the aisle while those at the end stood on the platform at the entrance. The conductor remained outside to ensure the process of cramming passengers in was undertaken with efficiency. On this occasion it appeared to Liz that he might have performed his task not wisely but too well, for there was no room left for him when it was all done. As he struggled to mount and gain at least a toehold, one of the passengers, through impatience, mischief or mere accident, rang the bell and the bus lurched off. The roars of anguish issuing from the stranded conductor were drowned by the cheers, jeers and applause of those being conveyed on the bus. Liz and Marie-Antoinette, sitting in front of the lower deck, had not been fully aware of these last events until the bus reached the next stop. The bus paused dutifully, several passengers struggled out, and an even greater number, by some magic of compression, were substituted for them. These could hope for a free ride for there was no one to take their money. This time, however, no one dared ring the bell and more hopeful passengers tried to get in. After a few minutes the driver alighted from his cab and launched an investigation. Finding his colleague, the conductor, missing, he went back to his cab and switched off the engine.

"What is happening?" Liz asked. "Why are we stopping?"

Marie-Antoinette rapidly apprised herself of the situation.

"The conductor has fallen off, Missy. The driver won't go without the conductor. It is against his union rules, Missy."

"Where do we get a spare conductor?"

"We have to wait for another conductor. Or may be the lost one will come in the next bus."

"Good heavens! We could be here for hours."

But the conductor arrived, as Marie-Antoinette had predicted in the alternative, by the bus following, and they resumed their journey.

The carnival itself was a colourful affair despite being put together, like so much else, in haste when it became known the land was going to be blessed by a temporary truce expected to run for seven days. The ramshackle organization meant only that there was no standard fee for entry. Marie-Antoinette insisted on buying the tickets once they learned there would be a variable fee for entry and that Liz, an obvious foreigner, would be at risk of being fleeced in these circumstances. Upon entry they found the universal currency of funfairs freely in circulation – merry-go-rounds, giant wheels and stalls of every description purveying fruit, vegetables, sweetmeats, household goods, arts and crafts.

Marie-Antoinette insisted they go into the fortune-teller's tent, where a wizened old man, surrounded by several personable young men and women, held court.

"Missy reading palm?"

"If you insist, Marie-Antoinette."

They parted with payment and the old wizard pondered Liz's future. Unfortunately, he spoke no English, and Marie-Antoinette added interpretation to her repertoire. "You have come from far," Liz was told without apparent irony. "You must wait and be patient. You have a bright future. What is happening to you now will bring rewards in the future. Keep calm and let the fates work for you. Do not fight them."

Her future decided, Liz went with Marie-Antoinette to the sweetmeat stall. There she saw things that she had been warned against, on pain of grievous illness they could perpetrate by themselves or through the germs they conveyed. Daringly she chose one, similar in appearance to a piece of Turkish delight but with a crisp covering and a cloying taste; once inside her mouth the sweet travelled like a piece of rubber. It had potency of a kind, for the hunger that was hinting beforehand disappeared and was replaced by nausea.

They noticed that security was intensive; the police were crawling everywhere, and there were more of them than at the match. It was as if the soothing properties of the game of cricket could subdue even the demons of violence but, now that it was night, and with the rest-day suspending the game, trouble was being anticipated.

Liz saw Marie-Antoinette drinking the juice of a young coconut. The boy in charge of the stall had taken a golden yellow coconut complete with its encasing husk, and with a knife shaped like a sickle had made a deft slash, slicing its top. He had offered Marie-Antoinette a straw to drink it with but she declined, preferring to drink it by inclining her head and emptying the contents of the coconut down her mouth. Still feeling the pangs of nausea induced by her sweetmeat, Liz averted her gaze as

Marie-Antoinette drank, and, as she did so, she spotted Bubb talking to a couple of policemen.

Excited, she ran to the group, remembered her maid had been left behind, stopped, shouted to her to follow, and resumed running. Bubb had not yet seen her.

"Bubb! I kept ringing you."

"I kept ringing you, too, but you must have left. I have something to tell you. But these officers wanted a word with me."

"What about?"

"It seems some members of the England party have been seen trying to exchange sterling for the local currency. That is unlawful." He turned to the two policemen still standing by his side. "That's fine, officers. I'll make sure your concern is conveyed to the highest levels. I'll make sure the authorities stamp it out."

Apparently content, the officers left them, and Liz could restrain herself no longer.

"Heard anything about Phil?"

"Yes. He's all right. They kept him in place of Freeman when they released him. He was back playing today."

"Where is he?"

"Freeman does not know. He was blindfolded when driven to and fro. But not to worry. He's well. They treated Freeman well, too. He was quite fit to take the field and club a few runs today."

"But why?"

"They took Freeman to ensure England won the match, you know. When it was pointed out to them that England were less likely to win the match without Freeman, they let Freeman go but insisted they keep Phil back."

"Why do they want him? Why did they take him?"

"They couldn't understand what Freeman was saying, you see. They thought he was resisting, not co-operating as he might; half hearted about victory they thought he was. And perhaps he seemed a marble short. He's from Somerset, but you don't know him, do you?"

"What made them take Phil?"

"I suppose they just picked up anyone able to interpret what Freeman said, and help to drill into him the urgency regarding an England victory."

"But it happened at school..."

"Good reason for suspecting Bark, who was lurking there that evening."

"But we must do something. I mean, they'll keep him till the match finishes, and if we don't win..."

"That's three more days."

"Can we win?"

"We looked set until that damned dog ran on. All life in the country came to a stop then. Well, we are even now. Anything can happen."

"You don't sound hopeful."

"One is never confident or certain when England are playing. There have only been bad results and worse results in recent years. But we have also been plagued by bad luck."

"You mean the weather?"

"Yes. But even more by top-quality fast bowling, bad umpiring, captains going to the fleshpots... I must say, the umpires are behaving themselves, there is no fast bowling to speak of, and Sainsbury appears to have taken the vows of chastity and obedience if not those of poverty."

"Bubb, we must get him out. You still don't want the police?"

"No, certainly not. Did you see the clowns who were speaking to me? While murderers, rapists and gangsters stalk the land, they were complaining of some England players getting small local change for their pound notes. These buggers have no sense of proportion. Accounts for the state of their country."

"But, Bubb, we can't take a chance waiting for England to win. We must help him now."

Bubb thought for a moment. "I'll try to find Bark. If I fail, I'll go to see a minister or someone high up in the Government. They are bound to have some influence with the Panthers in these days of the truce. But Bark is the key chap."

Marie-Antoinette had joined them but stayed demurely at some distance. Then all three walked the grounds, looking for all the world like an expatriate English couple taking the evening air with their faithful retainer. This idyllic scene was soon punctured by what sounded like a suppressed howl from Bubb.

"Bark!"

"Where?"

"There he is, with those two men."

"I see him now. Are those his bodyguards?"

"No, they are priests in mufti. That's how they go about when they are off duty. Isn't that right, Marie-Antoinette?"

"Yes, master. They are priests from the temple."

"Isn't it right, Marie-Antoinette, that we cannot get close to them until we are invited into their presence?"

"Yes, master. You must stand in front about ten yards. If they see and call you, you go forward."

"Fat lot of chance we will get invited into that circle with Bark among them."

"We must keep him within sight. The moment he leaves the company of the priests we shall be able to grab his attention." Walk steadily but not too fast. We don't want him to see us."

"I think it is too late. He has seen us. He is making a signal of some kind."

"Damn! But never mind, let's follow them."

"But don't you know where he lives, where he works, for whom he works? Would make much more sense to contact him there than follow him like a bunch of third-rate detectives."

"He's a mysterious little tick. No one really knows what he does or where he does it or with whom he does it. Stick close to him. There's nothing else to do."

Bark moved in the protective environment of a handful of priests. Liz, Bubb and Marie-Antoinette accompanied them at a respectful distance. There seemed no point in taking a chance getting any closer; they did not fancy creating a public incident – a contingency of great likelihood given the ubiquity of the police. So, when Bark's company paused, those following stopped, too, and watched discreetly. Bark showed no inclination to break away. Once they halted by the merry-go-round, where a young member of Bark's party, perhaps a novice priest, asked for a ride on it. He indulged himself alone while the rest of his group watched, and the trio following watched them. To Liz it all seemed fairly ludicrous.

The minutes slipped by and Liz thought impatiently that, while they may have gone somewhere, they had reached nowhere. Bark seemed to be beyond their reach. They had eaten and drunk twice over and they had made two complete circuits of the fairground.

By now Bark's party had reached the giant wheel yet again. The novice priest, wishing no doubt to extend his stock of worldly experiences, got onto the structure while Liz looked up wearily. When she turned round, she saw a couple of policemen emerging from the shadows. They went up to Bubb.

"We having problem," said one of them.

"What is it? An England cricketer found exposing himself?"

"Not that, sir. But it is a serious matter. It is gambling, sir."

"What is gambling?"

"England cricketers gambling, sir."

"Are they now? But why tell me? I'm not their keeper. I'm not even their manager. Mr Thistle, he's their manager. You should complain to him."

"They are not doing it alone, sir."

"Ah, a pity. Otherwise, gambling between consenting adults in private would have been all right."

"But no, sir, it is not private. They are gambling with our boys."

"Corrupting the young and pure in heart, are they? It is a shame. But it is nothing to do with me. I'm a humble layman in these matters. I can do nothing."

Liz and Marie-Antoinette stood and listened to Bubb's ironical protests.

"We would like you to come with us, sir, to let us explain the problem."

"But you have explained the problem clearly. It's crystal clear, in fact. Absolutely precise. Why do you want me to come?"

"If you do not come with us, sir, we shall have to arrest the two members of the England team. We will have no alternatives."

"But this is absurd. I'm not coming anywhere with you. Let's get that clear."

"All right, sir. We shall arrange to have the two England cricketers arrested."

"Wait!" said Liz. "Can we come with him?"

"Most certainly," said the man. "The two ladies can come with us."

He nodded to his companion, and the party of five set off together. They had proceeded about two hundred yards when, without warning, the man turned abruptly into the fortune-teller's tent.

"Are they here?" asked Bubb.

"Not yet. But I want to speak to you privately."

"What do you mean? Aren't the England cricketers gambling? Is this a ruse to lure us here?"

"Be patient. We have been sent here. We are not real policemen. We were told you would be here. It is about your friend."

"Mr Phil Smallbone?"

"It is him. He is well. He is happy."

"Did you take him away?"

"No, we did not take him away. We are looking for the man who took him away. Perhaps you will tell us this man is where."

"How do you know I'll know the whereabouts of this man?"

"Because we hired him to get the High Priest for us. You know about that?"

"I know about that. But don't you have the High Priest?"

"No."

"But Bark – that is the man you are looking for – said he knew where the High Priest was. I assumed he was with you."

"This Bark could have taken the High Priest. But he did not bring him to us."

"Where is the High Priest, then?"

"We do not know. But we do know we have been betrayed by this Bark. Perhaps you will help to find the man who has let you down and taken your friend."

"Well, I know where Bark is."

"Where?"

"He's on this fairground. We were following him. But we can't get to him. He is surrounded by priests. It seems it is improper to approach him when he is with them. They provide him with a cordon sanitaire."

"But we must get him. You to ask how he took your friend, we to ask where the High Priest we paid for is."

"All right, I shall point him out to you, but the rest I leave to you. I'm not involved or responsible. Remember?"

"Yes, sir."

The man went behind a partition in the tent and spoke to others. Four men in khaki police uniform, and a man in plain clothes, then emerged. Together they all went, the two women following behind, the plain-clothesman, who appeared to be their leader, and Bubb leading the pack. After they had retraced their path, they sighted Bark's party.

"There he is. With the priests."

"That is Bark?"

"Yes. You haven't seen him before?"

"No. We have spoken through intermediaries but we have not met. This is the first time we are seeing him. He looks like one of us, yes."

"One of you, yes. What do we do now?"

"We must take him."

"How?"

"I have a plan. We must break through the priests. It can only be done in emergencies. We are policemen. What kind of emergency can be there for us? Crime. We stage a crime."

"What kind of crime?"

"Any kind. A common one. In here it will be pickpocketing. Pickpocketing common in carnivals, yes?"

"Yes. But who is going to pick whose pocket?"

"That is easy. No one is going to pick anyone's pocket. We just give the impression of a crime, remember?"

"Right."

"Good. Now, you shout at top of voice when I signal, 'Pickpocket!' Two or three times, right?"

"Right."

He turned and briskly addressed the posse.

"I say one, two, three, right, and..."

"I shout pickpocket."

"One, two, three..."

"Pickpocket! Pickpocket!" yelled Bubb.

The four men in uniform rushed after their colleague in plain clothes. That man, chosen evidently for his speed, broke away and ran like a deranged hare towards Bark's party. The men in uniform rapidly gained ground and plunged into the group. The priests scattered like chickens escaping a marauding fox. Bark stood his ground and looked quizzically at the advancing man apparently been chased by a quartet in khaki. He made as if to move aside, but the lead man of the onrushing group crashed into him, felling Bark. There was a scrummage. For a few moments all was confusion, noise and dust. Eventually it all settled. They picked themselves up from the top of the pile, like a film of falling dominoes being played backwards. The last man to come up held Bark. Such was the speed and violence of the capture that he did not utter protest. The man in plain clothes was nowhere to be seen. The four men in khaki held Bark and then took him away with them.

Part Four – The Rest-Day

I

With Bark taken away, unquestioned by them, obviously the pursuit of Phil had to be switched to other tracks if any information was to be had. Monday was the stipulated rest-day at the match, when cricket writers and commentators paused, put their feet up, explained why their predictions had not materialized yet but could still come good in the two days remaining, and re-hedged their bets. The match itself, they all conceded, was evenly poised, with a sliver of an edge to the local team now batting again. England would have to bat on the last day, and for some hours before that, when the wicket, emotions and tempers would be most worn and fragile, and the umpires at their most frail and vulnerable to the temptation of being prised away from dreary neutrality.

By that morning Liz felt rested, having had the best night since the match commenced. It had gone past 8.00 when she rose, surprisingly keen and expectant, with a clear vision and no headache. She found that Marie-Antoinette, whether in hope or expectation, had considerately arranged breakfast for two.

"Missy sleep well?" Liz was asked in the kitchen.

"Yes, thank you, Marie-Antoinette. I feel better for it."

"There is no match today, Missy. Players taking rest. Getting strength up. Fighting to the finish on two last days."

"Yes, I understand. What are the chances for us, Marie-Antoinette?"

"England side winning, I think, Missy. Definitely going to win."

"Are you saying that to cheer me up, or are we really going to win?"

"England winning match. I hoping so. I praying so."

"Really? That's very kind of you to do that."

"Missy, I must tell you something. Before you waking up I hearing...I finding that Master sir keeping well."

"Really! Who rang? Was it Bubb?"

"No, Missy. Mr Bubb not ring. I hear...from small boy who come to door...very small boy."

"A small boy at the door? What are you talking about, Marie-Antoinette?"

"Small, small boy bring message from kidnappers...Panthers, Missy."

"Marie-Antoinette, tell me everything. What is happening to the master and what did you find out? I want the truth."

"Yes, Missy. I tell you. About six o' clock, Missy, while Missy still sleeping, I hear little knock on the door; only a little knock. I think it is milkman... maybe to get money. So, I wait – no hurry, no? Then I go and open door, and there is milk bottle, but full of blood."

"Full of blood?"

"Yes, Missy. One pint whole blood. It staying on top of little paper. Paper say, 'Mr Smallbone alive if England win match'."

"Where is the piece of paper?"

"I…throw it away, Missy. I not want Missy to frighten."

"I wish you had kept it to show me. It could have been important. Are you sure there was nothing else written on it?"

"Nothing else, Missy." Marie-Antoinette sounded hurt. "I can read English. I can tell."

"I'm sure you can. But it might have been evidence."

"It is just plain paper, Missy. In big letters. That is all it say."

"What did you do with the blood?"

"I thrown it down the rose bushes."

"Thrown it down the rose bushes? Whatever made you do that?"

"Blood come from man, Missy. It has strong food value. Vitamins and so on. Just like for chicken feed. Chicken grow strong. Plants grow strong. So I thrown blood down the rose bushes and wash bottle."

Liz rang Bubb immediately and he rushed over.

"I suppose it is his blood," said Liz quietly.

"Pretty odd way of assuring people someone is alive and well, I mean, sending a pint of his blood. It mightn't have been his blood, of course. Could have been someone else's. The High Priest's or an animal's, or just red paint. Cheer up, anyway. The important thing is he is well and is likely to remain so for at least the next couple of days."

"We need to act quickly. What can we do?"

"I wish I had managed to speak to Bark before they took him away. I think we need to speak to someone in authority."

"Who? And how do you go about it?"

"I think I know a way. Look at it this way. Bark was attached to the Minister of Culture's entourage. Well, he is now gone and the minister doubtless will like to know the circumstances in which he went."

"Will you speak to the minister?"

"I'll try. Perhaps I'll ring from here."

Bubb dialled the ministry and was told the minister would be late in arriving. Bubb insisted it was a matter of utmost urgency and that it was desperately important to speak personally, and in private, to the minister. No, he had said, he could not reveal either his name or the nature of the business. Very sorry, the ministry had replied, the minister was unavailable except through the ministry and its officials.

"Damn!" said Bubb as he put the telephone down. "We need to catch him before someone else gives him the facts. Or a version of the facts. Otherwise, the trump card we hold will turn into a useless dummy."

"How can we get hold of him? Can we get someone else to get the minister?"

"That will not work. Just a minute, I have an idea. I'll get Thistle to ring the ministry. Better still, I'll be Thistle. I have known him long enough, actually know him better than he does himself."

Catching his nose with his thumb and the forefinger of his left hand, and reproducing Thistle's slightly nasal tones, he spoke into the telephone again.

"Mr Thistle, England cricket team manager speaking. May I speak to the minister please? It is a matter of utmost urgency...a delicate situation has arisen...we are concerned about the safety of our team...one of our team members has been threatened. What do you mean, a serious threat? Is kidnapping serious?...perhaps it is not in your country, but in England and other civilized countries it is a serious matter, a grave matter...what do you mean, keep calm? I am keeping calm and cool, but not for much longer...there is a security threat to our team...we need an undertaking from the minister...we have been in urgent touch with Lord's and they seek immediate clarification...reassurance from the President...what do you mean, which President?...how many do you have? It is the President of the Republic, of course...he gave us the assurance our team members will be safe...we want him to keep his word...or the match is off and we fly back today...yes, I'm sure that Lord's will want...all right, I give you half an hour. If the minister has not got back in touch, I'll go directly to the President...right, I'm not at the hotel...I'm staying with friends...I feel safer with them...here's their number."

Within a few minutes the minister, in person, had returned the call and Bubb had concluded an appointment for later that morning at the ministry. Liz went with Bubb into the crowded streets. Despite dire predictions of a resumption in civil warfare, the truce still held. The Lions bided their time and the grateful citizens savoured normality. Although there was no play in the match, the streets on that rest-day assumed a festive air. Shopping was productive once more; fruit and vegetable produce could be picked in the country fields and sent up to town to arrive unmolested. Petrol was once again available off-ration. Even the air smelled safe. To an observer, strange as it might seem, a touring party of England cricketers had made a war pause and a people feel secure again, however transiently.

They penetrated the doors of the ministry with some difficulty. Their identification was sought and Bubb fished out a driving licence, but Liz had only a chequebook with her. Perusing these documents seemed to confuse the guard, who had evidently assumed they were man and wife. Moreover, the chequebook Liz carried actually bore Phil's name. The guard, raw and young, had to seek a superior's intervention.

"This chequebook belongs to Mr Smallbone, yes?" asked the superior.

"It is my husband's."

"This man here is not your husband?"

"No, he is a friend. My husband is away. I'm keeping our chequebook."

"Oh, I see. Are you a film actress?"

"No, I'm Mrs Smallbone."

"We have film actresses carrying on with their own names, not taking their husband's. You are perhaps not in that category?"

"No, I'm not. I'm Mrs Smallbone. This is Mr Bubb from *Roll Britannia!* We have come together to see the minister. We have an appointment with him."

"Right. I shall let you enter in your personal capacities, yes. Mr Bubb and Mrs Smallbone will enter separately, right? But we have a problem. We do not know you are Mrs Smallbone. You have no identification."

"But that's my chequebook."

"No, it is your husband's, as you say. We do not know you exist. You could be anyone."

"Could you take this up with the minister, please?" interrupted Bubb. "He's expecting us. He'll vouch for us."

Their inquisitor went away, and returned in a couple of minutes.

"The minister says he's expecting Mr Thistle from the England cricket team. He has no appointment for Mr Bubb or Mrs Smallbone. He cannot see you."

"I can explain. Can I speak to the minister?"

"Sorry. Security must be strictly observed. Only authorized persons are allowed in the ministry."

"The minister will see Mr Thistle?"

"Of course. The minister is expecting Mr Thistle and will see him in person."

Forced to withdraw, Bubb and Liz went out of the building and in search of a telephone. There was none that was undamaged among the several they tried in the vicinity of the ministry. They gave up and resolved to drive up to the England's team hotel and seek better prospects there. Bubb asked for Thistle at the reception.

"Mr Thistle not in. He go away," the murine male receptionist informed him.

"Go away? Where?"

"Today rest-day. He resting."

"For heaven's sake, can I have a word with him?"

"He not in."

"Do you know where he is?"

"He not leave details."

"Could you get Mr Sainsbury, England captain?"

The receptionist rang Sainsbury's room.

"Mr Sainsbury not wanting to speak to any damned journalist."

"But I'm not a journalist. I'm Bubb from *Roll Britannia!*"

"Sorry. Today rest-day. Mr Sainsbury resting."

With an overwhelming sense of exasperation, Bubb and Liz stood in the hotel foyer wondering what on earth could shift these rocks of obstinate officialdom. Then, Liz spotted what looked to be a working telephone within the foyer itself, and Bubb rang the ministry again. Liz listened closely.

"Mr Thistle is unable to attend for the appointment," said Bubb, now employing his own voice. "He has asked me to represent him. It is urgent."

"The minister wishes to know why Mr Thistle has not informed the ministry himself. His appointment was made as it was thought to be urgent. This is most improper. Gross discourtesy, we feel."

"No discourtesy was meant or intended," Bubb soothed. "Mr Thistle wished to speak to the minister very urgently about a matter of security involving the England cricket team. A member of the team has been threatened. There are doubts about continuing with the match. That is why it is urgent."

"Yet, Mr Thistle is unable to attend and unable to explain to the minister. This is most curious."

"Mr Thistle would wish most fervently to speak to the minister, but he cannot," said Bubb. Dropping his voice dramatically, he continued. "You see, we do not know his whereabouts. In view of the security situation we are alarmed. That's why I wish to speak to the minister on his behalf."

"Mr Thistle mentioned a threat of kidnapping. Perhaps when he was being kidnapped he very considerately made arrangements for you to represent him. Perhaps his kidnappers made this arrangement for him. How thoughtful! Wouldn't you say, Mr Bubb, we have quite splendid kidnappers who set an example by their behaviour to all the kidnappers in the whole wide world?"

"Look, this is very urgent. The security situation is very bad. Listen, I'll give you all the facts. An England cricketer was actually kidnapped. He was returned and another...er, Englishman was taken in his place. Do you understand what I am getting at, why it is urgent?"

"Mr Thistle is this second Englishman?"

"Well, he might be. I mean, he could be. But there is also another Englishman who has been seized."

"Mr Bubb, your Englishmen are being kidnapped one by one. And then they are being returned. Then another is being taken. This is most odd. Why are the kidnappers playing such games? What is in it for them?"

"They are making a point. They are also making demands. The first Englishman they took by mistake."

"Oh, I see. So, Mr Thistle might have been taken by mistake. Nothing to worry, I think, Mr Bubb. These kidnappers are only playing little games with you. They are perhaps bored by the truce and want something to do. There is no security problem. This is what we have been saying. Everything is peaceful and quiet. We must get on with our work. Today is the rest day. We catch up on our work today, and tomorrow we resume the match. I shall cancel the appointment with the minister and shall tell him it was just a false alarm. You must cultivate a sense of humour, Mr Bubb, and laugh at life's little peculiarities. Goodbye."

"Wait! What will you say if I tell you the kidnappers of the Englishmen have also got your Mr Bark?"

"Mr Bark?"

"Your minister's adviser, Mr Bark. We saw him being seized last night."

"Really, Mr Bubb? Mr Bark is not yet in."

"He won't come in. The Panthers have got him."

"Is this really true, Mr Bubb? If it is not so, this will lead to the most serious diplomatic repercussions. The minister will take a very serious view of matters if he is trifled with."

"I'm quite aware of that. I assure you, I can explain the whole of this complex matter to the minister."

An appointment was made there and then to meet the minister that morning. As they were leaving the foyer, Bubb felt a tap on his arm. Turning, he saw Groat, a journalist whom he had met fleetingly before.

"Couldn't help overhearing your conversation just then, old boy. Is it really so that Thistle has been kidnapped?"

Bubb, preoccupied, disdained to give an answer. Drawing Liz towards him, he sped to his car. This time they were admitted into the minister's presence without fuss. In there, Liz noticed the obtrusive details of that office, which gave out evidence of its habitation by a man of scrupulous religiosity. A large dog modelled in clay reclined on a table, a bowl of freshly cut flowers at its feet. A picture of another dog, origins uncertain, hung at the back of the minister's head. The minister himself sat behind a table massively carved out of teak.

"Mr Bubb and Mrs Smallbone?" He enquired from behind the table without rising when his secretary had ushered them in.

"That is correct, minister," said Bubb for them both.

"I know you. I saw you at the dinner the other day. Then I know you again. I saw you at the school drama contest. You were the man who made the people laugh."

"It is good of you, minister, to say so."

"But a serious matter now brings you to me, does it not, a very serious matter?"

"Yes, minister. There has been a very grave breach of security involving your assistant, Mr Bark."

"Mr Bark is not my assistant. He is merely an adviser on some matters of a cultural nature."

"Be that as it may, minister, Mr Bark is involved in very important political matters. That is well known."

"I've tried to contact Mr Bark today. He is not available. You wish to throw light on that?"

"You will find Mr Bark continues to be unavailable. He has been kidnapped."

"Kidnapped? Who by?"

"It is a long story, minister. Perhaps I shall outline it for you?"

"It will be better if you will tell us the end first. Very often the end throws light on the beginning. Mr Bark is kidnapped, you say. How do you know?"

"All right, minister, if you wish for the story in that order. Last night, we – that is Mrs Smallbone, I and several others at the carnival – saw Mr Bark being seized by several men. These men had spoken to us beforehand. They were dressed as policemen..."

"Policemen kidnapped Bark? This is serious."

"I did not say they were policemen, minister. They were only dressed as policemen. We had reason to believe they were not really policemen."

"Aha! That's a different matter. If they had been policemen that would be a serious business. The Minister of Home Affairs will have no business encroaching on my territory. Proceed!"

"Mr Bark was seized, as I say. When they spoke to us the men indicated they knew the whereabouts of Mr Smallbone, the husband of this lady here. We had reason to believe these men might have been kidnapped him, too."

"Why kidnap Mr Smallbone?"

"The explanation may be complex. Mr Smallbone teaches at the school where the drama competition was held, the one you presided at. He was seized there during the evening."

"What! Before my eyes?"

"Not literally, minister. But it was during the proceedings. We think Mr Bark might have been involved."

"Bark kidnapping Mr Smallbone? This is a great mystery. Why should Bark, adviser in culture to me, wish to seize a man, a foreigner, who is a teacher at the school? It makes no sense. I hope you are getting your facts right, Mr Bubb. These are serious charges to make against a public official, also one who is not able to defend himself. There will be diplomatic implications. I hope you have thought carefully, Mr Bubb."

"The facts, unpleasant and incomprehensible as they are, are, in fact, clear to us, minister. What lends weight to our interpretation is that Mr Bark was earlier involved in the kidnapping of Freeman, a member of the England team."

"What! Is this how Bark spent the public time and money, kidnapping people left and right? This is a terrible thing. If he is found, I'll sack him! How do you know this?"

"When Freeman was taken, minister, Mr Thistle, their manager, told me this. It seems it was an opportunistic kidnapping, unplanned. Mr Bark was apparently in the pay of the Panthers, or so we think. They paid him to seize a member of the England team to make sure England won the match..."

"The traitors! And they paid Bark, you say. You have proof? No? Yes? That is treason. If he is found, I'll shoot him!"

"But, you see, minister, the Panthers could not understand what Freeman was saying. He comes from a part of England where it is the custom not to speak clearly. His captors were confused. They thought he was being unco-operative, obstructive even. So they hit upon the idea of kidnapping someone who might be able to make him see sense. They asked Mr Bark to find someone. He was with you at the school drama competition. He loaned you the gun, I think, with which you so graphically demonstrated the importance of culture. We think he used the gun to take and hold Mr Smallbone that evening."

"But this is terrible, Mr Bubb. An official in my ministry has been involved in crimes and treasons like this. I cannot believe it. But I must act. I am going to act. But why wasn't I told before?"

"I think, minister, the England party feared for Freeman's safety if they were to go to the police. Mrs Smallbone here feared for her husband's safety for the same reason."

"But tell me, Mr Bubb; if I understand you correctly, the people who paid Bark have now grabbed him. Why is this so?"

"They are presumably displeased with him, minister. Maybe he did not satisfy them in some regard. Overcharged them, perhaps."

"I am in a terrible position, I might tell you, Mr Bubb. If it became known an official here was involved in these terrible crimes, my position will be in doubt. You must not tell this to anyone; is that clear?"

Liz, who had remained quiet right through the dialogue, now decided to have her say.

"I am very concerned about my husband, sir. He has been gone now for two days. Today we received a pint of his blood and a demand that England win the match. I am desperately worried about him."

"You will not need to worry any more, Mrs Smallbone. I am going to take steps to locate your husband. And loss of one pint of blood is not serious. We all donate a pint now and then. It is good for the body; gives it incentive to make more blood. That is no problem. And we will get him before the match finishes so it will not matter if we win it. My God! This cricket match has brought us more trouble than the troubles themselves. But please remain quiet and I'll do what is required."

"Thank you, minister."

They took their leave and went into the noonday sun.

"Well, we have put him in the picture. We can but sit and wait," said Bubb as they sat caught up in one of the many traffic hold-ups on their way back to the school. Liz did not speak, but then, spying the spires of the distant Great Temple, suddenly felt an irresistible desire to visit it.

"Just drop me there, will you? I'll find my way back."

The route to the temple, like all others in that city, was not traversed swiftly and it was another half-hour before she found herself within the temple gates. She had to leave her shoes at the entrance – to be guarded in the company of other pairs of footwear by an urchin in return for a handful of coins – and then, somewhat confused as to what she next had to do (perhaps cover her head, as she had read the women devotees of some Eastern religions did), she walked gingerly into the temple compound. In there she came upon a booth much like the type through which railway tickets are dispensed.

"There is no payment to get in, madam," said the man behind the partition. "But tourists feel free to make a donation. They think it might bring them luck. Would madam perhaps like a guide?"

"Yes, please, that would be nice."

"I shall find you an excellent guide."

The guide allotted to her turned out to be a young woman robed in red, as her male counterparts were. Liz had not previously known their religion permitted female priests to be ordained, but this one, seconded as a guide evidently on the strength of her proficiency in English, soon explained.

"You are perhaps surprised to see me dressed like this. Most tourists are. But we are not priestesses; we are nuns. We meditate and we contemplate. We also do jobs about the temple and we escort visitors."

They walked towards the outside of the sanctum. Within, Liz was puzzled, slightly disappointed even, to see that the sanctum was plain, its walls lacking the ornate carvings and figures found in the temples of some Eastern faiths. Her guide seemed to read her mind.

"You are surprised to see the simplicity of our temple. Ours is a contemplative religion. The ultimate truth to us lies in what we are able to think, and our oneness with God is achieved in another sphere. We eschew vanity, which is of this world, a world that is transient. We spend but a fraction of our journey through life in this world. So possessions are in vain. They are like the excess baggage which you must leave behind before you get into an aeroplane."

"You speak excellent English. How is that?"

"I was a schoolteacher before I joined our religious order. I was unhappy in my life with other mortals. Nothing seemed to go right, as they say. My family are poor. I was clever. They forced me to study. I passed examinations and I got qualifications. I trained to be a teacher. But it seemed destiny did not intend me for a life in this world. I spoke to my confessor, and he said the gifts I had been given were obviously meant for doing God's own work directly and not for indirect work in the world of other human beings. He asked me if I would like to join the order, and I did not hesitate. I took vows of charity, obedience, chastity and poverty. I renounced the world. My family are looked after by the temple. They will not want. But my work is here. For the first time in my life, I am content."

"Isn't it a lonely life?"

"Surprisingly, no. All sorts of people become nuns. Some have led a life of surprising worldly success and have been rich and famous. You would think they would be fulfilled but they are not. They yearn for something that is of another world, not of this one. But they must complete their tour of duty, so to speak, before they can seek that other world."

"Will you be judged by how you fare in this world, what you did, what you gave?"

"Most certainly. God has put us in this world to see how we conduct ourselves, and also to see how well we cope. You know, the next world may not be, what do you say, a bed of roses. It may pose challenges of other kinds. If you cannot cope here, you may not be able to cope there. So, you must give a good account of yourself in this world."

"It is indeed a very simple temple."

"It is. But, then, ours is a very simple religion. It is a religion of contemplation. The kind of right contemplation that will lead to right conduct."

"You seem gentle and contemplative, and yet there is savagery outside. You have heard?"

"Of course, we have heard. We look after the refugees from the troubles. Perhaps you wish to know why, in a land of such religious simplicity, there is so much hatred in the name of religion. But, remember, these are only the acts of men and women. They choose religion to be their shield and turn it into their sword. They are free to do so. But that is not our religion, which is about contemplation and the thoughts that lead to right conduct. That is how God intended us to live, and so He is not responsible for what people choose to do on their own account."

"Do you think God will punish them for their evil actions?"

"Our God is not interested in rewards and punishments. He is not a behavioural psychologist. These are the considerations of the mundane world. God is impartial, objective and detached. He has his own criteria by which you will be judged. That is, your conduct must be in keeping with your contemplation, which must have been properly exercised. You must be true to yourself. That is the test."

"If your contemplation produces results that lead you to kill your enemies, is it all right, then?"

"No, you are not correct there. If your contemplation is correct, you will not wish to kill anyone. Every being has a right to existence, a right to fulfil its destiny on this planet."

"And yet, men and women are killing one another."

"Of course. But they are killing to satisfy their own motives and desires, not to fulfil God's will."

"If you do not mind my saying so, your religion appears to be a rather theoretical one."

"It is indeed a theoretical one. If you look around at the practicalities of the world, would you not wish for a theoretical religion? My dear, we must go back to first principles, back to the drawing board, to sketch out another blueprint for life on earth."

By now, Liz was no longer surprised that there was little else to see. There was an inner sanctum guarded by a giant dog. Flowers had been offered to this gigantic creature; candles had also been lit, Liz was told, to aid contemplation, the puff of smoke being an especially potent aid to concentration, vindicating the contention of many a pipe-smoking philosopher. Otherwise, the simplicity of the temple was impressive. No one else seemed to be about – a mystery when Liz remembered all that footwear doffed in reverence.

"Do people ask for favours in here?"

"People ask for favours, and sometimes they have been granted them, but ours is not supposed to be that kind of religion at all. You know, when you think about it, that kind of behaviour is no better than young children beseeching Santa Claus for gifts."

++++++++

II

His captors having left him to sleep undisturbed, Phil had risen late that morning. He was wearing the clothes they had supplied and he drank from a cup of tea one of them, a man without English, had brought him soon after he stirred. Impatiently he waited for his watch to come around so that he could switch on the radio for the cricket commentary. It was fully half an hour, after listening uninterruptedly to *Housewives' Choice* whiling away the time by glancing out of the window on a gloriously lit day on which to rain would have been to commit an unnatural act, before it dawned upon him that there was going to be no play that day at the Test Match. He switched his mind over to wondering what Liz might be doing; then the leader came in and registered surprise at the silent radio.

"It is a rest-day today," explained Phil.

"What are they resting from?"

"It is traditional to take a break midway during a test match."

"It is a strange game, this. When we set up our country there will be no place for elitist pastimes like that."

"What will you have in its place?"

" In the first few years after the revolution there will be no time for leisure. All our people will be working hard to lay the foundations for our prosperity. We shall have no time for trivial games."

"Once your prosperity is assured, no doubt you will begin to think about sport?"

"We have no intention of letting our people get fat and lazy. Time on your hands leads only to mischief. You have doubtless had this in your own country. All the problems of the developed world are due to idleness."

"It does seem prosperity and leisure go together."

"We will try to limit our prosperity so that our people will wish to strive for more. That way they will not have leisure."

"And those that cannot or will not strive?"

"They will be eliminated. The weak in our society will be put down. That is kindness. That is nature's way."

"The Nazis tried that."

"The Nazis did not adapt nature. They were, in fact, an unnatural order. They were consumed by hate, not motivated by love or respect. There is no hate in nature, Mr Smallbone. Perhaps you have noticed that. In the state we shall create we intend to follow nature's way. By the way, what is the state of the match?"

"It is evenly balanced. England did well but you...the locals are catching up."

"And when will we know who has won?"

"There are two more playing days. Even then there may only be a draw."

"A draw?"

"Meaning 'undecided'."

The leader looked stern. "There can be no draw for us, Mr Smallbone. A draw, you say, but this is most irregular. Did not the founders of the sport not provide for a finish? There is no draw in nature, may I remind you? A fight to the finish, with a kill at the end. That's nature's way, you understand. We must hope England will inflict a humiliation on these usurpers of the nation."

"I hope so, too," murmured Phil, with feeling.

"And we think your wife will hope so, too. We have sent a bottle in encouragement to her today. With a message."

"You mean, you sent her a drink?"

"I hardly think she would have drunk what we sent her, Mr Smallbone, but we hoped she would drink in the message, so to speak. The bottle contained blood."

"Blood?"

"Yes, blood. Human blood. Thanks to you, we picked up the traitor Bark. And we have bled him. Last evening we undertook a mission, suspecting Bark would be there at the carnival. I think your wife was also there."

"Did you speak to her?"

"We spoke to Mr Bubb, who was with her. We told them you were well and likely to remain well until the match ended. Then they pointed out Bark to us. They had been following him, but it seemed he had the protection of priests and they could not approach him. We created an incident and then we picked up Bark."

"Weren't you noticed?"

"Of course, we were noticed. But everybody approved of what we were doing. You see, we dressed as policemen and we made Bark look like a pickpocket. It seemed like a lawful arrest, you understand, Mr Smallbone. We brought him here. He is in another room helping with inquiries."

"And you bled him?"

"It is customary for those helping us with inquiries to donate blood. It helps our boys. We find getting guns and ammunition and explosives easy. But getting trained men? It is not so easy. So, we conserve our strength and build it up when we can."

"You mean, you drink it?"

"We do that. Most nutritious food you can imagine. We are not superstitious, you know. We do not believe we get the strength of the man who gave us his blood. Anyway, what can a coward like Bark give? But the nutrients in his blood, they are the most natural and wholesome food in nature."

"But my wife, she must have thought it was my blood."

"That is no bad thing. It may lend an edge to her endeavours. She might be able to persuade England to win."

"It is not within her capacity. We have nothing to do with the England team. Personally, I mean. They are engaged in a sporting contest, and the matter will be decided between the two teams."

"Come, come, Mr Smallbone; if you think so, you will be showing a naivety we could not credit you with. What is this pure sporting contest you speak of? This is not ancient Greece, you know. The battle between the two teams is as real as the war between us and the usurpers of this nation. We offered a truce to them because we knew there would be other considerations besides sport. There is no pure sport any more, Mr Smallbone. There probably has never been. Remember Hitler's games? Remember the Moscow Olympics? The Los Angeles Olympics? Remember South Africa? Remember the ping-pong that was used to open up China to the West? My dear Mr Smallbone, sport is like the citizen of a country, a mere tool, to be manipulated to an end."

"She will be very worried," said Phil absently.

"Not as worried as Citizen Bark is at the moment. He has given us two pints of his blood. One for us and one for your wife. He has grown fat in the service of the state. He has bled them; so we bleed him. For once, that traitor's blood will serve someone else a useful purpose. But I must be going now. I must arrange a trial."

"For Bark?"

"Yes. Traitor though he is, he cannot be deprived of justice. We want to show you the quality of our justice. True revolutionary justice in the name of our people. Don't you agree, Mr Smallbone, that justice must be done?"

"Oh, yes. Justice under the law."

"There is law only under our movement, Mr Smallbone. The law of the state has collapsed under the weight of its own corruption. We are building our own order, with our own system of justice. And that is what we going to give our own Citizen Bark. Did England have a revolution, Mr Smallbone?"

"Yes. A small one, three hundred years ago."

"And did you not have a new political and legal order as a result of it?"

"Yes, we did. It was our Glorious Revolution. It was quite peaceful, though."

"Our revolution will be a trifle bloodier, Mr Smallbone. But a new political and legal order will be born out of that just the same. Mr Smallbone, you will be privileged to see the first offerings. Does not your heart beat fast to glimpse at the first fruits of our history?"

"I'm sure I'll be interested to see it."

"You must wait for a while, then. Enjoy your rest-day, Mr Smallbone. I have matters to attend to." He paused and grinned. "A revolution's work is never done, eh? And remind me to give you our recipes for the sanguinary dishes we make sometimes."

He left, and Phil could not help sensing that the temperature of their skirmishing, even though still conducted in good humour, had risen. Real menace was palpable for the first time. He had not long to muse, for the leader re-entered the room dramatically, dragging behind him a small, frightened man who looked as a rabbit might if it had been mugged outside its hutch.

"What are you doing to me?" the man implored. "Let me go, I plead with you. I have a wife and three children."

"You will be allowed to go once you have done the work of the revolution."

"Revolution? What revolution? I am a simple man. I have no interest in politics. I earn a humble living to help support my family. Let me go, please, I beg of you."

"This is Mr Bleating, Mr Smallbone. You will not notice it just now but he is one of the top lawyers in the country. Is it not so, Mr Bleating?"

"I am a humble lawyer, sir. I do my work. I serve my profession."

"Mr Bleating also serves the state, Mr Smallbone. He usually prosecutes."

"It is only a job of work, like anyone will do. I uphold the law. That's all."

"We thought we should give you some variation, a change to make things interesting for you. Today, Mr Bleating, you will defend."

"Defend, sir? But this gentleman looks like a tourist. He needs to go to his embassy first. He may not be within our jurisdiction, he may have diplomatic immunity."

"Calm down, Mr Bleating, compose yourself. The revolution believes justice, like charity, must begin at home. This man is not the accused. He is only a gentleman. He is Mr Smallbone, a schoolteacher. No offence meant to you, Mr Smallbone, but I believe the correct phrase is 'small beer'." He turned to Bleating. "The accused you will shortly be introduced to."

"What has he done?"

"That is what we shall have to find out. This is going to be a proper trial, not a show trial. When Mr Smallbone leaves us – after England have won the match, of course – he will tell *The Times* of London and the BBC that he saw revolutionary justice issuing from the Panthers, and that it was as good as anything that has come out of England. Wouldn't you like to do that, Mr Smallbone?"

"You flatter our system of justice, sir."

"Do I? The system of justice you left behind with us at independence has been corrupted by those whom Mr Bleating defends – those on whose behalf he chooses to prosecute, to be exact. But our revolution will return justice to the course from which she has been diverted. Mr Bleating, before you joined us, Mr Smallbone and I were discussing the English system of politics and law that followed their revolution. Did you know they have had a revolution, Mr Bleating?"

"I know nothing about that, sir. I am not interested in revolutions. I am a peaceful man. I am sick at the sight of blood."

"Their revolution was not at all bloody, Mr Bleating. It was peaceful, really. Not much happened. But a new order rose all the same. A lot of blood will flow in our revolution, Mr Bleating. It will be a river of blood and a lot of traitors will float in it."

"Can we get this...this trial over with, sir? And then, perhaps, you will let me go. My family will be waiting anxiously for me to come home."

"Families will have to take second place to the revolution, Mr Bleating. But you are right. We must start the trial." He turned in Phil's direction. "Get the ball rolling, isn't that what you say?" He returned his gaze to the hapless Bleating. "We must take you to the prisoner. Perhaps you will like a word or two in private with him. He is not a communicative man but do not despair. The revolution will enable the mute to speak."

"I'm uneasy, sir. We are usurping the properly constituted processes of the law."

"Are we, Mr Bleating? Who, may I ask, constituted this process of the law, as you call it? Are the Er people involved? They have suffered so much under it. It is your law, Mr Bleating. It is not ours. It is yours, and the traitor Bark's."

"Bark?"

"Yes, Citizen Bark we call him now. We thought he was one of ours. At least he took our pay."

"Bark one of yours? I thought he was a Government official. Is this the Bark who is adviser to the Minister of Culture?"

"The very same. We paid him handsomely to bring us the High Priest."

"So the rumours are right. You took the High Priest. It will be a great sin if you harm that man."

"We are not planning to harm the High Priest. We cannot harm the High Priest. We do not have the High Priest. Bark took our money; he took someone else's money, too. But the High Priest is elsewhere."

"I do not know what to say."

"You will defend Bark. That way you will get to know what he has done."

"How can I defend this man? He has committed a heinous crime. He has kidnapped our High Priest. I am not a religious fanatic, sir, but I have a simple faith. I respect the guardians of our religion. How can I defend him?"

"You must be true to your profession, Mr Bleating. You must defend anybody who needs your assistance. You would prosecute anyone, would you not? Is that not right, Mr Smallbone; it is the ethics of his profession?"

"Yes, I think that is the position."

"We cannot pick and choose the part fate has allotted to us. We must take what comes. So, Mr Bleating, you will be the defending lawyer. I, the Dark Avenger, will be the prosecution. And we must seek a judge."

Phil intervened. "It is customary, I think, to have a jury."

"It is customary, yes, Mr Smallbone, but these are not normal times. We are in the middle of a revolution, you are forgetting. It is like in Ulster. We shall not have a jury."

"But, sir, a man must be tried before a jury of his peers. That was the law of England after the revolution, and even before," Phil persisted.

"Jury of his peers? A fine phrase, Mr Smallbone, but – like all sentiments – not always realistic. Where can you find twelve men like Bark? This country has gone down the drain because of one Bark. Twelve Barks! Be realistic, Mr Smallbone. We cannot arrange for a jury. And also we must conduct the trial in English. Otherwise, how will you observe the fairness and impartiality, be able to tell the world what splendid chaps we are? No, sir, we shall not have a jury."

Phil responded quickly, determined to try to mitigate the gross injustice that now seemed likely to be perpetrated.

"You need a judge," he said, "someone who is impartial, fair and – well – judicial. Could I humbly apply for the position?"

Dark paused to reflect but Bleating, in his pedantic way, raised an immediate objection.

"But you do not know the law."

Dark interrupted him.

"He does not need to know the law. This is a revolutionary situation. We need unbiased judges. We need revolutionary justice."

"You will find, sir, that, if I am to report to the world how just and fair you have been in dealing with a man who has allegedly harmed your cause so much, I could do worse than sit in the judge's chair and force myself to be impartial."

"You will follow in the footsteps of the English rulers of this country who have traditionally been the arbiters in the disputes between *Ing* and *Er*," said Dark approvingly.

But Bleating was persistent with his objections.

"It seems irregular, if you do not mind my saying so, sir."

"What is this irregularity you speak of, Mr Bleating? You dispense justice according to your system. You think it is fair. We don't. Now we have justice according to our revolutionary system. We think it is fair. You don't. When in Erdom, sir, do as the *Ers* do. You will do well to remember that, Mr Bleating. The dawn of our nationhood is breaking. Be prepared, for the sake of your skin, at least. Now, it is time for the trial to begin."

He called out to three of his companions and they entered, all armed.

"We shall go into a more spacious room," Dark said.

They went into one lying two doors from that in which Phil had been held. There, Bark was found seated, scowling and silent, but retaining good colour despite the donation of two pints of blood. The three armed men took up their positions, one at the door and the others on either side of Bark. Dark motioned Phil to occupy a high-backed chair, easily the most impressive item of furniture in the room.

"Do you wish to speak to the prisoner alone, Mr Bleating?" asked Dark.

But it was plain a private conference between lawyer and defendant had not been anticipated, as the room had already been turned into a forum of justice, revolutionary style.

"All right, then. All ready? I shall make my case now," began Dark. "This man is Bark, a *None* but selling his services to anyone who wishes to hire him."

"Sir, I must object to that," said Bleating, rising. "You cannot prejudice the case against Mr Bark. It is not proper. It is not lawful."

"What is lawful or not is for the revolution to decide. Why cannot we state the facts? It is a fact that Bark can be bought for ready money. We gave him twenty thousand for the job. That is thirty pieces of silver index-linked over two thousand years."

"Judge, I really must protest," pleaded Bleating, with his pathetic eyes and simpering manner. Phil was embarrassed but felt he ought to stamp his authority on the proceedings lest they degenerate into lethal farce.

"Yes, Mr Bleating. Objection upheld," he said bravely, retrieving ill-filed knowledge derived from televised American court scenes. "The prosecution must state the facts, and only the facts, but the facts must apply to the charge being brought against the defendant."

"What is the charge?" asked Bleating, rising again.

"Bark is being charged with general treason."

"There is no such thing as general treason known to the law."

"Whose law are you talking about?" demanded Dark. "We are creating our own law. Bark is being brought before our justice."

"This is no justice. Judge, I must protest. There is no proper charge against my client. That is not right."

"Well, if you do not want a proper trial, we shall have summary justice, shall we not?" Dark shouted. He then barked some brisk order to the guards, who drew out their revolvers. "It will be simpler and cheaper to have him shot. We can deal with the lawyer afterwards."

"Gentlemen," said Phil quietly. "I do not think we should get too involved in the technicalities of the charge. Just yet, anyway. Why don't we agree on treason? It is something everyone understands."

"But treason, judge, is a crime against the state. My client has not committed an offence against the state..."

"How do you know that?" butted in Dark. "If we knew that we would not be needing to bring a case. I think, Mr Bleating, you have no case. You are putting forward an argument as secure as a mud hut in a storm."

"I must interrupt the parties again," said Phil joining in. "We will get nowhere arguing about technicalities. Mr Bleating, may I remind you your client faces a serious charge, however it is put? This is his only chance to clear himself. Give him that chance, please. The charge is treason, as the prosecution alleges. Let us proceed."

"Thank you, judge," said Dark approvingly. "The facts are simple. We had arranged a truce. The Government said we were only buying time.

But we wanted the match with England. We wanted England to win. But the Government scoffed at us. Said we had lost all our teeth, run out of ammunition and supplies and so on. We wanted the truce to find a means of humiliating the Government. If the match is held and England win, it is reported all over the world. It is a miracle. On the other hand, if we make an attack on the Government, no one takes any notice. We blow up bridges, schools, hospitals, army convoys, tanks; we raid banks and post offices; we kill policemen, soldiers, politicians. But no one anywhere takes any notice. But the country loses a Test Match – or England wins one – and that will be news. If the tour takes place it is news. Journalists come and they report. They interview. I have been on BBC *Panorama* and other programmes. You see, we need publicity like a seed needs sunlight to sprout. We also get a bonus of a Test Match defeat. So we do everything to bring the truce about. We swallow our pride. We accept that, for a whole week, we cannot shoot or blow up anybody or anything. But we abjure force for a whole week, like you give up something for Lent or Ramadan. But we do not wish for our determination to bring about a revolution or overthrow this corrupt state or create an independent Erdom, a nation for the *Er* people, to be forgotten or cast aside. A cricket tour will not succeed in making us soft. So we plot something else that will be talked about – or whispered, at any rate, for the press and the radio are as corrupt as the Government and will only do what the

Government tells them to do, or report – for the whole week. Something striking but for which the Government, having given its word, cannot go back on for fear of losing its face; especially abroad, for it has not much face to lose here. So, what do we do? Not burn another school or bomb another police station or hold up a post office. No one takes any notice of that. They have become commonplace and the people are bored with these things. We plan to do something that will grab the *Ing* people by their genitals – speaking figuratively of course, for most of them do not seem to have genitals, if you understand our meaning, judge. What do you think will really affect the *Ings*, really stir their blood? We decide to burgle their Great Temple and remove their High Priest. This is not easy for, though the temple is open, the High Priest is guarded as a dutiful father watches over the virginity of his daughter. We need an inside job done. We need someone high up. We need someone we can trust, someone who has sympathized with us, who has done jobs for us before. We seek advice. We are told Mr Bark is available. He will try to arrange it for us – if properly paid, of course. We say, 'right'. We rob a bank just to finance the business. Mr Bark thinks about it and comes back to us. The High Priest can be removed but how will they remove his guard first? We hear foreign mercenary soldiers are guarding the High Priest. They take orders from the President, not from anyone else; not, certainly, anyone else Mr Bark has influence over. Who are these foreign mercenaries? I will tell you. No offence to you, judge, but, when you gave up transportation to the Empire, you were stuck with people who are rotters; I mean those whose presence rots society. These are the men who vandalize your phone booths, rape your women, harass your immigrants, terrorize your elderly, mug your children, spoil your fun and despoil your country. Fortunately for you, there is some need for them in the Third World. Like London Transport double-decker buses, they can be reconditioned and put to use in the tropics. We buy them. These are the mercenaries. They are, though to say so will offend the people of this country, the dogs of war. Now, Bark, despite the sound of his name, has no control or influence over them. But he promises to find someone who has. He wants more money. We rob another bank. We get the money. Bark gets the money. Bubb gets the money. Yes, judge, your friend Mr Bubb happens to be the man with the influence. You may not know that Mr Bubb is a convicted football hooligan. He left your country when it got too hot to hold him. Several football clubs in your country would have given good money to see him secured vertically. But that man now promotes culture. But we cannot complain. Our own Minister of Culture is a notorious thug, not even reformed like Mr Bubb. So, culture is a very elastic term nowadays. Can mean all kinds of things. Anyway, it is arranged that Mr Bubb will persuade the guards to look the other way. Mr Bark will spring the High Priest and we shall have him for the duration of the truce, and perhaps even longer if things went well. The time came. The truce arrived. The High Priest went. But not to us. He went walkabout. Mr Bark had done some other deal. Someone else had got the High Priest. We did not know this at the time, judge, and so we were mystified. We, to our eternal shame, did not suspect the good Mr Bark. We thought the High Priest might have been moved for safe keeping. We might have dropped the matter. But Mr Bark got greedy. He opportunistically kidnapped an England cricketer and, to allay our suspicions, brought us this England cricketer. We had not wanted this cricketer. And this cricketer turned out to be a dud. We had been sold a pup. He could not promise us he could win the match. He could not even speak. We began to suspect he might not be a cricketer but a tourist of low intelligence attracted perhaps by the vice this land now offers to visitors. But when we told Mr Bark this, he insisted it was a cricketer and said he would find us a first-class interpreter. That was how, judge, you came to grace our humble surroundings. And that cooked Mr Bark's goose, for you told us how you had heard Mr Bark say he was holding the High Priest. The rest of the story is known to you, judge. The revolutionary council ordered the arrest of Bark, and there he is now."

With that flourish, Dark concluded the case for the prosecution.

"The prosecution will call its witness now," Dark then announced.

"Who is the witness?" asked Bleating.

"The judge."

"The judge cannot be a prosecution witness," Bleating protested.

"After the revolution anyone can be a prosecution witness. Even the defence. I will now put my questions to the witness. Sir, did you or did you not say the defendant Bark had kidnapped the High Priest?"

"I did not hear the defendant say it," replied Phil cautiously. "But he said, when asked, that the High Priest was safe."

"Who asked him?"

"Mr Bubb."

"And the defendant replied he had the High Priest?"

"Yes."

"That is all the prosecution wishes to know. Mr Bleating, your turn now."

"Judge, when did you hear Mr Bark say that?"

"At the party on the first evening of the match."

"I put it to you that you must have misheard...or you were intoxicated."

"No, I did not mishear. It is not the kind of thing one mishears. Moreover, Mr Bubb had been seeking to speak to Mr Bark the whole day about the High Priest. He bought Mr Bark a beer at the match. After that, Mr Bark expressed himself publicly and was forcefully contradicted by other spectators."

"He was attacked, you mean?"

"Yes."

"All this so that your friend, Mr Bubb, could find out about the High Priest?"

"Yes."

"Judge, why should my client seek to take the High Priest?"

"I have no idea, except for what we have heard just now."

Mr Bleating sat down. Dark stood up again.

"And finally, sir, you would confirm again you heard Mr Bark say he held the High Priest?" he asked.

"Yes."

"That concludes the prosecution case."

There was now a whispered conference between Bleating and Bark.

"My client does not wish to answer questions."

Dark rose. "Is that so? Well, he will answer mine. Mr Bark, stand up. Did you or did you not accept money to bring the High Priest to us?"

There was no reply, Bark remaining in sullen silence.

"Did you not get money to seek Mr Bubb's assistance?"

There was not a flicker of response from Bark.

"Judge, we are getting nowhere with the accused. Could we adjourn until we find out what the accused knows?"

"I must protest," said Bleating, on his feet again "What the accused knows must be ascertained in court."

"The revolution is not to be thwarted by a man mute of malice. We shall make him speak. Then we shall resume our sitting. What do you say, judge?"

"I have to agree," said Phil with resignation. "The accused must be given time to consider his position," he ended lamely.

The armed guards then hustled Bark away.

Part Five – The Fourth Day's Play

I

Much to her surprise, Liz had managed, once more, to spend a restful night. She had, furthermore, gone to bed at peace with herself. Strangely, and despite her scepticism that the Minister of Culture could keep his word to help spring Phil from the trap that had snared him, she also had hope. Besides, she had tried to put into practice what she had learned earlier in the day about the indigenous religion, that action must follow right thought and that thought should follow right contemplation. These insights led to her spending the evening in painful meditation, rehearsing her life's story before the harsh courts that are the memory and the imagination. Without claiming to aspire to anything like a full knowledge of her life until then, she nonetheless had seemed to learn enough to win a semblance of calm and contentment. She felt, at that moment of waking to a new day when reality has not quite intruded fully, that, if Phil walked in, then she could truthfully tell him that she understood him, even if she could not approve of all his ways or many of his actions.

This new-found enlightenment catapulted her from her bed. Often in the recent past she had risen with a dull throbbing ache at the side of the head, accompanying an irritable spirit and a not altogether clear mind. But that morning she swept into the kitchen, to startle Marie-Antoinette.

"Good morning, Missy," gasped the maid. "Missy looking well today."

"Missy is in good mood. That is why she looks well. How's your daughter, Marie-Antoinette?"

"She's well, Missy, but troubled. No baby yet. Several alarms, all false. I'm worried, Missy, if peace period not long enough."

"Nonsense. I'm sure the peace period will last long enough to bring your daughter her baby, and us your master."

"Hearing anything about Master sir, Missy?"

"We went to see the minister yesterday. He's hopeful."

"That good, Missy. I not trusting Panthers. They real savage. It in their blood."

"They have no reason to harm the master, you know. They just want England to win the match."

"I tell you something, Missy. I don't care now to win match. I want to see Master sir back. I pray for England to win match."

"How very kind and loyal of you, Marie-Antoinette."

"My place is with Missy and Master. What is cricket match? We can win some other time. Maybe we win in England. That even better. Maybe England umpires favour us as, what you say, below dogs?"

"Underdogs, Marie-Antoinette. You are right. What is this but a game? I have never even got the hang of it. And I tell you something else, Marie-

Antoinette. Yesterday morning, after seeing the minister, I went to your temple – you know, the big one. I learned something, I tell you. The nun made me think."

"What she say, Missy?"

"The use of right thinking. You know, when you really start thinking about it all, this seems so trivial. All these matches and finery and things. What is life for, Marie-Antoinette?"

"Life is for living, Missy."

"No, Marie-Antoinette; life is for living properly. All our preoccupations pale into insignificance beside that. We must think before we act, Marie-Antoinette. And before we think we must cast aside our preconceptions and prejudices. Our race, religion, country, family, school, club – nothing, but nothing, is that important. That is what your religion taught me, and I learned it all yesterday."

"Our religion excite you, Missy?"

"Yes, Marie-Antoinette. Your religion excited and intrigued me. It stated the obvious but the obvious needs sometimes to be stated. That is an axiom of life. To get at the kernel of truth, that is the thing. It is like when you are given a box of chocolates, all beautifully done up in gift-wrapping. You have to undo everything, go through the glitz and the chaff, the silvery dressing, to get at the chocolates..."

"It is same with coconut, Missy. Layer after layer after layer of husk, shell, water, meat and you get kernel."

"Exactly, Marie-Antoinette. That's the adventure of life. To go beyond meretricious posing, discarding veil after veil, dropping everything, cutting through everything, prising everything apart until you get to the box named truth."

"You doing thinking yesterday, Missy. Big thinking."

"Yesterday, for the rest of the day, I did nothing but contemplate, Marie-Antoinette. I put aside all our parochial concerns. I took a step back and peered into my life."

"Missy learning any secrets?"

"Well, I don't know if they are secrets. But I learned really to tell the difference between what is important and what is not."

"Today, Missy, what is important is for England to do well."

"You think so? For England to succeed in a piffling cricket match?"

"There is right thinking and right action, Missy. But if England not doing well, Missy, Master sir not coming back. That is why, Missy, though religion is so good, so uplifting, in real world not so practical."

"What do you mean, Marie-Antoinette?"

"I mean, Missy, religion very fine but it like music or book, no? Like a hobby. It not give you money. Master sir come back, say religion. But if religion right, why Master sir go away? He do no wrong. Bad men, not acting or thinking right, take him. They do what suits, not what religion say."

"Yes, Marie-Antoinette, I understand. There is a real world in which evil resides. But we must have hope. If we had no idealism, we cannot have hope. We will be consumed by futility. Your daughter's child, what will you expect it to have in this world if you cannot bless it with hope?"

"I tell you, Missy, the blessing I will give it even before it is born. I hope the child will be a boy, a grandson for me, Missy..."

"Really, Marie-Antoinette? What is wrong if it is a girl?"

"Plenty wrong, Missy. It will have no job. It will have to stay home. It cannot do hard work. It needing looking after all the time. When it grow up, its parents looking for money to marry it off. Girl babies, Missy, bring nothing but trouble."

"You really shock me, Marie-Antoinette. Here we are, two women discussing things, and one tells the other that an infant version of ourselves brings nothing but trouble! How can you say such a disgraceful thing, Marie-Antoinette?"

"Missy getting angry, I see. But, Missy, we are simple people. We have nothing. Our business on this earth is to live. We see hardship. We know hardship. We wish our children less hardship. Like all parents, Missy, we wish our children and our grandchildren to have a little more than we have, to do a little better. If you are born boy, you can hope for a little better life. If you are born girl, chance will decide. Who can tell chance, Missy? So we hope we have boy. Let someone else have a girl, who might come to our boy child with a little dowry. That way both may hope for a little better life."

"With that kind of attitude, nothing will change, Marie-Antoinette. The old corrupt habits will linger on."

"No, Missy, we are simple. We play parts God gives us. If God gave us star part, maybe we win Oscar. Change the world maybe. But we have no such part. We just read lines written for us, Missy. We think small. We expect little. Just we want to live a little better. Changing things too much, Missy, leading to unhappiness. Bombs and guns and blood required to change things in world. We coming into world unarmed. We just filling belly and thinking of doing it tomorrow and day after. That is enough for us, Missy."

"Well, there is something in what you say, Marie-Antoinette. The real world impinges, I suppose, on the world of unrequited hopes and painful disappointments, the world of sweat and tears as well as blood and adrenalin. I suppose that is the trouble with us. We don't know where the real world ends and the world of our dreams begins."

As Marie-Antoinette busied herself, Liz reached for the radio. She had no idea how to find the World Service, but she tried at random in an attempt to hear what was being said about the state of play in the Test Match, which was due to resume that morning. For several minutes she elicited only hums and whistles and crackles in between rival stations. The ones that sounded right turned out to be from everywhere except London; the accents of the BBC appeared to have penetrated more corners of the earth than even the Empire had managed. When a voice explained to her how guerrilla activity had intensified in southern Africa, she paused, only to leave that station with impatience when the voice identified itself as speaking on behalf of Radio Moscow. About to switch back to the known comforts of the local station, she caught the tail-end of what sounded like a cricket report. The match, it said, was evenly balanced but the advantage lay slightly with the local team who would bowl last. Rumours of the disappearance of the England team manager, Mr Thistle, had been discounted and London had announced he was safe and well and had also denounced the rumours as being completely without foundation. Back with the local station and its menu of an unvaryingly bland diet of songs and tunes scrambled together and seasoned with just a pinch of speech, she found its offering restful.

She put on a housecoat to answer the door when its bell rang. Mr and Mrs Grunt were on the outside, looking troubled.

"Sorry to disturb you so early, child. But we thought we should ask you about this matter without delay."

"Why, come in. We have been up…"

"You mean, he…"

"Oh, how silly of me. It is a habit of speaking. I'm sorry. Won't you come in? Marie-

Antoinette, a cup of tea for the headmaster and Mrs Grunt."

The headmaster and his wife sat themselves down but seemed embarrassed to be there. Mrs Grunt looked furtively around as if in an attempt to locate a lurking Bubb. Mercifully, Marie-Antoinette fetched the tea, which seemed, in time-honoured fashion, to ease the tension.

"We have heard of the England team manager's disappearance," began the headmaster.

"We were very disturbed. We thought the match might be called off," said Mrs Grunt.

"He disappeared yesterday, it seems. It is a rumour only, but what to do? It won't be reported in the press or on the radio," complained the headmaster.

"We thought you might have heard something from your...your friends," said his wife tentatively. "We are very worried for Roar."

"He didn't get much of a chance in the first innings. He played magnificently," said Mr Grunt proudly, "but then ran out of partners."

"He must be given a chance. The boy is so talented."

" And, of course, if the match goes, peace goes, too," said the headmaster glumly.

"I heard about the rumours, too," replied Liz. "But they are only rumours, and they are not true. I was listening to the news just now from the BBC, I think, and they say the story is completely without foundation. Mr Thistle is alive, well, free and able to play, or do whatever he does. The match starts again today."

"You are sure about that?" asked the headmaster from the edge of his seat.

"Absolutely. The TCB, is it...?"

"The TCCB. In London."

"The TCCB in London has confirmed it."

"Thank God for that!" said Mr Grunt, now visibly relieved.

"What a wicked thing to say." said Mrs Grunt. "It frightened all of us. I wonder who would say such a thing."

"I think the Lions must have had something to do with that. I was telling my wife they would do anything to disrupt the match."

"I think," said Liz, without thinking much at all, "they have confused Thistle with Bark."

"With Bark?" asked the headmaster incredulously.

"Bark, your man Bark. *He* has been kidnapped."

"Bark kidnapped? Who by?"

"Tell us, child."

"We saw him being taken away on Sunday night at the carnival," said Liz, sporting the pride of a newspaper editor revealing a world exclusive.

"Do the police know?"

"It was the police who took him away. At least, they were dressed like policemen."

"I think they must have been Panthers," said the headmaster grimly.

"Don't talk nonsense!" contradicted his wife. "Bark is in the pay of the Panthers. Why should they kidnap him?"

"How do you know he works for the Panthers? He works for the minister," argued Mr Grunt.

"Everybody knows Bark works for the Panthers," retorted his scornful wife. "He must have done some wrong to them, then. Anyway, it serves him right. He will now stop harassing you and trying to get you sacked."

"He brought me luck, you know."

"Luck! That's what you think! That man is your enemy. Look how he made Roar drunk?"

"We don't know that for sure."

"How much more do you want to know?" demanded his wife angrily. "When you are begging in the streets or lying shot dead in the ditch you will realize. You are too soft-hearted. It is a good thing to see Bark gone."

"I suppose they will shoot him."

"I hope they shoot him!"

"Don't say such things. It is not a Christian thing to hope."

"There is a time and a place for Christianity. This is not it. We are living by the law of the jungle now. We must behave likewise. When in the jungle do as the animals do. Don't you agree, child?"

"I don't know, Mrs Grunt. If he has done something wrong, I think he ought to be punished by the law," said Liz mildly.

"The law!" bellowed Mrs Grunt. "By the time the paperwork is done, the world will have spawned a thousand Barks. No, we must submit to God's will. It is God's desire that Bark be punished for the evils he has done. So be it!"

"Talking of law and justice," interrupted Mr Grunt, "we must tell Mrs Smallbone without delay about the other matter we came to discuss."

"Oh, I completely forgot that. I was so relieved when I heard Mr Thistle was safe. And so happy that Bark was taken away. We have a small problem."

"Perhaps you will let me explain the problem to Mrs Smallbone," said the headmaster, impatiently taking charge again. "You have a boy called Croaking in your house."

"Yes, I know him."

"His parents are very influential. That is the trouble, you see. The boy behaves very badly. He breaks the rules. He upsets people – staff, servants, other boys, people in the street, everybody. He is in debt to every boutique-keeper in the neighbourhood. But I cannot punish him because his parents are so very influential."

"His father knows everyone on the Board of Governors. And Bark," Emmeline turned to her husband, "your precious Bark used to go round and sneak to him."

"I had not thought of that," said Mr Grunt. "With Bark gone the business is in even greater muddle now."

"Maybe, with Bark gone, you can punish him now," suggested his wife.

"No, no, it is not that simple."

"What has Croaking done now?" asked Liz.

"He was caught smoking by one of the prefects," replied the headmaster.

"Openly smoking," amplified his wife. "Didn't even have the decency to hide behind the bushes when the prefect came. That boy is a law unto himself. Does what he wants. Goes where he wants. Nothing is out of bounds for him. He should have been sacked a long time ago."

"But his father is an old boy. Besides, he is influential," said the headmaster miserably.

"What was he smoking?" asked Liz with curiosity.

"Tobacco, thank heaven!" exclaimed the headmaster. "We are thankful to be quite backward in that respect. It is only tobacco that is smoked in this school"

"Only tobacco! Is this all you can say," demanded his wife, her temper flaring again. "It is time to assert yourself and sack Croaking. You know what the rules are about smoking. First time, warning. Second time, caning. Third time, sacking. Why can't we do that?"

"We came to ask if you could do something about it, he being in Mr Smallbone's house," said Mr Grunt, ignoring his wife. "We are sorry to be asking this, but Mr Smallbone is not involved in our petty affairs. He can do things without there being repercussions."

Liz could not think of anything to say.

"When he comes back after his ...er, break, perhaps you could put this to him. I am in a difficult position. Many members of the staff are of my wife's opinion that something must be done if good order is to be kept in the school. That is why I am coming to appeal to Mr Smallbone's wisdom and good sense."

"My husband is away, as you know."

"We knew that. But in the next few days, when he...er, comes for his things or something like that, we wondered if you could mention this to him."

"Perhaps you have not heard. But my husband has been kidnapped, too."

The Grunts were turned to something like stone, making them appear like a scene in a horror video with the 'pause' button pressed on the machine. Liz was able to continue.

"He has been kidnapped by the Panthers. They have sent messages. He will be freed unharmed if England win the Test Match."

"My poor child," said Emmeline, unfreezing and rising to her feet. "But what will you do?"

Liz shrugged her shoulders. "Nothing much to do. Pray for an England win, I suppose. I am told it is customary to plead to higher authority to seek success when England are playing."

"You are sure it is the Panthers?" enquired Mr Grunt.

"Oh, yes, as sure as one can be. They took Freeman, the England cricketer, first but found they could not understand him. Phil was invited, with some coercion, to interpret. When they discovered England actually stood less chance of victory without Freeman, they let him go and kept Phil behind as hostage."

"They did not understand the rules. That must be the Lions, then," speculated Emmeline.

"No, I tell you, it could be the Panthers," argued her husband. "Some of them are so ignorant. Typical, not understanding the laws of cricket. Shows what will happen to this country if they take over."

"And, to clinch the matter," added Liz, "Bark was thought to have been involved in the kidnapping of Freeman."

"Bark again!" exclaimed the headmaster. "Does the man pass the time seizing people?"

"That's what comes from working for that minister who is so ignorant of culture that he has nothing to do. So, I think he gets Bark to go around snatching people," said his wife with conviction.

"If you want to know," said Liz, contributing to the pot, "I have also heard Freeman was seized after he came to drop Roar off at the school."

"Freeman dropping Roar off!" The headmaster almost shouted in his amazement. "What is the meaning of this? We have talked of nothing but tobacco, kidnapping, killing, betrayal, alcohol...is there more? Already it is like Sodom and Gomorrah!"

"I don't think there is more. The England party might have had a hand in making Roar drunk that night."

"So, Bark was an accomplice, yes?" asked Emmeline hopefully.

"No, I don't think so. When the England party were at a loss to know how to dispose of the wrecked Roar, Bark stepped in to seize his chance," said Liz.

"But he got the wrong man."

"Freeman apparently wasn't the right one."

"My, my, what is the world coming to, child?"

The music from the radio, familiar and unobtrusively confined to the background, stopped abruptly, and the trio were made aware of a silent void that seemed to crave being filled. No music returned but heavy breathing was heard, as if its perpetrator was trying to compose himself after some bout of strenuous exertion. Soon the silence was broken.

"We are interrupting this programme to bring you an urgent public announcement. The Revolutionary Council of the Pride of Lions has issued the following proclamation. We shall endeavour to destroy the absurd, imperialist, elitist, so-called sport that is disfiguring the motherland. All spectators who have been foolishly seduced into watching this misguided spectacle are warned to keep away for their own safety. The traitorous truce is at an end. We shall fight to the finish. Long live the upcoming revolution of the *Ing* people and of the Pride of the Lions! Long live patriotism and our race! Death to the traitors!"

The voice went away as suddenly as it had come on. For a moment or two there was silence and then, without warning, it was replaced by a snatch of Bach.

"My goodness!" said Emmeline in a tremulous voice.

"This is bad," admitted the headmaster. "Somebody has seized the radio station. Security is so lax. How can they let it happen?"

"Did they really seize the radio station?" asked Liz.

"No, I now think it might have been an inside job. But it is bad all the same. It will panic the people. The Government must put out a statement immediately."

"Will it affect the match?"

"Not if the Government can clear it up immediately. Otherwise, there will be danger."

"Poor Roar," clucked Emmeline. "The fates are against him. Whatever we do, he seems to run into obstacles."

"His luck has held up to now," corrected the headmaster, "though his enemies seem to be everywhere. Let us pray he will get his chance."

As if in an answer to his prayer, the music came to an orderly stop and a voice with authority took over.

"We regret your programme was interrupted a few moments ago by an unauthorized announcement. We wish to repeat in categorical terms that the announcement was not made with any authority. It was a subversive act. The culprit has been apprehended and is being dealt with according to the due processes of the law.

Listeners are urged to take no notice of anything that was said. The Honourable Minister of Culture will address you shortly over the air."

"The Minister of Culture!" exclaimed Emmeline. "The clown! Can't they find someone with a little more authority?"

Her husband was evidently more mindful of constitutional proprieties. "They find the person responsible for the radio. That happens to be the Minister of Culture. But he must take a firm stand. Otherwise he will also be dealt with."

Emmeline was unappeased. "Yes, that idiot is responsible. Good thing if he gets the sack now."

"The main thing is the match. Why don't they say it can go on?"

"Well, they said not to take notice," Liz said.

"That's not the same thing. It may just mean the people must not take notice of all that revolutionary talk, the truce ending and so on. Anyway, if he is going to say anything, he must say it quickly and clearly."

"He can't do either of those things. That is the problem."

The headmaster sat up suddenly. "My God, your husband's fate also depends on the match, does it not, Mrs Smallbone?"

"I have just been thinking that."

"I wonder what happens if there is a draw," he asked.

"Those savages won't understand what a draw is," said his wife.

"They'll think we have struck a deal, or sold out."

"What have we done to deserve all this – I don't know," wailed Emmeline. "If the match goes on, the Lions will make trouble. If it does not, poor Mr Smallbone will be in trouble. And Roar will be disappointed."

Her husband said disapprovingly, "Roar's disappointment is nothing compared with Mr Smallbone's life. The match has now become a life and death matter."

Their deliberations were interrupted by the ringing of the doorbell, which heralded Bubb's entrance.

"Did you hear the announcement?" Liz asked.

"Couldn't help that. It was all over the car radio. But they recanted quickly."

"They arrested the man," said Mr Grunt. "They'll torture him. But it was a bold gesture all the same. I wouldn't like to be in the minister's shoes now."

"He was lax," complained Mrs Grunt.

"If the security at the radio station is so lax, what price the might of the Government?" enquired Bubb.

"Their enemies crawl at will."

"Do you think Phil will be safe?" wondered Liz, sounding the domestic note.

"He's getting forgotten in all this," agreed Bubb. "I think he is safe for the time being. I hope for his sake the minister is spared for the moment."

"My God, we had not thought of that," cried Emmeline.

"We have just heard of the sad plight of Mr Smallbone. Do you think I should put in a word with the President? After all, he's an old boy and will try to help a master at his old school."

"Can't do any harm. But I hear the President's office has already been contacted. They are doing what they can."

"What can they do?" asked Emmeline.

"They do have some clout with the Panthers these days, you know."

"But you can't reason with those savages," thundered Emmeline. "They call a truce to hold the match. Then they start kidnapping people left and right and putting the truce at risk. They are not reasoning."

"I don't think people like the Panthers are into reasoning very much," observed Bubb. "They get an idea and follow it through, come what may. One idea may contradict the one that preceded it."

"Like holding a cricket match and then seizing a player from the side they hoped would win the match."

"There you have the perfect example, headmaster. Dogma conquering logic and reason."

"Anyway, it will soon be time for the match to resume," said the headmaster. "We will have mixed feelings. We want our country to win but for Mr Smallbone to escape. We shall pray for guidance."

++++++++

II

Now that the reason for the missing Phil had been demystified to the Grunts, Liz felt she could sit alongside Bubb without exciting too much Emmeline's fantasies. She sat in the seat Phil might have occupied on the fourth day of the match if he had been free. Despite the fact that it was Tuesday, interest in the local team's prospects had gathered another large crowd.

The newspapers of that morning had made no reference to it, but the news of Thistle's alleged disappearance was still alive on the ground. A quarter of an hour before play was scheduled to commence the public address came to life. "Ladies and gentlemen," it called out, "the England team manager wishes to make a statement from the balcony." Thistle then appeared there, eliciting a cheer from Bubb and a few desultory claps from elsewhere.

"Looks alive to me," commented Bubb.

"You were responsible for his alleged disappearance, you know," replied Liz.

"Was I? How?"

"It must have been through that snooping journalist at the time you were using the telephone at the team hotel's foyer."

"Really? I didn't know that. Wasn't it Groat from the *Chronicle*?"

"You were implying that Thistle had gone missing to get to talk to the minister. Groat, or whoever it was, must have overheard you."

"I remember now. Good heavens! Never knew my handiwork could influence the course of a Test Match and appear in the news."

But Thistle had started to speak.

"Cricket-lovers, here I am, alive and well. The rumours of my going are false. Let's not waste any more time. Let's get on with the game."

"Hear hear!" yelled Bubb. Several more spectators joined the applause, and the festive atmosphere of earlier days was restored to the ground. Soon afterwards umpire Shrieker and his colleague plodded their deliberate way to the middle, and Liz found herself uttering a short prayer.

"For Phil's sake, let England win," she supplicated.

She was interrupted by Bubb.

"A beer?" he enquired.

"A soft drink."

The local team opened cautiously, in the hope of consolidating their position. England, for their part, resumed with their fast bowlers, but they gained little and soon Sainsbury switched to his spinners, Marks and Harrod, to extract any turn there might have been in the pitch.

"How are we doing?" Liz asked Bubb when he returned with their drinks.

"No real change yet. The locals are adding up, run by run, to get a big score and leave us fighting against a turner."

"Whatever is that?"

"On the last two days of the match the pitch gets worn, cracked and uneven. The ball keeps low and may turn a lot. Pitch could get dusty, too. Batting becomes more and more difficult and, since we have to bat last, we'll have the greatest difficulty."

"Seems unfair, I mean, us having to bat last."

"Luck of the toss, I'm afraid."

"You mean, when they tossed on the first day they were deciding who would bat last?"

"More or less."

"I suppose it is just like life. What happens to you early on could influence the rest of your life."

"I suppose you are right there. I had never thought of it like that."

"When will we know if we'll win or not?"

"Difficult to say. But by the end of the day we should have a clearer idea. But things can change quickly. A quick couple of wickets falling or a brisk fifty or even a dropped catch could make all the difference."

All through the morning the tempo set by the batting team was slow. The pitch, it appeared, had already been deemed untrustworthy, and the locals were labouring the point.

"Of course," explained Bubb, "there's a tactical advantage in the batting side, even at this stage, giving the impression that the pitch is more difficult than it really is. Sows doubt in the opposite side."

"It is a more devious game than it appears to be."

"As you said, it is just like life."

By lunch the local team seemed well stuck in. Bubb explained the position to Liz as they munched their sandwiches in gloom. Outside, with no Bark that day to entertain them, there was little scope for excitement, and the crowd remained sedate and good-humoured, taking on the characteristics of the play in the middle.

Having finished her lunch, Liz left Bubb and went over to Emmeline, to be met with immediate commiseration.

"My poor child, fate is against you. But a miracle can still happen."

"You mean, England could yet win?"

"I think so. I'm praying for it." She dropped her voice. "You know, child, what I'm praying for? I'm praying for Roar to do well and for England to win afterwards. That way we will both be happy."

"Is Roar going to play again soon?"

"Yes, Mrs Smallbone," Mr Grunt intervened. "He's next in. He's in good shape and in fine spirits. We are hoping he will do well."

"I hope he does well. Last time round he did not do so well, did he?" said Liz.

"He did quite well," contradicted Mr Grunt. "Very well, in fact. His spectacular batting was commented on. But he ran out of partners."

Liz, puzzled by this remark, attempted another perspective.

"Anyway, he was not feeling very well. He did marvellously considering how ill he was in the morning."

"It was due to that brute, Bark. God is now dealing with him," said Emmeline with fierce inaccuracy.

"You must excuse my wife, Mrs Smallbone. But she is not expressing Christian charity. We must not think ill of anyone or wish ill of anyone. We must leave all that to God."

"That's what I'm saying, no?" protested his wife. "I'm saying God will hold Bark to account soon. I don't care what happens. God will provide justice. Only this time He seems to have acted very quickly."

"Anyway, we were told it was not Bark that gave the boy so much to drink. Let's forget about all that and remember the kindness shown to Roar by Mr and Mrs Smallbone and their excellent friend, Mr Bubb."

"Oh, yes, child. We must never forget that. If Roar does well again today, it is you, your husband and your friend we must thank."

"Oh, it was nothing. We just did what we could."

"Your friend, Mr Bubb. He's a marvellous man," said the headmaster approvingly. "He's involved in so many things. I must thank you and your friend for another thing. The old boys were very pleased with the drama competition. It was in the rich traditions of our school. For all your effort and trouble, I must thank you again."

"Yes, child, and how nice it will be to see Mr Smallbone back and happy once again," sighed Emmeline.

"You know," she confided when Mr Grunt had turned away, "the headmaster's position is now so much stronger. The drama competition really thrilled the old boys and the parents. They said how civilized it all was. The headmaster is so pleased now and so relaxed. If Roar does well today no one can touch him. And with that creature Bark gone, he will be safe for ever."

"Bark may come back, you know. He's probably being held with my husband."

"No. No. He's going to be tried for being a traitor to the Panthers. There's no coming back from that, you know. It is now only the manner of his execution they will be deciding."

"This is horrifying. Will they really do that?"

"You mustn't worry about your husband, child," said Emmeline soothingly, as she patted Liz's hand. "He'll be perfectly safe. They just want to make a point about him. But, with Bark, they'll make an example."

When play resumed, little still happened. The score crept up slowly, and run by run the locals consolidated their position. England toiled and sweated but in vain. The beer and the sun conspired to make the spectators drowsy, and, when a rare four was struck or a landmark reached, they cheered as if in a dream.

"It's slipping away from us, I'm afraid," murmured Bubb in the middle of the afternoon. Liz did not reply but thought instead of Phil.

Suddenly it all changed. Marks had been bowling, and the batsman at his end was Roar, who had on several occasions sneaked a quick run by enthusiastic and legitimate backing up. This was annoying to the England fielders for he was running, when it counted, substantially less than the length of the pitch. Soon Marks and Sainsbury conferred in mid-pitch, and Sainsbury came on himself, replacing Marks. He bowled one ball without incident. The next he prepared to bowl. Then, instead of running fully to the crease, he paused, made sure Roar was out of his ground, and struck off the bails. A wild cry issued at this from the entire England team. Umpire Shrieker, who stood at the bowler's end, hesitated; then, confronted by twenty-two hostile English eyes, raised a sorrowful right index finger. Roar was stricken and looked imploringly at Sainsbury and then at umpire Shrieker. Neither man was moved. Roar had to depart.

It had happened so quickly that it was only when Roar had reached a point midway to the pavilion that full realization hit Bubb.

"He's out!" he shouted.

"Who is?" asked Liz.

"Roar."

Liz could not understand the technicalities but sensed the matter might be of decisive importance. She said no more in the momentary silence that issued from the paralysed crowd. In the next instant, however, there was pandemonium. A man had emptied the contents of a bottle of Coca Cola over Bubb's head.

"Cheaters!" the man screamed. "Bloody cheaters!"

The stadium had risen to a man, or woman. Bubb and Liz were surrounded by a sea of chattering, cursing, very emotional brown faces. In front of them a man, slightly drunk, tried to set fire to a pile of litter but his neighbour, more conclusively inebriated, kept dowsing his efforts with the contents of a bottle of *arak*. Then the pair stopped their skirmishing and seized each other by their throats. A few spectators threw cans over the boundary edge, from where the England outfielders had fled centripetally at the first whiff of trouble. To Liz's left a large black man with a trumpet attempted in vain to sound the *Last Post*. The noise, boos and jeers in continuous uproar had defeated him.

Bubb motioned to Liz to stand up so as to make themselves inconspicuous. Liz managed to get up unmolested, but the man who had poured the Coca Cola over Bubb now followed it up by hitting him with the empty bottle. Bubb swayed slightly, saw a few prancing stars but managed to remain upright.

"Stop the bloody match!" shouted Bubb's assailant.

"No point playing with these bloody cheats."

"Their manners have gone with their Empire."

"They are treating us like natives."

The England team huddled together in the middle of the pitch, the umpires conferred with the local batsmen, and a posse of policemen marched to the boundary.

From the players' balcony Thistle emerged to another chorus of verbally violent abuse.

"Kidnap the bugger," someone suggested.

Thistle ignored the crowd and made frantic gesticulations to the England players to stay put – a course of action they had already decided on unanimously, fearing a lynching if they had attempted to leave for the pavilion.

The furore went on for what seemed an eternity but, in fact, lasted only fifteen minutes. Like a flood abating, the disturbance subsided imperceptibly and finally disappeared altogether. When the danger of a malignant spread of the trouble had been aborted, the umpires took the initiative to restart play, Shrieker holding his arms above his head to beckon to the new batsman; when he made his way to the middle, the cheers he attracted finally mopped up the residue of the jeers and catcalls.

But the tide had turned in England's favour. Like a person who suffers what is called a mere breakdown, only to find he has completely lost his equilibrium forever, the local team could not regain their poise. The new batsman, unnerved despite the vocal support of his countrymen, tried a nervous sweep at Harrod and was clean bowled. The newer man, jumpy as the one he had succeeded, contrived to run out his partner. By teatime England seemed on the verge of retaking the initiative. Bubb and Liz stayed put in their seats, not risking another outbreak of opprobrium, which might have remained latent. They looked nervously about them but found that the locals, busying themselves in the acquisition and consumption of food and drink, had been rendered benign. In the background the music played softly again.

As the England team went back on the field after tea they were perfunctorily booed, but it was hard to detect any convincing malice. An orange thrown almost apologetically at Sainsbury missed him, and was fielded by Spencer, who threw little catches to his mates. When he threw a low ball to Curry, the latter jumped in the air and let the ball through his legs. The crowd's hilarity at this reprise of Curry's previous gaffe dissipated any remaining tension.

But England relentlessly pressed home their newly gained advantage. Sainsbury resumed with his two fastest bowlers, Freeman and Wilberforce, who were impelled to bowl at their limits. The wicket had turned slow but to compensate the bounce had become uneven, and when the ball hit the cracks on the crumbling surface it was now prone to take off like a demented hawk. Rumbelow caught a batsman at first slip and Sainsbury himself grasped a ball edged high off the handle of the bat. The local middle order was now disintegrating; an hour after tea their innings was but dust. The crowd grieved in silence.

"Here's our chance," whispered Bubb.

"You mean we could make it?"

"God and umpires willing," whispered back Bubb.

"Thank God!" murmured Liz gratefully.

Ten minutes later England began their quest for a victory that seemed within their reach. Their target was modest, the light good, the umpires apparently beyond temptation, and the wicket, though far from pristine, still serviceable.

"All we have to do is to keep our nerve," said Bubb.

"All Phil has to do, too."

"We can make it," he said, striking a palm with a fist.

"I hope to God we will."

As they were leaving the ground, Bubb and Liz almost collided with the Grunts, and fervently wished they had not met so unpropitiously soon after the Roar debacle.

The principals remained static, and afflicted by an embarrassed silence.

"England seem to be doing well," said the headmaster. "You must be pleased, relieved even."

"Yes, things are looking up for us just now," conceded Bubb, "but there is a whole day to go tomorrow."

"The glorious uncertainties of the game, eh?"

Mrs Grunt could remain quiet no longer.

"But you shouldn't have done that to Roar. That was not fair. It was not cricket."

"All very unfortunate," agreed Bubb. "Done in the heat of the moment. Probably best forgotten."

"It won't be forgotten if we lose the match. Why did you have to do that? The boy was only being keen. He wanted to run the first run fast. The laws allow that."

"I don't know why at all, Mrs Grunt. I don't support the action one bit. Bet it was done instinctively."

"If Sainsbury had made a mistake, in the heat of the moment, why didn't he call Roar back? He did it in the first innings with Growler."

"It is difficult, Mrs Grunt...to explain. But Growler was clearly not out. Roar was out, although only on a technicality."

"It is not fair. Gentlemen do not do things like that. I thought they were gentlemen..."

"They try to be, Mrs Grunt," said Bubb emolliently, "but, when the day is long and hot, the score is mounting and you have had little success, your judgement can fail you. You behave out of character."

"Gentlemen don't give into pressure, Mr Bubb. You are called a gentleman only when it is known you can conduct yourself properly under all the conditions."

"You must excuse my wife, Mr Bubb. She is a bit upset. You see, Roar is like a son to us. And doing well again, you know. This could have been his match."

"He's been unlucky in both innings," agreed Bubb.

"That's what it is. On the first day, when you thought we were little sprats, you gave us a chance.

Said ball had hit the ground first, called Growler back. But on the fourth day, when we get into winning position, when we are equal, you start playing dirty tricks. Shame on you English!"

"Come, come now. You must forgive my wife, Mr Bubb. You can't blame Mr Bubb or Mrs Smallbone, can you? They really are one of us, you know. They support Roar. What happened was one man's act. Is the whole world to be condemned because one man did something foolish? No, no. We must part on good terms. Good night, Mr Bubb. Good night, Mrs Smallbone. Let us hope your husband will return safe and sound tomorrow."

++++++++

III

His captors being away for the morning, Phil had been left undisturbed to listen to the commentary on the Test Match. His solitude only made his dismay more intense as the locals appeared, at first, to be remorselessly piling up their advantage.

For lunch he had been left some bread and what he imagined to be a version of soup, a banana and a rock cake that lived up to its name. Returning to the cricket, he had switched on and off in the vaguely superstitious belief that such an action might precipitate a fall of a wicket, but it had been to no avail; England, for all the progress they were making, could well have been engaged in an aimless game of beach cricket. Gloomily he tried to get to sleep, but was too restless to gain it as he kept imagining a wicket falling and went dashing to switch on, only to contract a fresh dose of disappointment.

Then Dark came without warning into Phil's room, and immediately Phil sensed that the cosy philosophico-political discussions of previous days had now come to an end. Dark looked grim, and the cool insouciance of manner displayed previously had given way to a set and almost hostile mien. The casual inquiry as to the prospects for England, previously the preface to the talks between the two, had also now been discarded.

"Prepare to leave. We are going now," he commanded. Turning to his comrades, he addressed them shortly in their tongue, whereupon three of them descended on the scarcely alert Phil and half dragged him from the room. The uproar issuing from the radio went unattended.

They took him into the room in which he had first been kept. There they secured his arms and legs, and gagged and blindfolded him. Two pairs of arms lifted him and he was carried outdoors, where he instantly experienced the distilled heat and the simultaneous cooling breeze as they impinged on him. From a height he was dropped onto a semi-soft surface, and, although he was blinded by cloth, he could just discern that there was no light outside, either; it appeared to be a container of some sort.

When it began moving he realized he was being removed in the boot of a vehicle.

They must have travelled for an hour or two. The road was bumpy, giving nothing like the smooth ride he had had from the rickshaw transit of a few days before; moreover, it was an irregular road – a country lane, he surmised. When he got accustomed to the jolting, he tried to make sense of things. Had his captors become alerted and alarmed, he wondered, by the possibility of attempts being made to free him and the other two men; he concluded it was the only logical explanation for their recent action. The match was no longer of primary importance for another variable had entered the equation. He recalled the hostages in Lebanon, and shuddered within the bounds of the embracing ropes when he remembered how long it had been possible to keep them alive but out of sight and contact. Death worried him less and, though normally not a praying man, he now opened his eyes, concentrated on the darkness before them and uttered the prayerful hope that the fates would come to a swift decision.

Eventually they stopped. He was pulled out of the car boot and deposited on a rough and cold floor, and his blindfold and gag removed. As he blinked against the murky light he saw that he was lying under the dried fronds of a coconut palm that hung over a makeshift wooden structure the walls of which were constructed of earth and mud. He was, in fact, inhabiting the simplest of mud huts. In the room, which contained also implements for digging, cutting, burying and carrying, there were two other men present as well. One of these was Dark, who now appeared a trifle more relaxed than when he had last addressed Phil.

"We have brought you here for your own safety. You will be secure here. We learned plans were being made to attack us. We would, of course, have defended ourselves vigorously. You could have been hurt in the process. It is also possible the Government will break the truce. They say the cricket match is going the Government's way. I think they might have tried to take you before they won. Alternatively, they might have been trying to rescue Bark or the lawyer Bleating. Well, we have taken care of you all. You yourself will remain here until further notice."

They gagged him again but spared him the blindfold. Phil lay back on the floor and thought about England's history.

++++++++

IV

Soon after Bubb had returned to his home from the match, having deposited Liz at the school en route, he found the telephone ringing. It paused to convey the voice in person of the Minister of Culture.

"Mr Bubb, very important developments are taking place. We must meet to talk. You free?

249

Well, in one hour I shall order a car to pick you up from your home."

Bubb, intrigued, rang Liz and told her to await news. When the minister's car arrived, it was a small, nondescript Ford Escort of an older vintage, its driver a dull, lizard-like man whose eyes darted out of control all the time. He conveyed Bubb without speaking, and they travelled to the suburbs, driving through a city calm and quiet and yet busy in the lit darkness following another day of peace. After about half an hour they reached a deserted stretch of road and Bubb, from his seat beside the driver, espied the spire of a distant church. This came nearer in his field of vision and, somewhat to his surprise, they stopped at the church.

The driver motioned with his head.

"You go," he said, in tones that were in all probability neutral, though to Bubb it sounded a peremptory order.

"Here? It is a church."

"Go!" It was now unmistakably an order.

Bubb got out and walked onto a path that led to the door of the church. He had gone but a few yards when he heard a sharp, hissing sound. Terrified it might be a snake he stopped in his tracks and, in his petrifaction, he could feel sweat forming beside his spine. There was no more sound but soon, from the bushes, a voice spoke, calmly and pleasantly enough, but managing in the circumstances to startle him acutely.

"Come with me," it whispered.

Bubb spotted a dark figure in the bushes and followed it away from the path, and they went to the side of the church. Hidden among the vegetation was the entrance to a steep flight of stairs to a basement. In the gloom, aided only by his guide's torchlight, Bubb cautiously descended the steps. The guide knocked on the door, and a man opened it, allowing diffuse light to filter from the body of the subterranean premises.

"Stay here," ordered the guide. Bubb waited outside for a minute until, out of the basement, there emerged a man of smart attire, with a beard and the indefinable air of prosperity – a model of a capitalist to warm any cartoonist's heart.

"Welcome, Mr Bubb," the man called. The voice seemed familiar to Bubb, but it was not light enough for him to identify the speaker.

"Hello, do I know you? I'm actually meeting the minister."

"Sshh! You don't recognize me? I *am* the minister. Ha ha ha! You are fooled. Of course, you are fooled. I am off duty. I am in – what do you say – mufti. But keep your voice down. No need to tell every Tom, Dick and Harry who we are. Let them think we do business, make deals. But, now, come!"

Bubb followed him into the interior. It was only marginally lighter inside, whatever illumination there was being compromised by a pall of smoke. The decor was unrecognizable but the walls were painted a garish pink, the carpets were of a loud pattern, the people inside misty figures – a collection of individuals rather than any definable group. Who they were, whether male, female or mixed, could not be determined by Bubb, to whom the place reeked of the atmosphere of an old-fashioned brothel as portrayed on a low-budget film set.

"First we have a drink," announced the minister as he led Bubb. "You'll have a scotch. I will have one also."

When they had reached a table they sat far enough from anyone else to be successfully identified. Bubb dimly noticed a group of men playing cards; another man on his left was poring over a newssheet with the aid of a magnifying glass. He heard the voices and saw the silhouettes of mysterious individuals speaking in low tones. Unmistakably, deals were being struck.

"You are surprised, yes. But this is where – what do you say – we let our hair down. We get away from it all. Change our clothes, have a drink, gamble. This is my club."

"It seems an extraordinary place."

"Of course, you see the church. That is why we choose this place. Very discreet. Very exclusive. We take no notice of anyone. No meetings. No committees. Just some important people doing deals, relaxing, breaking a few laws." He laughed with uncharacteristic restraint. "We choose the church. People think coming and going very usual. Perhaps Bible classes. Perhaps revivalist gatherings. No one taking interest in what people in here doing. Fine idea, don't you think?

Not much noise coming out of here, either. Even if it does, people thinking it is hymn-singing."

"People are drinking, too."

"Of course. People are drinking. Gambling, too. And some days there are girls dancing also. Everything available here. It is like duty-free shop."

"Do your colleagues come here?"

"Yes. I have seen one or two here. But they are all in mufti. People think they are big businessmen. So people take no notice. I look the other way though I am in disguise. But we must be discreet. You are a man of the world and an Englishman. So, I know you will be discreet. But you will call me Mr X for now. That is how I am called here: X31. That is my membership number and that is how I am addressed. We are all addressed by our membership numbers."

"To business, then, Mr X. What is it you wished to speak to me about? Is it good news about Mr Smallbone?"

"Yes and no. The bad news is that he has not been found. The good news is we are looking. But I wanted to speak to you about this man Bark."

"Yes?"

"You know him, of course."

"Well, yes."

"What do you know about him?"

"Not much more than others know about him. He was just a contact for business."

"He is a relation of the headmaster of the school where Mr Smallbone teaches?"

"He is related to the headmaster's wife, I think."

"And he has connections with the Panthers?"

"He might have. I am not sure."

"Is it not right that he was paid money to abduct the High Priest?"

"He certainly was looking for the High Priest."

"He could not get him on his own because the High Priest is guarded by the presidential guards, who are foreigners?"

"That might have been the case."

"And so he approached you, did he not?"

"I must protest, minis...Mr X. This is turning into an inquisition. I did not come here to be cross-examined. I thought you had information for me, sir."

"I do have information for you, Mr Bubb. I have learned Bark approached you with money to tempt the guards."

"I assure you, Mr X, I had nothing to do with the High Priest's disappearance. But later, when I asked Mr Bark, he told me – he assured me – that the High Priest was safe."

"I have not found where the High Priest is or who took him. But I know the Panthers seized Bark because he let them down. He has somehow taken the High Priest but not handed him over to the Panthers. But I will tell you this, Mr Bubb; this is a serious matter. This may become a diplomatic incident with very great – very, very great – repercussions. What is your position, Mr Bubb?"

"I'm manager of *Roll Britannia!*"

"Exactly. You are permitted to spread your culture. That is your job. What are you doing with business deals? What are you doing associating with men such as Bark? Is that compatible with your status?"

"But, minis...Mr X, he is your adviser. I have to deal with him, whether I like it or not. We have to write to one another and meet and speak, socialize, organize..."

"Don't talk about writing. You can't read or write, can you? Ah, you have gone quiet. I can tell the world – more importantly, your Government – you are bogus, not fit to spread culture. You are like KGB man spreading culture that he only knows from behind a gun. Now, I tell you and you listen to me. If you do not wish to be expelled from the country for activities not compatible with your status, this is what you will do. Is that understood?"

"Yes, sir."

"Bark is kidnapped. That is known. By the Panthers. That is known. But nothing about the High Priest must come to be known, you understand? Nothing. Panthers seized Bark, well, because he was Bark, a Government official, just like they took Mr Smallbone because he was an Englishman. You get me?"

"Yes, Mr X. I understand."

"I need your help. You will do public relations for me. You will get British media to support me."

"Yes, Mr X."

"Good. We can now relax and be merry. We must find Mr Smallbone, of course. But what is happening at the match?"

"England hold the advantage."

"Is that official? Can they win?"

"They should. But, of course, there is a day's play left."

"That is good for Mr Smallbone but not for us. We cannot afford to lose, unless we both win. I take it that is not possible in this game?"

"No, sir. Victory is for one side only."

"That is the trouble with democracy, you know. We need always to have winners and losers. Why can't we have a system like the Russian elections where everyone wins? But, I don't care. Maybe it will be an advantage for me if England win."

"Is that right?"

"It will discredit the Government and the present leaders. Changes at top possible. Can't say more. And I...well, X31 can hope to gain some advantage. So, I might be praying tonight, Mr Bubb. Lot of good comes out of prayer, you know. On the way out, perhaps, we can put in a prayer or two for the success of the mother country and for the safe return of Mr Smallbone. What you say, Mr Bubb?"

"I'll join in heartily, Mr X."

"Well, shall we leave now? I want Mr Smallbone returned, you hear me? I cannot tolerate a big diplomatic upset like that when I shall be having very important things on my mind.

Power is like Scotch, Mr Bubb. It goes to the head. It also stretches the bladder and irritates the genitals. Very exhilarating but needing an outlet now and then. You will excuse me before we get ready to leave."

++++++++

V

The Grunts had returned from the match and took time to allow Emmeline to cool down and for the headmaster, no less agitated inwardly, to regain his composure. The headmaster occupied himself with a diagram that he, since childhood, had set before himself for solution whenever he felt in need of a period of restfulness. Like true happiness or success, the solution to the picture puzzle appeared simple but was, in fact, fiendishly elusive.

The aim was to complete the diagram, starting from any point, without once lifting the pencil from the sheet of paper. For over thirty years Mr Grunt had contemplated solving the riddle, but one line or one curve always stood between him and the final resolution. Now, whenever faced with stress or disappointment, he took out pencil and paper and renewed his quest.

Mrs Grunt, whose habitual comforts were derived from the thought, preparation or consumption of food, took herself to the kitchen. She assembled the variety of ingredients and condiments that would be needed for an elaborate meal and tried to imagine what the finished product would look, feel, taste and smell like. She sought, as did Mr Grunt with his puzzle, the solution in perfection resulting from the acts of mind and body.

In time a modicum of restfulness descended on the Grunts as they pursued their respective leisure interests. The evening stretched before them, following on a day that had brought forth its disappointments. Roar's promise had been dashed again, but there was another day's play to come. And when there's play, there is hope.

Outside there was peace – precarious and assailed, but somehow still holding together. The school itself seemed to be at gentle ease, like some venerable old party that had escaped from the brutalities of the real world. The absence of Mr Smallbone was a worry to Mr Grunt, who felt a sense of duty for everything that happened on the premises, but at least the morrow would make his fate plainer. There was, after all, nothing more the headmaster could do. The forces of the Government were seeking his missing schoolmaster but he knew it would be God and fate that would eventually find him, if they were so minded to. A part of Mr Grunt's mind thought it improper to put pressure on these supernatural forces; God and fate were not to be chivvied like some procrastinating clerk in a government office. It was more seemly for them to be allowed to decide in their own good time.

As the headmaster mused, several cars drew up outside his home, which was set apart from the school and hidden among clumps of mango trees, temple trees and bougainvillea bushes. The house was as old as the school and had once been named *Thalassa*, which had also been the name of the headmaster's house in the school's original home by the sea. When it had been pointed out by some classical scholars that the school was now situated inland, miles away from the sea, a debate had broken out between the forces of tradition and those of literal-mindedness as to the appropriateness of the name of the headmaster's house. The argument had never been officially resolved, though the subject once featured as an item on the agenda at the meeting of the Board of Governors, but, notwithstanding that, the realists had scored a quiet triumph and the name had been, for all practical purposes, dropped.

Smartly dressed and amply fed men moved out of their cars and into the headmaster's house. As he saw the mob moving stealthily towards him, the headmaster abruptly dropped his soothing pastime and started playing host to myriad demons dancing in his mind. This was the scenario he had feared all along, and one that regularly succeeded in thrusting itself into his consciousness, in sleep as well as in wakefulness.

"Good evening, headmaster," they cried in unison, as if they had been rehearsing diligently all day.

"Good evening, gentlemen," stuttered the headmaster.

"We thought we would call on you," said the men.

Their pleasant, contrived casualness and their apparent good humour only intensified his suspicions. Mr Grunt could identify them all; without exception they were members of the Board of Governors. Except that there was no chairman; the Bishop, whom he would have welcomed as a restraining influence, was not among them. That man, thought the headmaster, at least owed allegiance to a superior power; the rest of them had no such obligation, being motivated entirely by earthly considerations. A quick glance at the men, who were by now spreading themselves over the chairs of his sitting room, confirmed to the headmaster that they, together, owned three quarters of the country.

"Could we have some tea, Emmeline?" called out the headmaster.

"I'm cooking. Come and get it yourself," shouted back his wife.

"You must excuse my wife," said the headmaster pathetically, and rose to his feet." But we have been away at the match. We have been busy. Excuse me." He fled into the kitchen and returned with a cowering Emmeline.

"I am so sorry, sirs. I did not know you had arrived," she said ingratiatingly, all but curtsying to them. "I will bring you tea immediately."

When she had returned with the tea and placed it on a table she retreated, but stood nervously at the door. The headmaster motioned to her to leave, and she left the house through the back door.

As the men drank their tea, Mr Grunt swallowed apprehensively.

"The drama competition came off very well," said one of the men, who was often portrayed in the subversive press as a diabolical captain of industry. "Our congratulations to all concerned."

"It was well done. It is nice to see in this deplorable age that our traditions have not all been lost. Once these are gone completely the barbarians will be at the gates and ringing the bell."

They laughed politely and Mr Grunt was marginally reassured. "I have passed on your thanks to all concerned," he said.

"Not to all concerned, surely. I heard your English master, I mean your master who is an Englishman, has vanished."

"He's gone away, but not permanently, I hope."

"Trouble here? Trouble with his wife?"

"Nothing of the kind, sir. He's just gone..."

"Kidnapped, then?"

"Well, we...we are hoping he is safe."

"Well, it is neither here nor there. You must deal with it in your own way. When Triller was Commissioner of Police, one could have a discreet word. An old boy, you know. Got his colours in five sports. Poor fellow had to go, of course. No chance for the *Ers* now. Now they can't be trusted an inch. The police, I mean. Now, this Englishman...what   is   his name?…Smallbore?…Smallbone?...will have to fend for himself."

"I have had a word with the President's office," said the headmaster. "They are doing what they can."

"Wonder what the President can do, if he can do anything. Not really with it, you know. The old boy is getting on. I met him six months ago and all he could talk about was how he used to climb over the wall and go out of bounds. While the country was falling to pieces, he insisted on showing me, with the help of a woodapple, three pieces of firewood and a few charcoal remains, how he had run someone out at the big match. When I pleaded with him to seek more British military help, he promised to write to Baldwin."

They laughed again.

"Poor fellow. I hope he retires and lives on his memories."

"He can't go yet. There will be anarchy."

"There is anarchy. We need someone more alert, not one who insists on presiding over Cabinet meetings in his first-eleven blazer."

A lively argument, holding no promise of conclusive settlement, was threatening to break out. It was the headmaster's devout wish – as he felt easier in his mind as every minute passed – that a quarrel would develop among them. As had sustained the Empire, divide and rule had been his maxim guiding the running of the school, and he could see no logical objection to extending the principle to divide and survive when it came to dealing with the old boys.

"Talking about cricket, we must, of course, congratulate you again on Roar," said one of the old boys eventually.

"It was a splendid performance, headmaster. Accept our congratulations."

"Thank you, gentlemen. Of course, the school itself has had a successful season already," Mr Grunt reminded them.

"Of course, headmaster. The best season since President Trumpeting was captain of the first eleven."

"All in all, headmaster, despite the problems facing the country, all the destruction, all the horrors, the school can hold up its head again, and set an example to the rest of the country."

"That is correct. That has always been the philosophy of the school. Where it went, the country followed."

"This country would not have got its independence if not for its leaders. And where would the founding fathers of the country have been if not for their school?"

"I hope everyone has learned his lesson. The age of the common man is all very good but the common man is, well..."

"Common?"

"Simple. He does not understand the intricacies of life, the mysteries of nature, the need to accept, to tolerate things that are not to our liking..."

"Or are like us."

"Perfectly correct. Tolerance went out of the window when democracy came in through the door. The country went to the devil when it took the path down democracy."

"Come, come, we must not exaggerate. But it is true. The path to salvation lies in getting back to that which our school helped pave."

"I'm so glad that you gentlemen are pleased with how things have gone with the school. I must say it is most gratifying."

"You have handled things very well, headmaster. We hope you will be at the helm of affairs, to guide the school, to keep it on the right track. The Board has been observing things and is well satisfied."

"That is very kind of you to say so, sir."

"And so we hope, indeed believe, you will, without too much difficulty, clear up a small matter."

"What is that?" asked Mr Grunt, with renewed anxiety.

"It is only the little matter of Croaking's indiscretion. A misdemeanour. Nothing very much, wouldn't you agree?"

"Oh, that, gentlemen. I had almost forgotten about that. A silly, boyish thing to do. And only tobacco. I mean, just look at what is happening in the world today. What does a pinch of tobacco matter?"

"We are glad you take it in that spirit, headmaster."

"As Dr Arnold would have told anyone and, gentlemen, as you will no doubt agree, a good headmaster is one who knows what to take seriously and what not to take seriously. I aspire to Dr Arnold's ideal, which is to exercise discretion."

"You have impressed us enormously, headmaster. May we wish you long life, good health, and a prolonged period as headmaster of our school?"

"Thank you, gentlemen."

++++++++

VI

When Emmeline felt she had to flee her home, she felt impelled in the direction of Liz's. Liz, dropped off back there by Bubb, was concerning herself with those trivial tasks that tend to get overlooked when one is preoccupied with attending a five-day Test Match. Marie-Antoinette had helped early on but had to leave after getting word her daughter was threatening yet again to go into labour.

When Emmeline burst in she found Liz dusting casually in the living room.

"Forgive me, child. But they just walked in."

"They?"

"Those men. Into our house..."

"Not terrorists?"

"Oh, no, not terrorists. These are much worse. They are old boys. They were just like those in those American films, you know, those gangsters with family connections, what do you say?"

"The Mafia?"

"That's it. Just like that. I hope to God Mr Grunt will be all right."

"You mean, they might have come to break...harm the headmaster?"

"Oh. no, nothing like that. But they came in a crowd in many cars. Why did they come like that?"

"Maybe they wished to speak about school matters. Maybe to congratulate the headmaster on something. The drama competition, or on Roar's performance. Cheer up! Have a cup of tea."

They sipped their tea and chatted desultorily; two women whose husbands seemed to be in indescribable peril.

"Anything about your husband, child?"

"Nothing. I'm just waiting for news."

They spoke of this and that while their thoughts were engaged elsewhere, and did not notice that Mr Grunt had joined them. He looked pleased, like a curate who has, for once, been given an egg wholly good for breakfast.

"The old boys were most pleased with the school," he purred. "They congratulated all concerned and approved of Dr Arnold."

After that it was an anticlimax and, as Emmeline fussed shamelessly over her husband, emotions of anger, envy and fear washed over Liz. She was glad to see them leave. She switched on the radio and received more anodyne music.

When, as before, she turned to the short wave frequencies and tried to find the World Service, several likely voices were heard, but there was no mention of cricket. Despairing, she left the radio at the station at which the EEC was being discussed. Then she heard a knock on the door; soft, hesitant, somehow strange. She first thought it might have been a gust of wind playing on the empty milk bottles left outside, but the tentative knock recurred.

When she opened the door a small brown monkey with black, bright, button-like eyes gazed at her as if pleading and seeking approval. In its tiny hands it clutched a piece of paper. Without waiting for Liz to reach for it, the piece of paper was handed to Liz and the monkey turned and scampered into the darkness. She lacked the acuity of vision to follow the disappearing creature's path. The message on the paper, hand-printed, was brief: "England win or he die."

When she returned to the radio it had broken into the news. She listened intently but did not take anything in until her attention was annexed by the cricket news. England were poised for victory with a day left, said the announcer. Liz fell on her knees by the radio and prayed aloud: "Please, God, let England win." When she came back to this world there was a commentary following the news and a man was discussing agricultural policy in the EEC.

Part Six – The Final Day's Play

I

Believing he had been abandoned there, at any rate for the time being, Phil lay on the mud-covered floor of his hut for the better part of the rest of the day. The sun went down and it grew cooler as the fresh wind penetrated the precarious walls of the hut. He was hungry and he was alone. What had happened at the match that day he could not know but he was convinced the result would now only be of academic interest as far as he was concerned; he would be rescued or he would die.

Later he tried to sleep, but all he got was fitful and racked by dreams. He dreamed that he was floating on a river of blood that rose as bodies were thrown in; that Dark, grown to a hundred feet in height, was laughing maniacally; that he was floating into a dark tunnel and shivering uncontrollably as he did so; he regained wakefulness when he found himself being kissed by the Minister of Culture. By now it was pitch black and, shortly afterwards, two men walked into the hut, Dark being one of them.

"Get up!" ordered Dark. "We are going."

This time Phil was not blindfolded, but was loaded into the back of a small van in which the driver's cabin was separated from the space at the back in which he lay; so he could see nothing. The van started and they travelled for several minutes, climbing, descending, and hitting ruts and holes in what was undeniably rough country. When they stopped, Dark opened the back of the van and beckoned to him to get down. To Phil they seemed to be in the middle of nowhere, perhaps in a place like a crater on the moon, but, when his eyes had accommodated the murk, he saw they were actually in the middle of somewhere that was enormous but finite; it happened to be a giant quarry. At that time of night it was deserted but the implements, the scraps of clothing and the paraphernalia associated with manual labour signified it had been worked upon recently. Amidst the vast open spaces stood three huts.

"You will work here today," proclaimed Dark. "They have been looking for you, so we must disguise you. You will appear to be like a workman in this quarry, you understand. Then they will not find you. It is normal for hardened convicts and reconvicted criminals to work here. The security services will not come here. The guards here are now our people. They are armed, of course, and they have orders to shoot anyone trying to leave. They shoot first and then they explain. These guards are simple men. They take orders. They ask no questions. They appreciate the power they have... You are perhaps thinking you could escape. Put the idea out of the head, Mr Smallbone. You will be watched closely. You are the only one left, you know. Bark has paid the supreme penalty; he has lost his head. And the lawyer, he has paid the supreme penalty for a lawyer; he has lost his tongue. There, you stand only to lose what you value most, Mr Smallbone. Perhaps you are thinking that your skin will stand out when they work bare-bodied at the quarry. We have a solution for that, too. Come with us."

They led him into one of the huts where a fire seemed to have died after having burned dissolutely, leaving half-consumed firewood remaining at its pyre. Dark poked the remains and crushed the burnt wood with his fingers, gathering the powder macerated with sweat in his hands and motioning to his colleagues to do the same. When they had all collected what they felt was enough for their purpose, they removed all of Phil's clothes and laboriously painted him all over with the powdered remains of the charred wood. When they had finished, the first light of the new day was seeping in, and Phil observed he had been transformed into a passably black man.

++++++++

II

At dawn that morning Liz rose and, much to her surprise again, felt rested. She had slept well; the accumulated exhaustion of several days' strain and several nights without sleep had taken their toll, and mind and body had given in. Where she expected to be anxious and fretful, she found herself to be calm and able to face what threatened, in all likelihood, to be a nerve-racking day with something approaching equanimity. She rose slowly and then came into the setting room to switch on the radio. She listened to the nondescript music as she dressed in her bedroom, and, then, realizing there was no noise issuing from the kitchen, surmised that at last Marie-Antoinette's daughter had slipped into her long-threatened labour. When Liz returned to the sitting room the music on the radio had given way to the news. It bragged that the truce had held; that the President would address a mammoth political rally later that afternoon; that the Minister of Culture had predicted that final victory would lie with the forces of law and order; that an interesting finish was awaited in the Test Match; and that the monsoonal rains were expected in a few weeks.

While making a cup of tea for herself – finding that she had no stomach for breakfast –she glanced at the daily newspaper that was delivered to them each morning, and confirmed England's advantageous position, the details of which had to be prised from the lengthy columns of critical exposition on the England captain's fall from grace. The editorial in the centre pages was headed 'Triumph, Decline and Fall', and said that never in the field of human endeavour had so much been lost so quickly for so little. Illogically, the piece then went on to argue that, as a result of that act, the match was now in England's grasp. However reprehensible Sainsbury's actions might have been, there seemed little doubt they had borne fruit.

More sympathetically, Liz read another account of Roar. On the first day of the match there had been much said about Roar's promise;

on the second day's play it had been about his brilliant cameo of an innings amidst the collapse of all around him; now, on the fifth day, it was about another scintillating performance cut down in its prime by the perfidies of people who had been exposed in their true colours. Not being able to resist the political metaphor, the piece went on to opine that Roar's fate was like the country's. Both had been born with auspicious promise but had fallen victims to the doings of evil men, and they hoped, like Roar, the country would rise to fight again.

It was all too melodramatic for Liz, who preferred to escape back to the familiar sounds of the popular music of the 1950s and 1960s that were coming from the radio. Bubb then rang and said he had received word that a unit from the President's guard had approached a few hideouts suspected of being used by the Panthers. Phil had not been seen but was believed not to be too far away. Bubb concealed from Liz the information that the forces had discovered a headless body at one of the hideouts; a body so dark it had to be of a local, but unidentifiable because the head which had been found in close proximity to the body, and presumably lately belonged to it, had had a blowtorch applied to it. It was literally the body of a faceless man.

Bubb arranged to pick her up and take her to the match.

"Remember England are winning," he ended cheerfully. "Not many times have we been able to say even that recently."

++++++++

III

"You will work with the other men in the quarry," Dark had ordered. "You will not speak to anyone else, not try to walk away – just work. If you try to do anything else, you will be shot."

Phil, suitably blackened, looked at the implements he had been given and found they were ramshackle: a spade writ large, a pickaxe and a rusty metal bucket. Quite clearly there were not enough instruments of labour to go round. He set to work, striking a couple of desultory blows, but the implements, despite their unpromising appearance, were uncommonly heavy and he wearied after those blows. The atmosphere, though still without sun, was deceptively warm and perspiration threatened his forehead. Involuntarily he wiped his forehead with the back of his hand, and removed a smidgen of the black that had been applied. He resumed work, uneasily, for a few minutes when a guard, eyeing him from a distance, walked up to him. Phil, thinking he was being thought slack, redoubled his efforts and contrived to strike a few more blows with increased vigour. The guard came up, looked intently at Phil's eyes and said a few words that Phil could not understand.

"White," the guard said, still peering at Phil.

"No, brown, I think," replied Phil.

"No, white," persisted the guard.

"You mean the surrounds?" said Phil, pointing to his eyes. "Yes, they are white. But is there anything wrong? I mean, they are white on you, too."

"No, no," said the guard in exasperation.

Giving up that unequal contest with the English language, he went away, only to return with a man who looked like a superior, possibly the foreman.

"Yes?" inquired Phil.

"You have gone white," said the foreman.

Phil continued to look puzzled.

"Your head has gone white," the foreman continued.

Phil put his hand on the top of his head.

"My God! It must have been the worry."

"No, no, here, here," said the foreman excitedly, pointing first to his own forehead and then at Phil's. Phil wiped his forehead again and more black came off in his hand.

"Oh, my gosh. I'm sweating."

"Yes, yes, you gone white. It is not good. Stop your work."

Phil was taken away from his manual labours and more black was applied to his forehead. In the hut the foreman addressed him again.

"You like me. You not work. You walk about. Slowly. Understand?"

"I do understand," said Phil, who could not stop himself breaking into a grin.

++++++++

IV

Brought to the match by Bubb, Liz again occupied what would have been Phil's seat. On that last day the ground filled up systematically but the atmosphere was subdued, almost funereal, the spectators taking their seats almost as if performing some duty, without enthusiasm. The bands were muted, too, and their music solemn.

"The day of judgement," remarked Bubb.

"When will it all be over?" asked Liz.

"By mid-afternoon, if all goes well."

"You don't expect a hitch?"

"None obvious. The wicket is not entirely to be trusted. The umpires could have had their patriotism given a boost overnight, of course, but they have been playing fair up to now. If anything, we are the bad boys in this match."

"You mean, what Sainsbury did? I read about it in the papers. They seemed to have gone to town over it. I didn't realize it was that serious."

"It isn't. I mean, gamesmanship of that order is more or less routine. Only this time it was a visiting team, and England of all teams. The mother country is still expected to set an example. I am told the writers and commentators lost no chance in drawing a parallel between the ugly incident, as they called it, and what is happening in England today."

"I suppose it was a political metaphor."

"Of course it is. God-given to the editorial writers, I suppose. A schoolboy batsman, raw and inexperienced in the ways of his more seasoned colleagues, backs up in his enthusiasm and pays for it with his neck. Opportunistic, ruthless, seizing the main chance, paying no heed to the traditions of the gentleman's game, etc. etc."

"You make Sainsbury sound like a contemporary stockbroker in the City of London."

"Which he probably will be when he leaves the game. My boss at headquarters was very upset. Kept me on the phone late last night for an hour, worried what this might do to the message we are supposed to be putting out about the wholesomeness of British culture."

"I think you'd be better off sticking to Shakespeare and the King James Bible and leaving out more mundane perversions like cricket. By the way, I hope all this will not affect Phil."

"It won't. You needn't worry about it at all. The Panthers are unlikely to be concerning themselves about the critical writings on the game or its etiquette. They will be interested in the result and nothing else."

"So the monkey said."

"That's typical of the way the natives behave," said Bubb, dropping his voice, "getting an innocent animal to do their dirty work. Veneration of animals also leads to exploitation of their innocence."

"I can't understand why they had to get an animal to do it. I mean, I wouldn't have recognized the man who might have brought the message anyway."

"I suspect there is little trust between individuals in that mob. They hunt in packs to deflect suspicion between factions. Far, far better to entrust these delicate missions to animals. After all, they never let you down. Moreover, there is an old tradition in this country – their ancient kings killed off their rivals by dragging them behind horses, or putting them into caves inhabited by bears, or dropping them into a sea full of sharks. You see, the line is a long one."

"Heavens! I'm glad they have stopped doing that."

"Only in a manner of speaking, of course. Since they aspire to the levels animals have reached, they are now doing what they got animals to do. Killing, I mean."

"Let's talk about something else. I can't wait for the hours to pass."

A roller bore down on the wicket. As it did so, the England captain, Sainsbury, and the manager, Thistle, raced down the pavilion steps in front of Liz. Sainsbury was shouting but, at the sight of him, the stadium had erupted, to a man and woman, into an uproarious cacophony of boos, defeating his voice comprehensively. Halfway to the pitch Thistle turned back and started waving to the local team's dressing room, managing thereby to attract the local captain's attention. In the meantime, Sainsbury, finding vocal protest of any kind unprofitable, was running towards the men engaged in pulling the roller. By now there was a considerable din. Liz then saw Sainsbury gesticulating in the middle of the field and the groundsman remonstrating with him. Thistle and his counterpart were conducting an alternative debate near the boundary line.

In the middle of the pitch Sainsbury demanded of the rollers, "Stop it, will you?"

"No, laws of the game must be observed," rejoined umpire Shrieker. "The rolling must go on."

"But it is my choice."

"You asked for a roller."

"I asked for a light roller."

"This is the only roller we have got."

"We were not told you only had a heavy roller."

"It is you who must ask for the kind of roller you want."

"How could we know you had only one kind of roller? This is a Test Match. We expect the facilities available at a Test Match."

"Sir, we are a poor country. We do not have the technology. We cannot afford various types of rollers. We have only one kind, large. No small or medium."

"Well, in that case, I am now asking for the rolling to be stopped."

"It has stopped, sir. Its time is up."

Liz had been bemused and mystified.

"What is happening?" she asked at length.

"I imagine they are quarrelling about the roller. It has happened before. You may roll the pitch before the match resumes each day. It is like ironing a shirt; it smooths out the wrinkles. But, as the match goes on, it is better to use a light roller so that it will not hasten the break-up of an already wearing wicket."

"So what is wrong?"

"They probably asked Sainsbury what he wanted. He very likely said, use the light roller, and they wheeled out the only one they claim to have. Sainsbury is incensed, poor chap. In his innocence he has probably failed to notice the pitch has been rather too well watered, too."

"Would they do that?"

"What have they got to lose? If England fail to play, the locals win by default. If England play, the locals win through doctored pitch. There will be a row, which everyone has budgeted for anyway, and Lord's, mindful of all the sensitivities, will just give in. We can't win."

"I hope you don't mean that literally, do you? Anyway, they can't help it, I suppose. These poor chaps have only one roller, presumably."

"You are quite wrong there. They have every kind of roller salted away somewhere. This situation has occurred before. That was how they beat Pakistan. When a row developed it was said their action had been based on the doctrine of delayed retaliation. The Pakistanis could not do much, of course, they being in a mote-and-beam situation."

"I didn't realize that so much skulduggery was possible in the course of a game."

"When a game stretches over five or six days one has to amuse oneself somehow."

Liz paused to listen to the polite applause that greeted the entry of the two umpires and, a minute or so later, the altogether more enthusiastic sounds that applauded the home team as they took the field. When the locals had reached the middle, they crowded around the wicket and appeared to inspect it closely. They poked it and one team member stretched out his hands out as if conveying the size of the apocryphal fish that had eluded his grasp. Another affected a pose that would have excited Rodin. Yet another looked mournfully towards the England balcony and shook his head with sad finality. One other played a forward defensive stroke with an imaginary bat and then jumped abruptly as if the ball had taken off from that dodgy pitch and stung his nose. It was altogether a consummate display of miming and the locals, without a doubt, had managed to draw first blood in the final day's battle of wits.

Soon the two England batsmen had joined them, mindful, that, well placed though they were, the psychological advantage had passed decisively in those crucial few minutes to the other team. In only the second over of play, a local spinner had utterly defeated and bowled a batsman; he had been seeking and playing for a turn on the ball which existed only in his mind; the spinner had not spun but the batsman, for all that, had been spun out.

From then on England were undeniably in retreat. The occasional ball turned, as it will at the end of most Test Matches, but the pitch was far from untrustworthy. However, the germ of uncertainty that had been planted in the England batsmen grew and multiplied and infected all. The locals intensified the pressure by exaggerating every deviation from the norm that there was. The result was that England slowly folded, and by lunch such had been their decline from their initial position of strength that they found themselves contemplating their demise. The escalating noise in the stadium battered at the spectators' eardrums. Liz, who had little idea of the specifics of each incident, could sense England were in disarray. At lunch she turned to the wordless Bubb and asked, "It is bad, isn't it?"

He said nothing in reply – which was sufficient confirmation of her worst fears.

++++++++

V

Whenever Phil tried to accelerate the pace of his walking, by however mild a degree, one of the guards in the quarry would call him to order.

"Slow. No sweat."

He walked mostly with a measured stride, and when the sun came out he was ordered to stop, rest in the shade and observe the gangs of men labouring in the quarries. As the sun climbed higher in the sky, Phil knew the Test Match would have resumed but he felt no urgency in seeking out what was happening; he was resigned to the thought his fate was now yoked to other events.

Then, having shone brightly for a couple of hours, the sun slid behind a cloud. Two or three clouds, at first no bigger than wisps against the bright sky, coalesced, and soon turned sombre and then black. As Phil watched this negrifying process with fascination, the clouds found it impossible to contain themselves any longer and first leaked a drop, then two, then more; soon they burst, incontinently unleashing the torrent of water they had been harbouring. The rain now drove relentlessly down. At first the men at work in the quarry ignored it, then they welcomed it for the respite it afforded against the fierce sun. But, after a few minutes, they could resist its force no more, and fled to the refuge of the trees dotting the quarry. But the trees in turn became wet and their flimsy leaves and threadbare branches could themselves offer no protection against the elemental power of the rain. Drenched, they huddled together, and Phil observed them at the same time as he watched the black on his body being washed away. No one else noticed his transformation, for the rain was now pouring down in sheets and no one could see clearly through that cascade. As the rain drummed against the rocky ground, a shaft of lightning and a burst of thunder were orchestrated from above. The monsoonal scene was truly awesome.

Phil fled from the arbour of trees – a dangerous port to be in a thunderstorm, as he was aware – and ran as fast as he could from the quarry, beyond the huts, which were now concealed behind the many layers of the rain, and beyond the perimeter. He kept running, forcing himself against the rain as it battered his body, and he had to screw his eyes up to see where he was heading. After fifteen minutes or so of exertion he reached a road on which puddles of respectable dimensions were gathering. He turned left on the road and kept on until he reached the comforting scene of a traditional red telephone box. Frantically rummaging in his trouser pocket for change, he found none. Despairing, he suddenly remembered he could ring the emergency 999 number for free. He dialled, but there was no sound; the storms had already unhinged the telephone system. He had to resume his passage, and, another quarter of a mile or so onward, he reached another, newer telephone. He tried it and found it worked. As he was poised to dial, he remembered he would need to identify himself and his whereabouts, and then doubt crept in. Were the police to be trusted? Whose side would they be on? Had the Lions or Panthers infiltrated their ranks? Indeed, could there have been a *coup d'état* while he had been away? Not remotely knowing the answers to any of these questions he desisted from using the telephone, and, after a moment's further reflection, replaced the instrument and resumed running. The rain had, if anything, increased in ferocity. He stood by the road – his clothes soaked, his body wet, the rain lashing against him – but he felt where he was to be as safe as any place could be at that time.

Nothing moved on that road; nothing was there to move. For about a quarter of an hour, breathing with labour, for the rain assailed his nose and mouth, he simply stood. And then he saw in the distance two misty lamps, looking like candles spied through a glass window. As he watched they came nearer and he could just perceive the outlines of some amorphous structure. In time it turned out to be a large motorized vehicle. Excitedly Phil waved his arms and, fortunately for him, he found himself on the driver's side of the road. Spotting him, the vehicle lurched to a halt, and Phil was able to clamber in through the door behind the driver's cabin. It looked to him like a single-decker bus, and he noticed also that it was empty. The driver turned round.

"No fare," he said magnanimously.

"Thank you," stammered Phil.

"No fare because school bus this."

"Thanks. I have no money anyway."

"You catching rain. You hippy?"

"No, I am a schoolmaster, actually. At St Mark's."

"Ah, big, big school. Big people going there. You training for marathon, then?"

"Not quite. Do you know where we are going now?"

"Me? Me going to school. Small village school. No like St Mark's. This is tiny, tiny school. Like sprat to a shark. That's my school."

"We are going there now? Can I use the telephone there?"

"Pardon?"

"Telephone?" said Phil, miming.

"Telephone. Yes. You use money not paying for bus ride, yes. Then you can use telephone."

He drove skilfully through the rain.

"Monsoon come. Flood come. If rain no stop, children no going home. They stuck in school."

"You picking up schoolchildren?"

"Yes."

They reached a vast compound in which, scattered among brick-built structures, were several palm-thatched huts. They stopped by one, and Phil could see within tables, chairs and a blackboard, but there were no occupants.

"No good. They all going to office. Me not stopping bus. It starting not again. So me going to office and stay there, engine running. Right?"

They pulled up by the office block and, as the driver had predicted, Phil saw a multitude of children standing there like so many battery chickens, but singing, waving and shouting as they joyously celebrated this feat of nature. Phil, soaked to the skin, rushed into the building to the sounds of the cheering horde.

Evading their patting hands he located a schoolteacher.

"Could you direct me to the headmaster, please?"

"No headmaster. We democratic. We having head teacher," she replied sternly, and pointed to a door at the end of the passage.

When Phil knocked and went in he met a neat, small man dressed in a starched white suit.

"I'm sorry the monsoon has come early. I fear the tourists could not be warned in time," said the head teacher. "Perhaps you will like a towel and some hot tea."

"Thank you. May I use your phone?"

"Certainly. There it is," he said, and went in search of towel and tea.

Phil dialled his school's number and was greeted with voluble good humour by the bursar.

"You are safe, Mr Smallbone!" he cried.

"Yes. Listen to me. Where is the headmaster?"

"Headmaster's gone away to the match. But he gave instructions to get in touch with a man at the President's office in case of need. Where are you?"

Rummaging furiously in the contents of the head teacher's desk, Phil located a letter pad of the school and gave the bursar the address and telephone number.

"Oh, my dear, you are far, far away. How did you get there?"

"It is a long story, but I promise I'll tell you that over a beer if you will get me safely out of here."

"Righto, straightaway."

"Hang on. What is happening to the match?"

"England are losing. But the rain has saved them. You are lucky devils, you English. Always the weather on your side. Cheerio for now."

The head teacher had returned with towel, tea and a pair of workman's overalls.

"Put this on, sir. You will be dry. Then drink this herb tea. It will preserve you from a cold."

++++++++

VI

Liz, watching the match resume after lunch, sat with a leaden heart and failed to notice the gathering stormclouds. Bubb returned with a beer and remarked, "It looks like rain, to add to all our other worries."

"What will happen to the match?"

"It will be drawn. No decision."

"Will it upset them?"

"Probably. A draw will not exactly be an England victory."

She said nothing but returned her attention to the play. There, England's fortunes did not revive, and two more wickets fell in rapid succession. But, strangely, the crowd seemed no longer to be exultant; it was as if the rain had already seeped into their consciousness and dampened their expectations.

"Real spoilsport, the rain," muttered the man on her left to his neighbour.

"The monsoon coming early. It is not a good sign. Perhaps peace will not stay."

"At least it makes the explosives moist. The bombs will not go off if they are wet. Perhaps it really is a good sign."

"These days you don't know what is a good sign and what is a bad sign. Everything is so jumbled...so..."

"Topsy-turvy."

It was only about twenty minutes since lunch, but it had already become clear that prospects for any prolonged play were bleak. A few drops of rain began to fall. An England batsman, conscious of his back being to the wall, looked ostentatiously at the clouds but did not succeed in convincing the umpires. A whip-like flash of lightning suddenly suffused the ground and galvanized the local team to move more briskly so as to get in as much play as was possible. They started running at the end of each over to the places they needed to occupy for the next. But it was to no avail. The clouds broke and a torrent descended over the ground. The two England batsmen, not bothering even to look at the umpires, took to their heels. Even as they ran a cataract drenched them.

"That's it," said Bubb glumly. "The ground will be flooded in minutes."

"We can't lose then?"

"Well, I suppose there is that to be said for it."

Bubb was proved right when a few minutes' worth of rain rendered the pitch unplayable. But no one stirred from the still-dry seats. After several minutes of silence, Liz spoke again.

"What will happen to Phil now?"

"He will be safe," said Bubb, with a confidence he did not feel. "Don't brood about that. Come on, let's go and meet Thistle."

Things were quiet in the England dressing room. Liz could not help thinking of the comparison Phil would have made – with Dunkirk, when a lot of water had previously saved England from defeat by way of an honourable retreat.

"That's justice for you," they heard Thistle thunder as they entered. "Rain just in time to stop these bastards winning by cheating."

"Harsh words, Thistle," admonished Bubb.

"Did you see them doing us over this morning?" asked Thistle, who did not seem in the mood to be placated. "I thought they were gentlemen – ones we could trust."

"All in the game, Thistle. All's fair in love, war and overseas cricket."

"I hope they have learned a bloody good lesson. This will teach these superstitious savages that cheats come to no good."

"The mills of God grind slowly, or maybe I should say, roll slowly."

"Don't mention rolling to me!" spat out Thistle.

++++++++

VII

Phil had settled with tea and dry clothes in the head teacher's study.

"So, you are a teacher at St Mark's? What do you teach?"

"English and history."

"We try to teach English and history also. But our standards are not good. Our children are not very interested. They wish to have jobs as clerks. What use is history to a clerk? He will simply be disappointed, fall into despair, when he learns how little things have improved."

"Your country had a proud history before the invaders came."

"We were famous before the invaders came; we have become infamous after they have gone."

"These are teething troubles, headmaster. A nation needs time to grow up."

"Time, yes, but how long much? We have been independent for forty years. How much more time does a country need? If it were a person, it would be called a lost case. A suitable case for treatment, the social workers would have said."

"You must not despair. England took centuries to develop. You may call her a particularly late developer."

"What about us who are individuals? I was a small boy when independence came. I went to the celebrations. All the singing, dancing and the...the...hope that was there. It has all vanished. We had no one but friends then; everyone wished us well. We have no one but enemies now. I sleep at night not knowing whether the Lions or the Panthers or the Government will be coming for me. What will I tell my children and their children?"

"They must have hope. Out of chaos and destruction come renewal and regeneration. Take more recent examples. Look at Germany and Japan. They rose triumphantly out of their ashes."

"No, no, my friend, I too have studied history. These countries were destroyed by enemies from outside. It is helpful to know who your enemy is, to be able to identify and, even in a way, be able to trust him. When he lays down his arms, you know it is safe to get up. Now, how will we know when our enemy has given up, for we do not even know who our enemy is? My enemy may be my next-door neighbour."

A clap of thunder distracted them from their deliberations.

"But you will have another cup of tea, yes? But you have not told me what you are doing here, all this way from St Mark's."

"I was lost."

"You mean, you were out walking in this weather?"

"In a manner of speaking, yes. But it was fine when I started."

"You thought perhaps it was the way to the cricket match?"

"Yes, I did. Pity it has been washed out."

"Yes, that is a pity. But thanks to your countrymen we have had a week's peace. When they go back tomorrow, the quarrel here will begin again. Perhaps you will say it is just history repeating itself."

Amidst the intermittent booms of thunder and the echoing cheers of the schoolchildren, another distant rumble could also be heard. It got close when the prolonged applause of the schoolchildren drowned all other sounds.

"Perhaps it is your party come to rescue you," said the headmaster, cocking an ear.

No sooner had he said it than an impressive figure in khaki sauntered into his office.

"I'm Debbit. You are Smallbone, I presume."

Phil nodded.

"I have been asked to pick you up. Are you ready?"

"You would not care for some tea, sir?" asked the head teacher.

"Thank you very much, sir. But we ought to be moving."

"Who are you?" asked Phil.

"We are the President's auxiliary force. We have instructions to collect you. Let's talk on the way. We have another collection to make."

He let Phil climb into a truck, one of a convoy of three, to more cheers from the excited schoolchildren,

"This is a bit unusual, isn't it?" Phil asked as they moved off in the still-heavy rain.

"We are used in special operations by the President."

"You sound English."

"I'm English when you get behind the sunburn."

"Are there many of you?"

"More than the three trucks you see."

"I didn't know we were still here. As an army, I mean."

"Not you. It is just us. Private individuals with a military background. The proper term for us is mercenaries. I'll say it for you in case you feel too embarrassed to say it yourself."

"You guard the President, then?"

"More or less. Officially and for public purposes the President and the Government are protected by the crack Tiger Regiment. But next to the skin, so to speak, we lie."

"They don't trust their own soldiers?"

"Don't blame them. One of them looks very much like another. Unless you look into caste and pedigree you can't be certain. Even then you can't be sure, for they might have been bought by one side or another. At least we do what we are paid to do."

"I see. Are we going back to town?"

"Once we have picked up this other chap. By the way, how did you get up here? It seems a long way away."

"I ran."

"You ran?"

"They had me up in the quarry. When the storm broke, I made a dash for it."

"The quarry up there? They are just convicts up there doing hard labour. I suppose they were trying to conceal you among them. Where did they keep you before that?"

"In two places. But I have no idea where they were."

"You were picked up at the school, right?"

"Yes. By a chap under a white sheet, almost certainly someone called Bark. You know him?"

"Yes. And he is lying under a white sheet just now. I suppose they killed him. I think we very nearly got you before, you know. We were searching for their safe houses one by one when they got whiff of us, panicked and ran. Shot Bark, mutilated the lawyer and sent you into the hills."

"It is a savage business, this."

"You should see what happens when the fighting is really on."

They had reached a turning off the main road; at the foot of this path there stood a house.

"Our pick-up is in there. You stay here."

As Debbit collected his revolver, several other khaki-clad men with rifles jumped off the three trucks and ran to the door of the house. Debbit and two of his men remained at the door while the others surrounded the house. Debbit knocked three times on the door, but elicited no reply. Then one of his men hit the door with his rifle butt, but found no response either.

"Let's go in!" cried Debbit.

The two men with him broke down the door, and the three of them disappeared into the house. Phil anticipated gunfire and commotion but none ensued. Instead, after a few minutes, the three reappeared with a fourth man in tow. This man, a local, was large and squat, dressed in a shabby suit, and wearing dark glasses and a picturesque blue turban on his head. He looked anxious and bewildered as the men helped him into the front seat of the truck alongside Phil and Debbit.

"This is Trotsky," said Debbit to Phil by way of introducing the fat man, who settled uneasily into his seat, blinking and twitching in resignation, looking like a rabbit nervously awaiting despatch.

"Thank you so much, sir," the newcomer trilled. "It is kind of you to come all this way."

"Not at all," replied Debbit cheerfully. "Glad to be of assistance, Trotsky."

The radio in the truck crackled and Debbit spoke to it.

"Very good, sir. We shall proceed there." He turned to his two passengers and said, "Change of plan. We are ordered to go to the mass meeting the President is addressing. We'll drop you both off after the meeting."

As they retraced their path to the main road leading into town, Phil, intrigued by his neighbour, tried to draw him into conversation.

"Very wet today," he remarked.

"It is so," agreed the fat man. "You must excuse our weather but it is not always so unreliable. The monsoon is early."

"It has been raining for several hours now."

"Unfortunately that is so. The river will be in spate, there will be floods. Our poor country is so full of misfortune. The time is not good for us."

"You can say that again, Trotsky," said Debbit. "More misfortune for your country today. The rain washed out the Test Match just as you were going to win."

"Pardon? I do not understand."

"Test Match. Cricket match," Debbit explained, miming a bowler's spinning action with a right hand taken off the steering wheel.

"Oh, I see. But I am not a sporting man. I do not know about these things. But no doubt our country has suffered more bad fortune."

"What do you do, sir, if I may ask you?" enquired Phil, who was moved by the dignity and nobility of bearing of this otherwise unprepossessing man.

The fat man hesitated. "I am a man of simple habit. But you must be an Englishman."

"I am. We are," Phil corrected himself to include Debbit. "I am a schoolteacher, also a man of simple habit."

The fat man laughed. "It seems it is we men of simple habits who find themselves rescued by armed soldiers."

"The world is a funny place."

"So I have found, sir. The world is full of simple men but it is very complex."

They travelled in cramped discomfort in the unceasing rain for a few miles more. Then, Phil, feeling emboldened by his freedom, asked the fat man, "Forgive my asking, but I'm intrigued by your name. Why are you called Trotsky?"

"It is not the name I have chosen, sir. I was asked to assume the name. Perhaps our friend here will explain."

Debbit shrugged his shoulders. "I know nothing about it. I didn't decide to call you Trotsky. I was simply ordered to pick up Trotsky at the address given. I'm doing no more than a taxi-driver's duty."

"It is very kind of you, sir, all the same. I don't know what I would have done if you had not arrived."

"I was escaping from the Panthers," explained Phil, in the hope that his confession would help draw out more information from Trotsky.

"The Panthers, sir? My God, you have had a lucky escape. Not many come back from the jaws of the Panthers alive and to speak of their experiences. You are a lucky man, sir."

"Luckier even than you think, Trotsky. The Panthers would have wanted to kill me if England had not won. Well, England have not won, and yet – here I am."

"England to have won? This is a surprise. Are they fighting a war?"

Debbit chuckled. "He means the cricket match, Trotsky."

"If England had not won a cricket match, the Panthers would have killed you? I did not know they were such serious sportsmen."

"I didn't, either, but there you are."

The fat man mused for a few moments.

"It is a puzzle, this world. The Panthers wanted to take me also, you know. We came to hear about that. They wanted to disrupt the peace, I think. But luckily the President, I am told, had an idea and he got me sent away. You see, I had long wanted to see the world – the real world, the world in which people actually live their lives. I had asked the President a long time ago, but he had said it was not safe then."

"Why do you need the President's permission to let you see the world? Have you no passport?"

"No, sir, I have no passport. But that is not what I mean. When I say the world I mean going into town like an ordinary person.

"You are not an ordinary person, then, Trotsky?"

"No, sir, I am a man of simple habit. I took the decision about the simple life all those years ago when I was a boy. The world has changed. People have changed. I no longer understand them. I thought I might understand my people better if I knew about the world they were living in."

"You sound like one of your ancient kings."

"In a manner of speaking, yes. But my power is not temporal anymore. It is spiritual. You see, I am the High Priest."

"So it was you they thought had been kidnapped?"

"The rumours were started to explain my absence, sir. When the truce came I got my wish to see the world. I went out into the world, what do you say, incognito."

"But why are you now being rescued?"

"Frankly, sir, I could not manage. I would not have survived. My flesh was weak, sir, but I found my spirit was even weaker. I had to call for assistance and these good soldiers here have come to help me."

The High Priest removed his dark glasses and his turban. His shaven head glistened through the bristles, his face revealed the ravages of a few days of unbridled living, and his eyes were moist.

"I came to the world. I saw the world. And I was defeated. So Trotsky I had to become and call for help."

"And where did we find you?"

"That, sir, is or was a house of ill repute. The occupants were all arrested this morning. I feel sorry for them, but, when I told the authorities where I was, they were discovered. The police came early this morning and seized them."

"Why didn't they take you?"

"I was hiding under a bed, sir. Besides, the police were not meant to know about me. So they did not look for me."

"You really have gone to town, Trotsky," laughed Debbit.

"I betrayed them, yes. My flesh is too weak for the demands of this world, sir."

"I dare say you are right, Trotsky," replied Debbit. "It needs constant use for the flesh to keep up its strength. I suppose things have atrophied through disuse since you were a boy, Trotsky."

The three of them with the accompanying troops arrived at a large, open-air stadium at which the presidential meeting was to take place. Trotsky had replaced his turban and dark glasses, and the three, in the company of the all-white armed mercenary guards, went to the end of the park and situated themselves behind the dais on which the President was to appear.

"It is an important rally," explained Debbit. "It was planned weeks ahead. Let's hope it all goes right."

The soldiers scattered and busied themselves making the dais and its environs safe for the President. It was still raining steadily, and Phil wondered if the crowds would brave the weather and gather in strength.

"The people will come," Trotsky assured him. "They expect the President to exhibit supernatural powers and banish the rain. They have confidence in him. That's why he has so much power."

"He will need an awful amount of power to quell this force of nature."

"He has that power, sir. He is very old and very frail but the power is in his spirit. It is not of this world."

"Is it anything like your power?"

"Not quite. My power is spiritual. It is in me because I have inherited it from my forefathers and it has come down from the founder of our religion. The President's power is not spiritual but it is of the spirit. He has inherited it from no one. It has been given to him by the grace of God, the spirits and the stars. No one will have it exactly like what he has after him. His own son is a very ordinary man, devoid of his father's great gifts."

"How do you recognize it? I mean, how do you know who has it and who lacks it?"

"Only by its effects can the presence of this power be known. It is like identifying a tree by the fruit it bears. The people recognize it. That is the source of temporal power."

"The people will know who has these qualities? It is like charisma, you mean?"

"You may call it what you like. If a man or woman moves the masses, he or she has it."

"Hitler and Mussolini had it."

"I did not say the power of this spirit is always benign. It is a power that can be used for good or ill."

The current holder of this power arrived shortly afterwards. The crowds had started to gather, coming in a trickle at first, then in larger groups and eventually by loaded buses and lorries. Like a warehouse being systematically packed with goods, the park filled with human beings. Phil watched, fascinated. Then the limousine containing the President drew up, eliciting a gigantic cheer; the spectators chanted and applauded, waved rattles and blew whistles. Even the rain eased.

The President's movements on disembarkation confirmed that he was a very old man. A wheelchair was taken up to the car and he was helped into it. Dressed spotlessly in white, he, too, wore dark glasses. A crowd of helpers gathered around the wheelchair, which was pushed directly onto the dais, on which rested, supported by a table, a microphone and a tape recorder. As his minders stood solicitously by, the President remained seated in his wheelchair. On seeing him on the dais the crowd roared again, the sun peeped through the clouds as if to pay nature's respects, and the people broke into the national anthem.

As the noise ebbed, Phil noticed one of the men surrounding the President switch on the tape recorder. Within moments the amplified voice, familiar in local politics for over half a century, boomed out to the masses. It spoke in a local language and Phil could understand no word of it, but the pauses, the cadences, the resonating exhortations and the pleas were all familiar to him, for addressing the multitude is always done in a universal style. To all appearances this was a speech capable of having been made at Nuremberg, except that physical frailty on the part of the speaker precluded too much by way of the physical manifestations of raving and ranting. For about fifteen minutes the crowd listened with devout intent, occasionally punctuating the address with outbursts of fevered cheering. However incapacitated the old man might have been, his grip on his people still seemed to be firm. The spirit the High Priest had spoken of with awe, if not the body, appeared to be firing on all cylinders.

Then the sun went in, the clouds closed and the rain resumed. The crowd took on an air of collective outrage at this effrontery of nature and seemed to expect the old leader to reassert his authority. But his powers had obviously waned, for the intensity of the rain only increased. From a brisk drizzle it went on to lash down at a fair pace, and the winds picked up, howling as they did so. Thunder and lightning joined in. The dais swayed, a stray chair was blown over, and then a rogue gust of wind struck the President's wheelchair. The man supporting it fell over, and the wheelchair rushed backwards and fell off the dais onto the ground, depositing the President in a sitting position where he remained, like some mummified remains, on the grass. Over the sound effects of machine and nature the collective gasp from the crowd was palpable. The President's disembodied voice still came out of the obstinately functioning tape recorder.

"Good heavens!" cried Debbit.

"My God!" shrieked the High Priest. "He is sitting down. Is he hurt?"

"He is dead!" snarled Debbit. "He has been dead for some time. We have been conned. They have tried to get a corpse to address the masses."

"What is going to happen?" asked the High Priest.

"Trouble, without a doubt. Where are his advisers?"

"They have scattered," replied Phil.

"We'd better do the same," said Debbit.

"Don't you have to see if there will be any trouble?" asked Phil.

"No. My orders are to guard the President while he is alive. Keeping order is their business. Let's go. Come on, Trotsky."

"Should we not take him with us?" enquired the High Priest.

"Better not touch him. The mob will be upon us any minute. Let's go! Come!" ordered Debbit.

They ran to the three trucks. The soldiers had already got in. They started the engine and set off.

++++++++

VIII

At the match, as the rain poured relentlessly down, to Liz it appeared as if the heavens had decided to wash off, on a single day, the past sins of the

304

country. Other spectators resigned themselves to seeing play being abandoned, and after about half an hour it became clear that no further play was feasible.

"It is only a matter of time now," remarked Bubb, but Liz was too preoccupied to enquire what he meant

For an hour or more after that the torrential onslaught of the elements persisted, and then the public announcement system crackled into life and said play was being abandoned. Such was the inevitability of that fate that when the announcement came the dejected spectators did not even care to hoot or jeer.

"That's it," said Bubb.

"We wait for the first shot," the man on Liz's left said cryptically. As if in response to him a violent clap of thunder was visited on them.

"What do we do now?" asked Liz.

"We'll have to sit and wait till it eases a bit."

"I don't like it like this."

They had to sit and wait for two full hours, with the ground by now under water, before they attempted to move.

"We'd better risk a soaking," suggested Bubb. "This is as much as it is going to ease."

Liz agreed, and they dashed out of the stadium into the muddy car park. Their car started with reluctance and crept out cautiously. The streets, such a colour of activity only that morning and for the past several days, were now deserted. The bursts of thunder that punctuated the rain-laden air frightened Liz. She recalled the neighbouring spectator's ominous remark in the stadium and wondered if the violent excesses of heat, light and water they were experiencing were a portent of unnatural excesses to come.

They arrived home and Bubb came in with Liz.

"It is a question of waiting now, I suppose," she said despondently.

Marie-Antoinette had been deliriously scrubbing the kitchen floor, and leapt like a galvanized frog when Liz came in.

"My daughter had a baby. A boy, Missy."

"You must indeed be happy, Marie-Antoinette."

"I give thanks to God, Missy. A boy – that is what he has given us. And before peace period coming to end. We could not ask for more, Missy."

"Your daughter must be very happy also."

"She is so happy, Missy. Because it is a boy. So much responsibility, no, for girls? Finding a dowry so big a problem, no? And so much going wrong with a girl. One leg short, one tooth crooked, one eye squint, and dowry go up by ten thousand. No end to problem. Boy, Missy, grow up, grow strong, he work, he earn. And, if not able to do anything even, he join army. He not problem; that is why we pray for boy, Missy, and God and fate give us a boy."

As Liz was leaving the kitchen, Marie-Antoinette called out, "Master sir coming back, Missy?"

"We have not heard anything, Marie-Antoinette."

"England not winning match. That not good. Maybe Panthers seeing rain fall and not blaming England."

"I'm told, Marie-Antoinette, that if the rain had not fallen England would definitely have lost the match."

Back in the sitting room, having tuned the radio to the World Service, Bubb rang the President's office. They would not reveal anything and, in fact, were quite short with him. He next tried the Minister of Culture, but he was unavailable.

"When will he be available?" asked Bubb.

"The minister is busy. He is preparing a campaign speech."

"Campaign? What campaign? Is there going to be an election?"

"We cannot say more. You will hear about it soon. We are very sorry."

Bubb replaced the telephone.

"Very strange goings-on at that ministry. The minister is closeted with his aides, it appears, planning a campaign. Is he plotting to seize power?"

"It would be a strange way to go about it by telling the world first."

"But we are told we shall hear about it very soon. What is happening?"

Having no more inspiration, they sat in the sitting room and listened in gloom to the radio.

Outside, the thunder and lightning had ceased, and even the rain was easing. There came a knock on the door; it was the headmaster and Emmeline.

"Have you heard the news," beamed Emmeline.

"No, what is it?"

"Your husband rang, child..."

"He made the call to the bursar while we were away at the match," interrupted the headmaster.

"Where is he?"

"He was calling from a school in which he was taking refuge," explained Mr Grunt.

"What are they doing now?"

"I had left instructions for the bursar to ring the President's office. The message would have been taken and relayed to the special forces."

"So, your husband is back on his way, child. What a pleasant surprise for everyone. He will be back soon and all will be well," said Emmeline, patting Liz's arm. "Sit down, child. We will all have a cup of tea."

She marched into the kitchen and shouted, "Marie-Antoinette, tea for all of us. We are celebrating."

Liz remained in silence in the sitting room.

"Pity about the match," said Bubb.

"Not to worry. It is only one match. We will win the next time," said Emmeline, still excited.

"And Roar has proved himself. He will get another chance. They are speaking of him as a future captain already," said the headmaster, with quiet pride.

"And what of us?" asked Bubb.

"We must wait and see," replied the headmaster philosophically. "A miracle has happened already. The truce has held for six days. Will it go on, we must ask."

"I'll have to go back to monitoring the BBC to learn what is happening here," joked Bubb. "But, seriously, headmaster, is there an election campaign coming on?"

"An election campaign? No, no. I do not think so. How can one hold an election campaign in the middle of so much disruption? Where did you hear about that?"

"I rang the ministry just now. They let slip that the minister was in the middle of a campaign meeting."

"That stupid man is probably plotting a coup. It is a party game. A fantasy," intervened Emmeline.

On the radio a raucous comedy from the BBC came to an end and the news followed. The lead item was an account of the death of the President. A commentator in London sketched a brief background and commented that a new period of uncertainty was now bound to follow in that strife-torn ex-British colony. The news ended by noting that the Test Match had been washed out.

"My God!" cried the headmaster. "We did not know this. Our radio will not say anything."

"So that is why the minister is planning a campaign. It all makes sense now. He wants to be President," said Bubb.

"That man has no shame," remarked Emmeline scornfully. "Even before the President has grown cold, the man gives vent to his ambition. After all, the President was an old boy."

"The minister is ambitious but he has no chance," said her husband more temperately. "His caste is wrong. All his ambition will not help purify the tainted blood that flows in his veins."

"Anyway, he is going to give it a try," said Bubb. "I think we are going to live in interesting times again."

"But today we must be happy," said the headmaster, beaming at Liz. "Mr Smallbone will soon be back amongst us. For that we must thank God and our stars."

Liz rose and went to the curtains in the room and drew them apart. The sun was now beating down, gloriously, as if it had not gone away at all, and across the horizon the tops of the mountains could be seen clearly. The trees looked lush and the birds, released from a watery confinement, were taking off vocally into the sky. There was a happy chatter about nature.

ABOUT THE AUTHOR

The author is a consultant psychiatrist, barrister, law tutor and company director. He writes regularly on medicine and law, and his previous books include *Uncommon Men of Medicine*, a study of – among others – Rabelais, Locke, Keats, Conan Doyle, W.G.Grace and Maugham. This is his first novel.